Notes From

MW00799536

Fascinating and Thought-Provoking,

From Hope

"I found this book fast-paced and compelling, as well as illuminating. Several times I caught myself reading with my mouth agape…your book awakened my understanding of the spiritual unseen realm in helpful ways. It was a much needed awakening, for which I am very thankful.

Great job!

From Maegon

"I can't put it down! I have read this book 2-3 times already! Great job!"

Thank you…

From Sara

"Thank you for helping me to the way of the light."

I could not put it down…

From Johanna

"I could not put it down until the end. Of course, I saw a lot of your experiences in the story, and even my own time in the New Age Religion and the joy of being set free from it and forgiven of all my sin."

It was wonderful.

From Shirley

"I just finished your book…it was wonderful."

Western Witches & Warlocks; A Journey Into Eternity

Second Edition

Sarah Sheena

Published by Sarah Sheena
Morgan Hill, California, 95038, U.S.A.

Although it is based on true stories, this is a work of fiction.
Names, characters, and incidents either are the product of the
author's imagination or are used fictitiously and any resemblance
to actual persons, living or dead, business establishments, or
events is completely coincidental.
Cover photo by Sarah Sheena
Cover Art by Maegon Jewel Mitchell and Sarah Sheena

Copyright 2014 Library of Congress # 1-1727728351
All rights reserved. No part of this book may be reproduced,
scanned, or distributed in any printed or electronic form without
written permission. Please do not participate in or encourage
piracy of copyrighted materials in violation of the author's rights.
Please purchase only authorized editions.

Scripture taken from the HOLY BIBLE, NEW INTERNATIONAL
VERSION, Copyright 1973, 1978, 1984 by the International Bible
Society. Used by permission of Zondervan Publishing House. All
rights reserved.

978-0-9908020-1-3

Dear Reader,

"I keep asking that the God of our Lord Jesus Christ, the glorious Father, may give you the Spirit of wisdom and revelation, so that you may know him better. 18 I pray that the eyes of your heart may be enlightened in order that you may know the hope to which he has called you, the riches of his glorious inheritance in his holy people, 19 and his incomparably great power for us who believe. That power is the same as the mighty strength 20 he exerted when he raised Christ from the dead and seated him at his right hand in the heavenly realms, 21 far above all rule and authority, power and dominion, and every name that is invoked, not only in the present age but also in the one to come."

Ephesians 1:17-21 NIV

"For this reason I kneel before the Father, 15 from whom every family in heaven and on earth derives its name. 16 I pray that out of his glorious riches he may strengthen you with power through his Spirit in your inner being, 17 so that Christ may dwell in your hearts through faith. And I pray that you, being rooted and established in love, 18 may have power, together with all the Lord's holy people, to grasp how wide and long and high and deep is the love of Christ, 19 and to know this love that surpasses knowledge—that you may be filled to the measure of all the fullness of God.

20 Now to him who is able to do immeasurably more than all we ask or imagine, according to his power that is at work within us, 21 to him be glory in the church and in Christ Jesus throughout all generations, for ever and ever! Amen."

Ephesians 2:14-20 NIV

Sincerely,

Sarah Sheena

Dedication

First and foremost to the one who made this story possible:
You will always be first in my life!
I love you, Jesus, the Christ.

To my dear children who have always believed in and supported me in this dream. May you pursue first the Love which is eternal. May you be encouraged to be bold enough to follow your dreams wherever they lead.

Acknowledgements

Thank you to all my family and friends who have given so much support and love through it all! I could not have done this without you.

A special thank you to those who are obedient to the call even when you don't see the fruit. Your willingness to reach out does make an impact.

CHAPTER 1

Sheena ran around the house, preparing supplies for the trip. She stopped and scanned the kitchen table and counters. "The list, where is the list?" She asked in a panic.

"Here it is." Sergio said soothingly as he picked it up from the coffee table and held it out to her.

"I don't know what I would do without you." Sheena stated as she turned and gave Sergio the smile that melted his heart. She took the list from his hand and looked it over. Finally, convinced she had not forgotten anything, she nodded to Sergio. Sergio took the supplies to his 1980 Ford Mustang Cobra. He knew Sheena loved driving the car as much as he did, so he handed her the keys when she came out of the house. Sheena smiled and kissed him on the cheek. She skipped over to the driver's side and shouted, "Let's go!"

Lisa climbed in the back seat with anticipation, wondering what the night held for them. This was the first time she would go to Rebel Hill.

That evening, as they drove up the winding highway, Lisa began feeling a little uneasy. Something about this trip was wrong, but it was too late to turn back now. They were almost to the hill. The sun was beginning to hide behind the ridge they had just come over.

As they turned onto the road that revealed an isolated hill, Lisa took in the view. It stuck up all by itself in the middle of a small valley splitting the valley almost in two. The little valley was surrounded by a huge ridge that stood far taller than the New York skyline. The drop into this little valley wasn't as sharp as the Drop of Doom but was four times a long. Rebel Hill stood in the middle of the valley and was roughly 500 feet (almost 100 ft higher than the famous ride). It was covered with a forest mixed of Blue Oaks, Pines, and a dense variety of shrubs. The valley was a grassy meadow which exploded with color from wild flowers this time of year. A couple of the Blue Oaks stood like lighthouses in the sea of flowers. The mountains surrounding the valley were forested with Ponderosa pine, Incense-Cedar, White Fir, and Sugar Pine. The sky was streaked with pink and orange.

The scene nearly took Lisa's breath away. The air refreshed her senses with the light scent of pine and cedar intermingled. Lisa wondered out loud, "How magnificent is God's creation."

Sheena looked in the review mirror, a smile engulfed her face, her eyes filled with sparkle, and she shouted, "You haven't seen anything yet!"

"What could be more beautiful than this?" Lisa asked waving her hand across the back seat as she kept her gaze focused out the window.

"Just wait!" said Sergio with a big Cheshire cat grin.
The trio talked about the area and the name of the hill as they drove down into the valley. Sergio knew the names of the ranchers that had homes here on the west side of the hill. They ranched in the old family style. The Ferguson's and Metcalf's split the valley and raised cattle. Neither raised cattle on a large commercial scale. They both had small herds to provide for the local community need. During the summer both families planted a garden, tended it, and harvested it together. The women canned together in the fall. The families also had businesses and homes in the Fresno/Clovis area.

Children were playing in the yard. The smell of a barbeque dinner reached the road and made Sergio's mouth water.

Sheena suggested crashing the dinner and the three laughed. The cattle lazed about the pasture. There amidst the cattle were a small herd of deer grazing on the tall grass that grew in between the wildflowers.

Sergio said, "Those deer will soon be jerky if old Metcalf has his way. We bought some once at the little store in town. It was good. Have you ever had venison jerky, Lisa?"

"No, and I don't think I want to try it," Lisa retorted, her nose wrinkled and lips turned down with disgust.

"Why not? It's really better than beef," remarked Sergio

"I just can't stand the thought of eating Bambi," Lisa replied.

Sergio began telling Lisa about the Native American tribe that lived on the east side of the valley. The forest was home to a Monache tribe. The tribe was known for isolationism. They did not want to interact with curious tourists. The turn off for climbing Rebel Hill was about a hundred feet before a sign that warned trespassers of the private reservation.

The dirt road was the sight of post cards. Oak trees canopied the road as far as Lisa could see. Just to the left sat a collection of four mailboxes. Rebel Hill was host to four homes which were not visible from the main road.

Shortly after beginning the ascent, there was a smaller dirt and gravel drive that veered to the right. The road wrapped around the south side of the hill where the home was nicely tucked away. A few hundred yards later there was a drive off to the left. The home could be seen sitting in a small flat area that faced west.

There was just enough room to the east of the house for a couple of vehicles to be parked. The wall of the hill climbed steeply from the home. The climb began to get steeper and the car bogged down a little. The road curved to the east. Lisa could see straight down the side of the hill. There were no protective Oaks standing guard against the elements here.

3

The wall side was sheer weathered granite with a ditch dug out along the base to direct runoff water away from the road. The road was rough from overexposure. They were only about 200 feet up and it looked so far down. There was barely enough room for their car. As they passed the rock wall Lisa could see a small A-frame home in area just in front of them.

The road twisted around the north side of the hill and suddenly there before them was a road that was almost straight up! Sheena gunned the engine and then kept it steady at the higher rpm.

Lisa was getting nervous as the back of the car was sliding to one side then the next. Back and forth the rear swung as the car slowly climbed; tires slipping, sliding, then gripping.

Slip....slide....grip....slip...slide....grip....slip...slide....grip.

The loose gravel loudly crunching as the car inched its way precariously up the 75% grade. Lisa's eyes were filled with fear. Sheena and Sergio had been up here several times and were used to it. They laughed as they looked back at Lisa. This was just the first of many firsts for her tonight.

Sergio thought about the Mustang. He loved this car, but was thinking he should get a Bronco II. The Bronco II had just come out a couple of years before. The four wheel drive would make trips up Rebel Hill a lot easier. Now that he was out of high school and working full time, it would not take him long to save up for one. His parents let him keep all but $200.00 a month. Besides, replacing the tires on the Mustang was expensive.

Finally they reached the top of the wretched road and made a sharp right turn. Just a few feet away lay a large flat area. There was the desired destination. The flat on the top of the hill was perfect. They could see both valleys and over the low point of the surrounding ridge into a large valley floor between two different mountains ranges.

Lisa was elated; she felt like she could see almost the whole world from up here. They had been right. This was a much more spectacular view. Lisa slowly turned around, taking it all in. Within a half an hour, the sun had set, it became dark, and lights were coming on in the valleys below.

Sheena began setting out the blankets. She set Lisa's away from theirs against a large rock but where Lisa could easily see everything that was happening. Their blanket she set in front of a small set of rocks stacked to look like table legs. Sergio put the long board on top of them and completed the table. Sheena carefully arranged the crystal oil lanterns.

It was completely dark now. Sergio lit the oil lanterns and they knelt together in front of the homemade alter. The two of them began to chant and meditate. Lisa had never seen anyone worship outside of church before.

Lisa felt a little strange being there with them, but she had been drawn to them from the first time they had met at school. As she began hanging around them she discovered they were different from everyone else she knew. There was a confidence that seemed unique about them. They weren't particularly interested or uninterested in anyone else around them. If you wanted to be around them cool, if not, cool.

The more she came to know them she found out the thing that seemed to be behind all the difference was their belief in the Spirit Realm. They seemed to be in a close relationship with the spirits. They knew things that no one else knew. They were able to do things the others weren't. Sheena had healed a sick cat and Sergio could make objects lift of the ground. They said they would grow in strength as they got older, followed the spirits, and practiced more.

Lisa looked over at them. They were humming some old sounding tune she'd never heard before. Sheena and Sergio look so much more spiritual than the adults that sit like stone figures at church, Lisa thought. She began to look up at the sky.

There were millions of stars. More than she'd ever seen anywhere else. They looked almost like they were close enough to grab.

"Praise you God for creating such a glorious sight." She wondered what it was all for. She'd heard all the Bible stories since she was a child. God created the stars and the earth for his plan, whatever that meant. He had given us rule over the earth and everything in it. Why would he make everything so beautiful for us? she wondered.

Suddenly she was pulled back to what was happening there by an excited cry from Sheena. Sergio and Sheena were both about two feet in the air. They looked like they were lying flat but nothing was under them.

It was as if they were being held by gigantic hands and she could almost see the spirit cradling them as if they were babies. They both seemed to be talking with the being but not with their mouths. Their bodies, their minds, and their hearts were actively engaged. Lisa couldn't see what Sergio or Sheena could see.

Sergio saw himself holding the Pegasus under its neck with one hand and petting it with the other hand. The Pegasus sent thought into Sergio's mind, "Follow me and I will lead you into a rich and exciting life."

Sergio was a little unsure now and questioned, "What would I have to do?"

Pegasus reassured him, "I would never lead you into anything wrong for you." Sergio responded with a laugh of delight.

"If you will ask for direction, I will guide you always. I will show you how to be a powerful person. I will draw people to you. I will give you great wealth." promised the Pegasus.

Sheena was able to see herself getting on the back of the Pegasus and riding it over the whole earth. Before this she had only been on short rides. She was not leading it however.

She was fully submitted to where it would take her. She had given herself over to it and now she was ecstatic. An elder had told her no-one was ever able to get on the Pegasus and ride it anywhere.

She knew this meant she was special and would have a great deal more power than her elder had. As Pegasus carried Sheena over oceans, mountains, and plains, he promised, "I will take you higher than anyone before you. You have a great future in store. I will make you the high priestess of my following. Everyone who wants to come to me will have to come to you. You will lead them and guide them. I will give you the world."

Lisa was getting a little frightened. She had always been taught that it was wrong to worship anyone but the Lord God Almighty. Yet, she had never seen anything like this in even the most emotional of churches. The intrigue drew her in. She had heard some of the Pentecostals talk about seeing visions or having dreams, but no one she knew had ever floated while they were getting these visions. She began to feel a presence there with her on the blanket and prayed, "Oh Lord, help me," with a halfhearted cry. There was a strong desire in her to experience what Sergio and Sheena had. She would have never come with them if she hadn't desired their confidence.

Soon, Lisa felt as if a hand was on her back and she heard pleading thoughts in her mind, "Come to me and I will give you what you seek. I'll take you places you never knew and I'll teach you the mysteries of the universe." The thoughts continued to wash over her. Again and again Pegasus was calling to her.

She finally gave in, as to a persistent lover she no longer wanted to deny. The being enveloped her entirely and she felt it surrounding her with its large powerful presence. Slowly and gently, the spirit entered into her very soul and she knew she was his. She began to feel remarkably excited and the feelings grew into pure bliss as this spirit consumed her. "I am in love with him! Could that be right?" she thought. It was almost sunrise as the feeling began to diminish within her.

As the first streaks of dawn crested the east ridge she relaxed into the blanket. Lisa sensed a new feeling of satisfaction deeply within her.

She now had to go back to the meaningless world of normalcy. Yet now, like Sergio and Sheena, she would go back to normal life knowing that wasn't the whole sum of their lives. She couldn't wait until the next time she could meet with Sergio, Sheena, and her Pegasus.

Lisa remembered her family as the sun peaked over the highest range. They will never understand. They are strong Christians and will think this is horribly wrong and evil, she grieved. They had always worshiped Christ alone. For several generations they had all been Christians. Her aunts, uncles, and all her cousins were Christians. Most of her friends belonged to the church her family went to. She decided she had to keep this a secret life.

Surely as she grew in this she would someday be able to tell them, but not now. Today she could just rest and take it easy with Sergio and Sheena on top of Rebel Hill. It was beautiful. Maybe the most beautiful place in the world and she now knew bliss.

Lisa turned to where Sheena and Sergio lay on their blanket with another over them. They were sleeping soundly. Lisa wondered how long their love fest had lasted. The last time she had noticed them they were still two feet off the ground and completely enveloped by Pegasus.

Content to be there the rest of the day, she wrapped her blanket around her and lay beneath an Incense-cedar pine breathing in the delightful scent. The fallen pine needles were rounded, short, thick, and flat. Layers of the needles had gathered under the tree. They made the ground a little softer. Lisa looked at the tall tree that reached straight up towards heaven. "Thank you, God, for making such wonderful angels to be with us. Thank you for this enchanting place." she whispered. Lisa lay down and quickly drifted off to a deep sleep.

A few hours later, Sheena could feel the warmth of the sun radiating on her cheek. She smiled and slowly opened her eyes to see that the sun was a little to the right of the center of the sky. The sky was very light, almost white, blue.

No clouds floated above to soften the brilliance of the sun. It must be at least 10:30, Sheena thought. She stretched her right arm back while rolling over and reached for Sergio. His place was empty. She sat up to look around and saw Lisa asleep under a tree, but did not see Sergio. She continued to scan the area until she spotted him. On a large boulder, Sergio was preparing their breakfast.

The small fire pit next to the boulder had a simmering pot of hot water ready for hot chocolate and instant oatmeal. He set out the Styrofoam cups and bowls with plastic spoons. There in the center of the rock was the round dark brown wicker basket full of Gala apples that gleamed with the sunshine.

Sergio's face mirrored the bright morning. Sheena had not seen him so happy in several months. What had Pegasus shown him last night? she wondered. She knew not to question him, but she was curious how she would be leading someone as strong as Sergio. She questioned, why would Pegasus choose me instead of him?

Sheena scrambled to her feet and strolled up to him. Sergio's back was to her so she quietly slipped her arms around his waist. He turned towards her and embraced her. They stood holding each other without a word spoken for several minutes. As Sheena stepped back, Sergio gently brushed her long red hair from her face.

"Good morning, did you sleep well?" Sergio asked lovingly

"Never better. You?" Sheena replied cheerfully.

"Great, but not long enough," Sergio answered honestly.

"I could stay up here forever!" Sheena said wistfully as she took in the sight of her handsome man in the mountain top scenery.

"Me too. Breakfast is ready," he announced.

"I'll go wake up Lisa," she said and turned towards where Lisa lay sleeping. He gently pulled her back into himself not willing to let her go just yet. She gladly leaned back and relaxed against his strong chest. For a few minutes they just enjoyed each other.

Sergio released Sheena and said, "She looked pretty deep when I came back."

He smiled as he recalled, "It was still dark, but the moon was already way to the West."

"She was still in it when I came back too. Let's see how she is doing," she said thoughtfully. Sheena walked over and lightly tapped Lisa on the shoulder.

"Lisa, wake up. Breakfast is ready," Sheena said gently.

"Already, don't you guys sleep?" Lisa groaned

"Not as much as we used to." Sheena laughed. "Come on, get u p, and come eat."

"Sounds great. I could eat almost anything," Lisa admitted. Lisa hopped up and the girls headed over to the makeshift breakfast bar. Sergio had already fixed his and sat down on a smaller rock. There were five more of these rocks, perfect camp chair size, arranged in a circle. There was a larger circle of similar rocks surrounding the inner circle. Lisa had not seen these the night before hiding behind the big boulder. From their vantage point they could see down into the side of the valley which they had come through. Four huge knotted Blue Oaks spread their twisted branches over the circles, but the trees where just far enough apart to leave the center of the inner circle clear. Sergio envisioned building a fire pit there.

"So what do you think?" asked Sheena.

Lisa smiled and her face lit up. Then she looked down shyly. Sheena thought she could see traces of a blush. "It was the most fantastic rush I've ever felt," Lisa admitted.

"There is nothing like it," Sergio declared, "Believe me; I've tried just about everything."

"It gets better too," Sheena encouraged her, "The more you go there the more intense it gets."

"Now I know why you guys always seem so happy," Lisa said with a sense of new knowledge.

"We know where to go.......for everything," Sheena stated with absolute assurance.

"Pegasus promises to lead us through it all, if we will ask," said Sergio.

Lisa's smile turned down into a frown. Sheena looked back, tilted her head, and lowered her eyebrows into a questioning look.

10

Lisa furrowed her brow, and asked, "Do we have to come all the way up here? I mean it's beautiful and all but...."

"No, we can talk to Pegasus anywhere, anytime," Sheena answered with an understanding smile and then told her, "This is a special place though."

"Yeah, I feel him and all when I am other places, but up here...." Sergio leaned back, spreading his arms wide with a grin to match, and proclaimed, "...it's like nothing is holding me back."

"I get that too. I am totally free up here," Sheena agreed.

"Free from what? What is holding you back anywhere else?" Lisa intently questioned.

"You know; the everyday stuff," Sergio said.

"Oh yeah," Lisa acknowledged.

"It's not as easy to focus there," Sheena explained

"I get it," Lisa said as she thought of everything that made up her everyday life. She could see how it would be difficult to be in a spiritual mind set while going to school, playing a game, or simply being with friends and family.

"We better start packing up," Sergio said as he checked the time.

The three friends got up and began getting everything in the car. Lisa went one more time to the middle where she could see in all directions and she turned around slowly for one last view. Sheena walked up next to her. Sergio then joined them and they turned together, slowly, silently, taking in the beauty of this special place. Then, in unison without speaking a word, they quietly went to the car. As Lisa and Sheena climbed in, Sergio started the car. They began the drive down, ready to go back to face the everyday. Sheena looked back at Lisa an enjoyed the look of contentment upon Lisa's face.

Sheena thought back to the first experience with the spirits she could remember and smiled. She was only six years old. A bright light woke Sheena up.

Sheena could tell by the slow, deep breaths of her sister, Morgan was soundly sleeping. There at the end of her bed stood a woman. The woman was the light that lit up the room.

The rest of the room was still pitch black. Sheena became paralyzed with fear. She dare not move and draw attention to herself. She lay as still as she could, holding her breath, watching, waiting. The woman then looked into Sheena's fear filled eyes with gentleness. Though no sound was heard, Sheena could hear the woman say, "Do not be afraid." The thought and the "voice" in Sheena's mind were soothing, but still she did not move.

Suddenly, the woman was gone. "Wait! Who are you? Don't go." thought Sheena. There was no response. Although she was a little disappointed, she was also relieved.

Sheena slowly relaxed and went back to sleep. The next morning she thought to herself, it must have been a dream. She told no one about her dream.

A few days later, Morgan asked her, "Did you see what I saw last night?"

"No, I was asleep. What did you see?" Sheena asked curiously.

"I saw a woman with a child," Morgan replied.

"Where!?" Sheena asked with puzzled expression.

"In our room, right by the foot of your bed," said Morgan with a serious tone.

"You were just dreaming!" Sheena exclaimed.

"I was wide awake," Morgan declared emphatically with a hand on her hip. Then she explained, "I woke up because of the light"

"What light?" Sheena questioned. She was more curious than she wanted to show.

"The light from the woman and child, they were all white with light. They seemed so nice," Morgan answered as she remembered the pleasant experience.

Sheena became pale and Morgan knew Sheena had seen something. Morgan prodded her for more. "What did you see?"

"I thought it was a dream," Sheena said with shock.

"What was a dream?" asked Morgan.

"I saw the woman just like you described her," Sheena answered with surprise.

"I thought you said you were asleep," Morgan challenged with annoyance.

"Not last night, before, only the child wasn't with her," Sheena admitted.

"When?" asked Morgan as she leaned forward in anticipation.

"Oh, a few nights ago," Sheena explained. Then she seriously stated, "She spoke to me."

"You heard her talk." Morgan said with a tone of disbelief.

"In my head, not my ears," Sheena tried to clarify, "She told me not to be afraid." She added as she recalled the meeting, "She had kind eyes too."

"What else did she say?" Morgan probed for more.

"Nothing. She left," Sheena said with an unmistakable disappointment in her voice.

Morgan stopped questioning Sheena and the two girls sat quietly on their beds for several minutes until they heard their mother calling them to breakfast. Neither of them talked about what they had seen in their room with anyone else in the family. As they walked to school, the two sisters talked again of their visitors.

"Maybe they are angels." Morgan said.

"You're probably right," Sheena agreed, "Ghosts aren't that nice."

"Except Casper." The girls giggled.

"Maybe it is your mom," Morgan said more thoughtfully a few minutes later.

"What do you mean?" Sheena asked.

"Maybe she can come from Heaven to watch over you now," Morgan said with a sense of hopefulness.

"Maybe," Sheena replied hopeful, but unsure.

"That must be why she stands by your bed and not mine," reasoned Morgan.

"Do you think so?" Sheena asked hoping for Morgan to be right. She really admired how smart Morgan was.

"She talked to you too," Morgan's reasoning continued.

"But were you really scared when you saw them?" Sheena asked sincerely.

"A little, but she didn't talk to me," Morgan admitted and then questioned, "Didn't Mom and Dad tell you that your mother had a baby that had died?"

"Yeah," Sheena's head dropped, "They said the baby died before it was born. The baby was born dead," Sheena confirmed.

"Well....that is the one that looks like a child," Morgan continued with self-assurance in her reasoning.

"You think so?" Sheena said doubtfully.

"What else could it be?" Morgan challenged Sheena to give another explanation.

"You're right," Sheena agreed a few minutes later when she couldn't think of any other reason, "Wow! My mom is watching over us. That's pretty cool," she declared.

"Yeah, really cool," agreed Morgan as she took off running. "Last one to the crosswalk is a rotten egg!" Morgan yelled back as she bolted towards the crossing guard.

Sheena yelled, "Not me," and began running as fast as she could. She barely caught Morgan as the crossing guard smiled at the girls and said, "Good Morning." The girls both panted a greeting in return.

They never really talked about the bright white lady or child again. With the simplicity of childhood, they simply accepted what had happened. Sheena often looked back to that memory with fondness and sadness. It was the beginning of a new and exciting world that she was privileged to be a part of. It was also one of the last meaningful memories of her sister who'd died just a couple of years later. Her family had not been the same since.

Sheena's thoughts jumped to memories of times she tried to talk to friends about the spirits. She had found as she became older that not everyone could see the spirits. She had to be careful. Now, she was to lead the people Pegasus led her to. She was to show them, teach them.

Sheena looked over at Sergio. He had also known the spirits since he was a child. Their meeting must have been on purpose. It simply could not have been an accident. She admired him. He was strong; he had moved all those large stones into the circle himself. She enjoyed watching him work. Even now as he drove them home, Sheena enjoyed watching him. He looked so relaxed. His muscles rippled gently, almost effortlessly, under his bronze skin. The serene look in his deep dark brown eyes as he focused on the road drew her in. She wondered what was running through his mind as he maneuvered the car around one curve and then another.

Sergio kept his mind focused on the road. He looked ahead about half a mile and then quickly back to the road only a few feet in front of him. Occasionally, he glanced in the rear view mirror, just in case. Then back again to the distance. He loved to drive the windy mountain roads. It was a challenge to keep the ride smooth and not over use the brakes.

Sergio felt Sheena watching him. He looked over, smiled, and then looked back to the road. He thought I am the luckiest guy in the world. With her reassuring smile, he knew that everything was right.

He was glad the ladies were content and quiet right now. He didn't want to try to talk. He couldn't quit thinking about the night before. He was excited about the promise Pegasus had made to him. "I will follow you," he silently declared, "I will follow you anywhere."

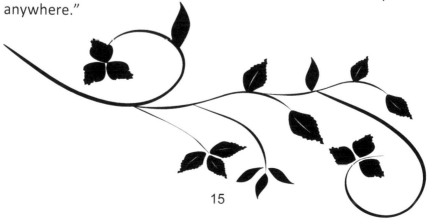

CHAPTER 2

"Good morning sleepy head. It's time to get up," Lisa's mom, Tina, said in a sing song voice, "Come on now. You have to get going....You must have been up late last night....Well you'll have to go to bed early tonight......Let's go. The sun is shining and you should be too."

The room, bright with sunlight, was shocking to Lisa as the covers suddenly pulled away from her face. She blinked her eyes and groaned. Her mother's voice seemed distant, but her voice was persistent and running out of patience. "Lisa, get up. You're going to be late."

"What time is it?" Lisa half moaned.

"7:15" Tina stated.

"Oh no!" she cried. Lisa jumped out of bed and scrambled to the bathroom. Within fifteen minutes she was running down the stairs and heading out the door. As she quickly walked to school, she was thinking about her new friends. She had so many questions and her emotions were a tangled ball of twine. How did they meet the Pegasus? Could I learn to float like that? Were there other things they could do? What would the Pegasus give me? Should I tell anyone else? What about my parents? How can I keep them from finding out? They will kill me. When can I meet with Pegasus again? How come it felt so wonderful to let him in? Were there others who worshiped this way? What were they like? Where did Pegasus come from?

16

Her mind was reeling with curiosity, guilt, fear, bliss, and amazement. She had to be cool though. She couldn't just start drilling them with questions. She would just wait for the right time and ask one here or there, space them out. Lisa was so wrapped up in her thoughts she walked right passed her best friend.

Maria reached out for her, smacked her on the shoulder, and demanded, "Hey! What's up?!"

Lisa looked at her with a blank stare for a few seconds and then replied, "Sorry, I was just thinking."

"About what?" Maria asked.

"Nothing" Lisa replied, but she couldn't hide the anxiousness in her voice.

"Are you nervous about the test?" Maria empathetically questioned her.

"Yeah, I forgot to study," Lisa answered with some conviction. It was at least half true, and she didn't have to lie to her best friend. She was relieved.

"You always do really well on the tests. You don't have to study," Maria encouraged.

"That's what you think. What about you?" Lisa replied.

"I studied, but I still don't get it." Maria said with desperation.

"What part?" Lisa asked.

"All of it. I'm lost." Maria responded with hopelessness.

"Sorry." Lisa stated, dropping her head in shame.

"That's ok." Maria replied. Then she curiously asked, "Where were you this weekend?"

"Camping" Lisa said, picking up her head and smiling in remembrance.

"You're mom said you were with friends. Who'd you go with?" Maria pried a little more.

"Sergio and Sheena," Lisa replied nonchalantly.
"When did you start hanging out with them?" Maria questioned, putting her hands on her hips and tilting her head.

"First time," Sheena clarified.

"How was it?" Maria asked with just a hint of sadness in her voice.

"It was beautiful." Lisa replied as she looked up in the sky, saw the place in her mind's eye and remembered the experience. Lisa did not catch the tone in Maria's voice and began to describe Rebel Hill and how it seemed as if she could have just grabbed one of the millions of stars. Yet, Lisa was careful to avoid anything about Pegasus. It felt strange keeping something from Maria. They had shared everything since third grade. Maria's expression of disappointment became painfully obvious. Lisa suddenly was aware she had promised Maria she would help her that weekend with math. Her smile turned down and with remorse she stated, "I'm sorry. I forgot."

"It's alright. I probably wouldn't have gotten it anyway," Maria responded with a shrug and a slight frown she added, "I just wish they would have invited me, but that'll never happen."

"You don't know that," Lisa retorted.

"People like them don't hang out with people like me," Maria's head dropped as she stated what she just accepted as fact now.

"They hung out with me," Lisa said in an attempt to encourage her.

Maria replied shaking her head back and forth, "They'll never give me the time of day."

"Maybe they will. I will introduce you," Lisa said cheerfully.

"You'll get dropped," Maria sadly stated.

"They're not like that!" Lisa retorted, unusually defensive.

"You'll see," Maria said looking her best friend directly in the eyes as if it were already true.

"You just don't want me to have any other friends." Lisa shouted. Then, Lisa turned around throwing her head and shoulders back and stomped off towards class.

Maria dropped her head and walked slowly, stiffly, and with a slight limp in the same direction. Her best friend was going to leave her behind, just like everyone else. She wished she could stomp off angrily and leave Lisa behind.

Lisa couldn't believe Maria was acting like that. She doesn't know them. They're different. She'll see. Maybe I won't introduce her. That'll teach her. Maybe Pegasus could help her. Jesus certainly hadn't. The thoughts screamed through Lisa's mind the way she had screamed at Maria. Lisa was angry.

She was angry at Maria for accusing her friends. She was angry at her parents for lying to her. She was angry that she had to be in school right now. She was angry at Jesus or the people who made up the Jesus story. Suddenly she stopped dead in her tracks. Parents lying? Angry at Jesus? Made up? Lisa felt confused. Why? The warning bell rang and Lisa was jolted from her train of thought. Back to every day, she thought, Pegasus, they said you'd help with the everyday. Please help. She was no longer angry but she was already tired and class had just barely begun. Lisa quickly slid into her seat as the tardy bell was ringing.

Sheena was sitting across from her and asked in a concerned whisper, "Are you okay?" Lisa nodded she was. Sheena whispered, "We'll talk at lunch," because the teacher had begun discussing the day's assignments.

Each class seemed to drag on for hours rather than the forty five minutes they were scheduled. Although Lisa was usually interested in school, today the teachers sounded like the "Peanuts" teacher… "Waaa wawa waaa wa wa waaaa." She could not focus on anything being said. Her mind was spinning with the thoughts she had encountered that morning. As the lunch bell rang she thought, Thank God, and she walked to the cafeteria as if she had been beat relentlessly the night before. Her head down and exhaustion overwhelming her, it was all she could do to walk.

Sheena watched her walk in the cafeteria door and was worried. She had never seen someone so down after meeting with Pegasus. What in the world is wrong with her? Is she sick? Sheena thought. Sheena walked over to her and gently asked, "Do you want me to get your lunch?" Lisa said, "Sure," and sat down at a table in the back of the room, away from everyone else.

While Sheena was getting Lisa's lunch, Maria walked in and pretended not to see Lisa. Maria was still hurt and angry with Lisa. She got in the lunch line without even looking at Lisa. Once she had her lunch she went to the quad outside and ate lunch alone.

Lisa was so wrapped up in her own thoughts she never noticed Maria coming in or leaving the cafeteria. Sheena returned with Lisa's lunch and sat down next to her.

The two girls ate together, quietly talking about all that was running through Lisa's mind. By the time lunch was over, Lisa felt better. She did not have all the answers to her questions, but she knew Sheena was going to help her learn to reach Pegasus at any time. Sheena promised Pegasus would help her with the questions and everything else she wanted to know or do. They agreed to meet right after school, under the big white oak tree, on the east side of the campus. There they would be free to talk and pray. No one hung out over there, and Sheena had met with Pegasus there many times. The place had become a sacred ground.

Lisa was able to focus a lot better in the last three classes. Yet, this day she was excited and interested in one thing only. Meeting with Pegasus again was the only thing she cared about.

Maria could see Lisa was pre-occupied and with the morning's argument fresh on her mind she decided to leave Lisa alone. Maria thought, this is just something she's going to have to work out on her own. I am not going to be her charity case or beg for her friendship. I will just make friends with someone else too. Maria glanced around the classroom thinking about who she might befriend. What girl in the class would be willing to hang out with me and not make fun of me or play mean tricks on me? she wondered.

She spotted a girl who had just recently started attending their school. She looked smart and nice. She had not won a spot in the popular crowd right away. That was a good sign. I will ask her if she wants to get some ice cream together before we go home.

Maria looked back over at Lisa, and gave her a "Whatever" look when Lisa half smiled at her.

Lisa knew Maria was hurt, but she figured Maria would come around. The bell rang and Maria got up, turned away from Lisa immediately, and walked over to the new girl.

Lisa smiled, grabbed her bag, and headed for the oak tree. Lisa had to wait about ten minutes for Sheena to get there. She laid back on the grass, looked up at the sky, and asked, "God are you there? Jesus, are you real? Or are you just a made up story? Why would my parents and so many other adults lie to me? I know Pegasus is real now. I have seen him and felt him. Yet, I have never felt anything different when I was in church. I have never felt like that when I prayed to you Lord. I have never heard you answer me. Why? If you are real, are you even listening?"

Finally, Lisa heard footsteps rustling through the grass. She sat up and saw Sheena just a couple of feet away. "What took you so long?" Lisa was unable to hide the stress in her voice.

Sheena looked at her sympathetically and answered, "I had to talk to Mr. Hernandez about the science project."

"I was beginning to think you forgot," Lisa replied.

Sheena's eyes grew as big as saucers and she shook her head back and forth exclaiming, "No way! You need help,"

"That bad?" Lisa half smiled at her response.

"You looked like something the cat drug in at lunch. I have never seen anyone so down before. You look a lot better now though." Sheena smiled a soft, kindness showing through her eyes.

"It was a pretty rough morning. I have never been so confused or angry," Lisa admitted.

"Well then, let me show you how to call out to Pegasus so he will come and help you," Sheena replied as she put her hand gently on Lisa's shoulder.

"Okay." Lisa replied.

Sheena dropped her back pack at the base of the tree and sat on her knees. Lisa copied her. "First, hold out your hands like you're getting water from the facet without a cup." Sheena held out her hands in a cupped position and Lisa followed without saying a word.

"Then, picture a lake or pond in your mind. Reach the water with your hands and fill them up. Imagine you are drinking the water and then say, "Pegasus please come, share with me your water. Fill up my empty hands." Sheena watched Lisa go through the motions and said, "Now do this until you can see the Pegasus standing there by the lake." Lisa continued going through the chant and motions for about two minutes. She was getting frustrated. Sheena said, "Stay calm or you will miss him."

Lisa sighed and whined, "How long do I have to do this?" Sheena hesitated, took a slow deep breath, and then calmly said, "Until you see him. He may not be able to get to you right away. Your own frustration and confusion may be blocking your spirit's ability to go there."

Lisa cried in anguish, "Please Pegasus, come to me. I cannot go to you yet." Suddenly, she could see the Pegasus in her mind. The image was not sharp but she could see. "I can see him," she stated with excitement.

Sheena smiled with relief and replied, "Good. Now ask him to help you with these questions."

As Lisa began communing with Pegasus, Sheena relaxed and began her own meditation. Lisa began throwing all the questions and thoughts that had ran through her mind that day to Pegasus.

Pegasus nodded and told Lisa to slow down. "I will reveal the answers to you, one at a time. You must be patient and trust me."

Lisa agreed and said, "Okay, then tell me first, why would my parents lie to me?" This was the thought that had plagued her the most. This was what made her angrier than any of the other thoughts or questions.

"They told you about Santa Claus," Pegasus simply stated.

Lisa suddenly felt a calm overtake her troubled mind. They had told her about Santa Claus. The whole world told little children the story and even had people dress up like him.

They did this to convince children to be good, so they would get presents. Was this the same thing as telling children about Jesus, she wondered. They did the same thing with the Easter Bunny. She mused, they sure go to a lot of trouble for these fairy tales. They do the same thing with Jesus, so we will be good. Lisa thanked Pegasus and reached out to pet him.

"That is a good girl." Pegasus whispered to her, "You are so smart. I will be able to teach you many things. You must go now." Pegasus backed up and quickly flew away. Lisa opened her eyes. She felt good now. It was as if a whole new world was opening up to her.

Sheena looked over at Lisa, her eyes questioning.

Lisa smiled and assured her, "I feel so much better now." Sheena let out a sigh of relief as they got up and headed home.

"So any time I need to talk to him I just do that chant?" Lisa asked with uncertainty.

"That's right, you meditate. As time goes on it will get easier to reach that place in the spirit realm," Sheena assured her.

"How long have you been with Pegasus?" Lisa inquired

"About 5 years," Sheena stated and then added, "He was not the first spirit I talked to."

"There are others? How many?" Lisa asked amazed.

"More than we can count. It would be like trying to count all the people in the world that had ever lived." Sheena told Lisa in a matter of fact tone.

Lisa was intrigued. "Why did you choose to follow Pegasus?" she asked curiously.

"Really, I think he chose me," Sheena confessed.

"What do you mean?" Lisa asked.

"You have an incredible curiosity. That will help you go far, but you need to be careful," Sheena cautioned.

"Why?"

"Not all spirits are good," Sheena's eyes furrowed, and her mouth straightened.

She stopped, put her hand on Lisa's shoulder, looking her straight in the eye, and said, "Some are out to hurt us or others." Then she turned and began walking again.

Lisa stood still for a few seconds as she took in what had been shared, then double timed her steps to catch up. "How do you know which ones are good?" Lisa, somewhat bewildered, asked.

"They reveal themselves pretty quickly." Sheena replied.

"So what did you mean...about Pegasus choosing you?" Lisa asked intently.

Sheena looked at Lisa for a moment, wondering if she were really ready for all of this. Yet, in many ways it was too late to back up. Lisa had already experienced the reality of Pegasus. Sheena thought maybe the more of her questions I can answer, the easier she'll adjust to all of this. She determined to answer as many of her questions as possible.

"We can ask them to come and show us, but it is their choice."

"How was I chosen?" Lisa questioned.

"Pegasus told me to invite you," Sheena replied calmly.

"Why? What does he want me for? I am nobody," Lisa responded in bewilderment.

Sheena smiled and encouraged, "He sees something special in you. Maybe it's your questioning. I don't really know."

"Will he tell me, or you?" Lisa curiously asked.

"He will....when you're ready."

"When I'm ready? Lisa threw her arms up in exasperation, "How will we know when that happens?" Lisa replied.

"He will know." She was relieved to see a soda shop and take the conversation a different direction. "Hey let's stop for some ice cream.....my treat," Sheena excitedly changed the subject as the idea crossed her mind. She liked Lisa's inquisitiveness, but she didn't feel truly prepared to teach someone else just yet.

"Cool." Lisa responded enthusiastically.

They turned and went into the place.

The building had been built in the late 1950's about two years after the school had been finished. The shop was kept in the fifties style. The outside of the old hangout was painted a clean basic white. The floor was a checker board pattern with black and white tiles. A few feet in front of the doorway was a long wrap around bar surrounded with chrome barstools. The barstools were topped with a thick pad covered with pink vinyl. The bar ran the entire length of the
shop and gave the inside an L shape. There was one break in the bar for the waitress to go back and forth between the tables and kitchen. The kitchen order window was to the left end of the bar, just behind the break in the bar.

The front wall was lined with large windows and booths. The pink vinyl was trimmed at the base with a chrome molding. The booths were just big enough for four people to sit together. Because the L shape made the right side wider, there was space for a dance floor.

Of course, just beside the dance floor was an antique juke box. The owner kept many of the popular 50's songs in the juke box, but he also had the top 40 songs of the previous year.

The shop was busy as usual shortly after school. This was the closest and coolest place for everyone to hang out. All the booths were filled and so were most of the barstools. There were a lot of teens hanging out in the parking lot, sitting on their cars. Some of the girls were going from one table to another, talking to almost everyone. Someone had put some money in the juke box. The old thing still had a decent sound. Several couples were dancing. Sheena and Lisa headed for the barstools at the end of the counter. Maria and Lisa spotted each other simultaneously. Lisa turned to Sheena and said, "Hey, I want you to meet someone." Sheena looked a little concerned and Lisa assured her, "I haven't told her." Sheena smiled and the two girls walked over to Maria's table. Maria was shocked but gracious.

"Maria this is Sheena, Sheena this is Maria," Lisa said proudly as she remembered the conversation that morning.

"Hi. It's nice to meet you?" Sheena said genuinely with a friendly smile.

"Same here," Maria replied with a pleasantly surprised smile. Then she held her hand out towards her new friend and said, "This is Tenicia."

"Hi." all three of the other girls said at the same time.

"Do you guys want to join us?" Maria asked.

Lisa looked at Sheena, and Sheena replied, "Sure."

"So Tenicia, you're new to the school right?" Lisa asked.

"Yeah, we just moved here about a month ago," Tenicia answered.

"Where from?" asked Sheena.

"San Diego." Tenicia replied without much thought.

"Wow! I would love to live in San Diego," Lisa said as her gaze turned out the window in a daydream.

"I miss it." Tenicia admitted with a hint of sadness.

Maria jumped in to the conversation asking, "Where you guys close to the beach?"

"Naw, we lived about ten miles away." Tenicia replied.

Sheena thought a minute and said, "I bet the shopping is awesome there."

Her eyes rolled and her her lips pursed, Lisa said with disdain, "Anything would beat this little town."

Tenicia thought a moment and responded, "I don't know. We sure didn't have a place like this so close to school." She had become rather fond of the quaint little city which felt so safe.

"Are any of you going to the baseball game?" Sheena asked with excitement.

"I am. Charlie's playing. He is sooooo cute." Maria gushed.

"That third baseman is pretty hot too." Tenicia added.

"Tenicia, if you go, I'll introduce you." Maria said slyly.

"Maria......*You* know Isaac?" Lisa's face showed her surprise. How did she not know this? Suddenly, she didn't feel so bad she had gone camping without her. She felt like she could keep some things from Maria now.

Maria grinned, and with a tone that implied it's not a big deal, she confessed, "We're neighbors. He's like a brother." She also felt a sense of satisfaction that Lisa didn't know everything about her.

Sheena grinned and said, "Too bad for you he's not more like a 'kissing cousin." The girls began giggling. Then she suggested, "Hey, we should all go."

"That would be awesome!" The girls chimed in agreement.

"I could get Sergio to pick us up," Sheena offered.

"Could you? That would rock." Lisa replied with excitement.

The girls agreed to call each other later that night to make plans. Maria was surprised that Sheena was so nice. Lisa grinned at Maria with a "See, I told you." Look. Maria felt bad for misjudging her. Maria nodded just a little so only Lisa caught it. Maria was still glad she had invited Tenicia though. She had thought about it a time or two, but had been too afraid. Maria knew it was right to make someone new feel welcome, but she thought Lisa might get jealous or Tenicia would laugh at her. Tenicia looked like she would be one of the "untouchables". Maria was surprised they hadn't been all over Tenicia.

Lisa was glad that Sheena was so cool with Maria. She didn't want to lose her best friend.

Lisa also thought it was amazing that Sheena was able to keep the conversation about normal stuff. It was as if she just turned off the water spout and walked away. Lisa thought, I hope it doesn't take me long to learn to do that. She could barely think of anything but Pegasus now. Lisa knew it would be hard to keep something so major a secret from Maria for long, but she must keep it as long as she could. Having others around her would help.

Lisa's train of thought was suddenly broken as she heard Maria saying, "Well I've got to go. I can't be late. My mom will ground me." Everyone got up from the table, paid the cashier, and began walking home. They all lived in the same neighborhood so they walked together for the first few blocks talking about school, hair, their families, etc. One by one they turned off onto their streets. Sheena lived two more streets past Lisa, so the two of them walked the last part alone.

Lisa told Sheena how glad she was that the Sheena had been so cool with Maria. She told Sheena how they had been best friends since the third grade when she had stood up for Maria.

Another girl was making fun of Maria for the way she walked. Lisa couldn't take it anymore. She felt so bad for Maria. The two girls became very close after that. They did everything together.

Sheena listened silently as they walked the last two blocks before Lisa's street. Finally, just before Lisa had to turn down her street, Sheena said kindly, "I think it's great you two are such good friends. Wait to tell her about Pegasus though. She's not ready."

Lisa agreed and then asked, "When can you teach me more?" The two agreed to meet under the sacred oak every day, right after school. Lisa said "See you later." and turned to the left.

Sheena replied, "Later gator." and kept walking towards her street. Sheena kept thinking about Maria and Tenicia. She had the feeling Maria would not be ready for a long time, but Tenicia on the other hand. There was something there. She asked Pegasus, "Is she one?" but heard no reply. She had been with Pegasus long enough to know that silence did not mean anything but to wait; for the answer would be clear soon enough.

With Lisa and Maria being friends, Lisa might be able to bring her in slowly.

But she would try to keep Lisa from it until Lisa was ready for whichever way Maria would respond. She was not expecting to be the teacher so soon, but she knew she must do her best and rely on Pegasus to help her. "The spirits reveal themselves to us."

Sheena was now a little nervous about Maria but she didn't know why. There was certainly something different about Maria, and it was not her limp. Yet, Sheena could not quite figure out what the difference was.

Sergio left Automart rushing home to call Sheena. The thing he missed most about high school was spending more time with her. He could hardly wait to hear her voice. He was looking forward to the game tonight as well. He missed playing ball too. Watching the game was not as fun, but the team this year was hot. They were heading into the league playoffs on top.

He figured it would probably never happen again either. Five of his team mates had been offered full ride scholarships and were now playing at college.

He thought about his team mates. We were incredible together. I wonder how they are doing this year. If my rotator cuff had not ripped, I would be at UCLA or U.C. Santa Cruz. I am so glad Pegasus helped me through that. He told me then he had a better plan. Now he is promising me power, wealth, and an exciting life. I wonder what could be more exciting than playing pro-ball, he mused as he pulled into the driveway. I better hurry now. I need to pick up Sheena before the game.

After a quick shower and phone call, he was rushing back out the door to pick up *all* the girls. His remaining friends would be glad to see him.

As they pulled into the parking lot at the stadium, Sergio spotted Mark, now a junior, and pulled in next to him. Mark and the other boys grinned as the girls poured out of the back seat of the Mustang. This game was looking more interesting by the second. The group joked and laughed as they headed into the stadium. They were there at a good time and were able to get a great section on the third row of the bleachers.

They talked about everything from who they thought would win tonight to which teacher was the worst. At last, the crowd was called to stand for the National Anthem. Finally, the familiar shout came, "Play Ball!"

Mark looked at Lisa. He was thrilled to be sitting next to her. He had noticed her at the beginning of the year in Geometry. He remembered the way she looked the first day. Her sleek blonde hair ran to the middle of her back. She had a black velvet headband keeping her hair out of her face. She wore a pink dress with the puffy sleeves. When someone called her from the back of the room and she turned around, the glimmer in her brown eyes and the sweet smile on her face made her seem like an angel. She sat in the front and middle. She was smart, but not stuck up.

She seemed kind and willing to help anyone in class. Now she was here sitting next to him.

"STRIKE 2!" yelled the umpire, shattering Mark's thoughts. He looked to see who was up to bat. Oh good, he thought, it's the other team. He watched intently now as the pitcher wound up and released the ball. Wow, that ball must be going 80 miles an hour, he thought.

There's no way this batter is going to.....Crack! The ball went flying to deep left of center field! The center fielder was running with all his might to get out there and catch the pop fly. The short stop had moved to cover second as the second baseman was set for the relay through. The batter rounded first, running straight for second. He didn't look to see where the ball was or if they could catch it. He stayed focused on second and bolted even faster.

The center fielder had been able to get under the ball and it looked as if it were a sure catch. Suddenly he turned his head slightly. As he tried to dodge the glare of the sun in his eyes, his glove dropped a tiny bit. No one could even tell his glove had dropped, but the ball slipped out of his grasp and fell to the ground. Now, the runner was heading for third. The center fielder recovered quickly and threw hard to the second baseman. They could not let this guy get a home run.

The crowd in the bleachers was on their feet screaming, "Throw home! Throw home! Stop him!" A small crowd on the other side of the diamond was cheering the runner on. He had rounded third and was going for home. The second baseman threw to the shortstop and he quickly turned to throw it home.

The catcher was just in front of the base, ready for the ball. The ball was rapidly approaching the catcher, as was the runner. It was too close to call from the bleachers. The runner started into a slide just as the catcher received the ball. The catcher quickly turned to tag the runner and got him just inches before the runner's feet touched the plate. "Out!" yelled the umpire. The crowd was wild with excitement. The boys in the dugout were jumping and cheering with the crowd. This was going to be a great game!

The team was good, yet they still couldn't touch his senior year, he determined. No other team had ever gone to the playoffs undefeated in the history of the school.

As everyone sat down again and the next batter stepped up to take the plate, Mark determined he would ask Lisa to the dance on Friday. He took the opportunity while everyone was still talking and he tapped her on the shoulder.

Her beautiful face gleamed with the excitement of the game. He asked her, "What are you doing Friday?"

She told him she didn't have any plans. So he quickly asked her to go with him to the dance, before he lost his nerve. She just looked at him for a moment, like she didn't hear him. She was shocked he was asking her out. She nodded her head yes and said she would as a pink blush spread across her round cheeks. She turned her eyes back to the field. They watched the game together, but hardly said a word after that. By the time she made it home, she was elated yet exhausted. This day had been full of so many wonderful things. None of this would have been as wonderful without having met Pegasus, she thought. As she went to sleep that night, she marveled at the day. She had gone through every feeling imaginable. She went from agony to happiness to excitement to a feeling of tranquility. She had never felt more alive.

CHAPTER 3

The bright warm sunshine streaming through the window stirred Sergio from his sleep. He looked at the clock and saw that it was 6:00 am. It was going to be hot today. The guys are home for summer vacation, he thought. Sergio called up his old team and made plans to go hiking together. He thought it would be just like old times and was looking forward to hanging out with them again. They agreed to meet at 9:00. Sergio was glad he had bought the Bronco.

The Bronco was only a couple of years old and in great condition. He couldn't wait for the guys to see it. The body was shaped like a pick-up truck with a seamless permanent camper shell. This Bronco was an "Eddie Bauer Edition." The two tone paint job had drawn him in. The maroon red with the tan trim on the bottom looked sharp. The interior was just as stylish as the exterior. The back seats even reclined. They would fit comfortably with plenty of leg and head room. The storage compartment in the center console was a great place for his favorite cassette tapes. They could rock out all the way up the mountain. The Bronco had a 351 W six cylinder. This was enough power although he would love to have more. The SUV burned more gas than his Mustang, but with the four wheel drive it was perfect for driving in the forest.

The guys loved the Bronco just like Sergio thought they would. The ride was surprisingly smooth even off road.

With the cassette tapes playing their favorite songs from last year, they reminisced the great times on the drive up. Now they were ready to catch up on current events. As they scrambled out onto the flat, the young men were excited to start the 8 mile climb to the top of the mountain.

Aaron asked David, "So what are you majoring in?"

David replied, "Engineering. What about you?"

"Business. I think I want to start my own someday," said Aaron thoughtfully, then he asked, "How did you do on finals?"

"Awesome!" David replied proudly, "They were pretty brutal though. A few guys think they failed," he added for emphasis.

"What kind of business do you want to start?" Sergio asked Aaron.

"I'm not sure yet, but I know I want to own one," Aaron replied.

The guys continued to catch up as they made the climb. As they neared the middle of the mountain, Sergio began to feel like something was wrong. He couldn't quite figure out what it was, but something was not right.

He began looking around to find the reason he was getting such a bad feeling. Everything seemed to be normal. He focused on the forest sounds. He could not hear anything that would make a dangerous situation either. He began looking at the ridge to the east of them.

He could see a boy and his dad about midway up the mountain right next to the one they were climbing. Suddenly he saw huge granite boulders crashing down on the pair like a movie playing before him. He shook his head and looked again. They were fine. No rocks falling. Yet, the sense of danger was stronger than ever. He looked up at the top of the mountain. It was granite. He saw that there had been rock falls before. There were boulders all over the side of the mountain. The forest grew up in between them. There were several places where the crashing boulders had stripped wide swaths through the Evergreens. The man and his son were reaching the granite strewn forest.

Sergio began yelling and waving his arms wildly. The pair looked over at him and could barely make out what he was screaming. "Run! Run!" Sergio shouted repetitively. The man looked up the mountain to see what was causing such a reaction from this kid on the opposite ridge.

Suddenly a gigantic slab broke loose from the mountain. The first crash was deafening. The granite broke into several massive pieces. The man grabbed his son and ran to the closest boulder from a previous slide. The boulder had some fallen trees piled in front of it. The trees had formed a bit of a cave beside the enormous stone. The man pushed his son into the shelter and shoved himself in behind the boy. The tumbling pieces of slab thundered through the forest. Terrified, they crouched together, covering their ears inside this retreat. They all hoped it would be enough protection from the falling rocks. The guys were frozen in place as they watched helplessly. They could do nothing, but wait.

As they stared at the immense rocks crashing down the mountain side, they could hardly breathe. They saw the towering trees broken like toothpicks. They knew if one of those huge boulders hit the hiding place just right, the pair could be crushed. Several stones hit the tree cave and kept rolling. The shelter seemed to be strong, but would it be strong enough?

Josh implored, "Sergio, let's go get help. I noticed a ranger station on the way up."

Sergio refused boldly, "No. I need to stay here."

"Come on! They're going to need help!" Josh pleaded.

"I know." Sergio calmly replied.

"We can't do anything for them if we just stand and watch," Josh added with bewilderment at Sergio's seemingly stubborn nonsense.

"I'm staying here," Sergio replied coolly.

"Are you insane?! Come on! Let's go!" Josh exclaimed.

Without even looking him in the eyes, Sergio held out his keys to the Bronco he was so proudly showing off just a couple of hours ago and said firmly, "Here. Go."

Josh grabbed the keys from Sergio. He looked at David and Aaron. They both were fixated on the thunder storm of granite.

34

Josh turned and began the descent alone. He weaved through the trees at a full run. He had become the hunted deer, running for his life. His heart raced with fear for the man and boy. He could not understand why Sergio would stay. What could they do just watching and waiting? He thought. David and Aaron were in shock. They were useless, but Sergio consciously chose to stay. He simply could not understand why. He knew he had to focus on getting to the station now. He knew he had to get help. It didn't matter what the others were doing, he assured himself.

Sergio became focused on a particularly colossal rock that was increasing in speed as it rolled through the previously stripped swath straight towards the man and his son. Sergio stretched out his hand and pushed all his energy over the trees protecting the pair. Neither of the guys could believe what they saw next. The boulder hit an invisible bubble and bounced over the burrow. The stone smashed into five large rocks when it landed just a few feet from the hideaway. The new smaller boulders kept rolling. The force felled forest foliage. Several trees splintered into tender that would fuel the next fire.

Hopefully, the boy and his father were still uninjured. Sergio suddenly sat down. His strength was gone. He could not even watch the rest of the slide. He dropped his head to knees and prayed. Pegasus was his only source now.

Josh was making good time. He reached the Bronco in 20 minutes. Boom! He shuddered and almost dropped the keys. The incredibly large boom shook the forest. His hands were now shaking as he strived to open the door. He got the door open and jumped into the driver's seat. In his urgency, he raced the engine as he started the Bronco. He could still hear rock plummeting down like a giant hail storm. What about the pair in the middle of the squall, he wondered, would they survive? How bad would it be? He threw the Bronco into gear and raced back down the mountain.

The roaring rock slide began to subside. As the forest became eerily quiet, Sergio could feel his vigor returning. When they could see that Sergio was okay, Aaron and David said in unison, "Let's go." The three boys began working their way over to the pair now trapped in their cavern. The gang had to climb down the mountain they were on, cross a small stream, and climb up to the father/son team. Debris covered the refuge. The guys did not speak. There were no words. They could only hope the man and boy were okay.

Josh was just pulling into the parking lot of the ranger station as the other guys moved towards the wreckage. He ran inside, and with a trembling voice, described the horrific scene he had left behind. Though the rangers did not say it out loud, they were sure of what they would find. No one could survive one of those rock slides. None the less there was a job to do.

The chief ranger began organizing his crew. The rangers assured Josh that he had done the right thing. They sent him to a waiting room in the back, and gave him some water and trail mix. One ranger stayed with Josh to calm him down and get as much information as possible. The helicopter crew was ready in 15 minutes.

The trio made it to the bottom of their ridge and looked up the mountain before them. Instinctively, they took a break and rummaged in their backpacks for something to eat. They sat together quietly. They still had no words.

The three knew they must get to the two trapped people on the side of this mountain. Just as soon as they finished a few handfuls of trail mix and jerky, they began the climb. It only took about forty minutes to make it to the site. Having been a team before, they knew how to work together. They were no longer individuals. They became a unit. The three of them began dragging away brush and rolling away stones. It would not take them long to uncover the refuge. However, there was a sense of dread. They were not sure what they would find once they uncovered the cave. Aaron paused and looked at the sky.

The sun would be dropping behind the western ridges within another three hours. Even if they uncovered the hole, they would be descending in the dark, possibly with two injured people.

36

It would get cool in the night air. If the man and the boy were hurt, they might go into shock. Sergio wondered where Josh was. Had he made it to the ranger station? Would there be more help on the way? He kept working with his team. They had to get to the boy and his father. Relief came quickly. They could hear the man and boy. Aaron shouted to them, "Are you alright?" The man affirmed they were okay. This gave the guys renewed energy. They would be releasing two people that were alive instead of unburying the dead.

The boy stood up and looked at his father. The man could almost stand in their small safe haven. Amazingly, they were unharmed. The father hugged his son and assured him, "We will get out of here soon. They heard us. They will help us." The man grabbed his back pack and got out their meal. "Now is as good a time as any to eat. Are you hungry?" The boy nodded and they ate their picnic lunch while they waited.

The sun was sitting on the top of the ridge. The day was still bright, but the sun would sink fast from this point. Darkness would cover the mountains before long. As if an answer to prayer, they could hear the search and rescue helicopter approaching. The guys all breathed a sigh of relief. Help was on the way.

David always carried a few flares in his backpack. So he stopped working on the debris long enough to get the flares out and lit. He remembered how his dad would say, "You must always be prepared for the unexpected." Then his dad would review the list and check his supplies with him. A few years ago, he felt like saying, "I Know, Dad." He was now glad they had repetitively repeated this drill over the years.

The pilot grinned as he saw the flares. He was glad someone knew what they were doing. He thought about how many more lives could be saved if people were just prepared. He pointed out the small flames to the copilot and they began to look for a drop point or possible safe landing spot.

The copilot shouted to the rescuers to get ready. The men began the routine they had been through thousands of times. Although actual rescue attempts were rare, the procedure was automatic now.

The slide had in reality helped them out. There was a large area in which the shrubbery was completely flattened. They were able to land about 300 yards away from the two trapped under the trees. They quickly made their way over to the young men who had been clearing debris for a couple of hours. Much of the work had already been done. The guys were close. The men all nodded to one another and continued the job. Directions being shouted occasionally broke up the sounds of foliage being drug off the shelter.

The man suddenly felt cool air rushing into their small sanctuary. The last rays of light came streaming in through the new hole. He and the boy shouted for joy. The rescuers also let out a resounding cheer. They worked as quickly as they could to make the hole big enough to get the pair out. Another cheer went up as they lifted the boy off of his father's shoulders and out into the evening air. The rescuer checked the boy from head to toe. Once he was confident there were no immediate needs, he handed the boy to Aaron. The boy clasped his arms around Aaron's neck in a tight hug as Aaron carried him to the helicopter. Aaron reassured, "It's going to be okay now."

Just a short time later another cheer went up as the father climbed out of the shelter and onto the rubble. The news crew had arrived just in time to catch the man's exit on film. They hovered over the scene continuing to capture the moment of victory amidst the devastation. Once every one was in the rescue chopper, the news crew flew ahead to the station to set up the cameras.

The reporter grew anxious as he thought of the opportunity. He had to choose his questions wisely. He would only get one chance for this incredible exclusive. This once in a lifetime report could certainly set his career in the right direction. None of the major network reporters had any idea that the star had taken his son hiking. His team would be the only ones to capture the rescue of Hollywood's prize performer.

He realized he owed a huge favor to his friend in the ranger station now. He began bouncing ideas with the team as they approached the ranger station. The whole team was excited at the prospect of meeting Rod Gray.

The rescue chopper ascended into the sky and everyone felt an intense release. "Thank you, for everything." Rod said to the men.

"We were happy to be able to help," replied the captain.

"If it weren't for these young men and their friend, we would not have known you were in trouble," said the pilot.

The father turned to the boys and gratefully said, "I cannot thank you enough,"

"You're welcome." David and Aaron said in unison.

"I am glad we were there." Sergio replied

Remembering Sergio screaming at them moments before the rock slide, Rod asked, "How did you know?"

"I saw it," Sergio replied with that sense of remembering a bad dream.

"You saw the rock about to fall?" Rod questioned further.

"I saw the slide, and you, and the boy." Sergio's face became somber as he remembered the vision.

Rod had heard of people able to see the future before, but he'd never met anyone that he knew undeniably had seen a real vision. He was intrigued and encouraged Sergio, "Tell me what you saw."

"It was like watching a show on the big screen. Although I knew it was real.....it wasn't real yet!" Sergio explained.

"Go ahead, what happened."

"The slate of granite broke loose and began falling. Rocks started crashing down the mountain. You and the boy were right in the path of a huge boulder and........" Sergio dropped his head.

"That's when you started yelling?" Rod questioned, trying to keep Sergio talking.

"Not quite. I looked around first. Thinking, I don't know....What....Is this real? It seemed so real, but yet I knew it wasn't." Sergio continued with the confusion and concern he'd felt when he'd first seen the vision.

Then Aaron asked with interest, "What made you start yelling?"

"I saw you guys," Sergio looked at the father and son as he answered, "You were exactly like the vision.....the same clothes, the same place; the same....everything was the same as I had seen it." His tone expressed the surreal feeling he'd experienced as he remembered, "I suddenly realized it was about to happen."

"You knew the vision was about to happen?" clarified the pilot.

"Yes. I knew it was going to be real if I didn't do something." Sergio replied, expressing the urgency he'd felt.

"How did you know?" David asked.

"I just knew." Sergio said, not wanting to tell them anymore.

"That is quite a special gift." the father declared.

David could not take his eyes off of the man they had freed. His face was so familiar. Finally he figured out why and asked the man, "Aren't you Rod Gray?"

"Yes, I am. This is my son, David." Rod answered smiling at the recognition.

"My name is David also," David said smiling to the boy. Then he looked back to the father, "I loved your last movie."

"Thank you," replied Rod genuinely, then added with a big grin, "We had a great time filming it."

The captain interjected, "When we land the reporters will already be there. Mr. Gray, we can block them for you if you'd like. We can insist you have to be immediately flown to the hospital to be checked for internal injuries."

"That would be great," admitted Rod. With sincerity he added, "I don't want David to have to deal with reporters after this."

"Boys," the captain called, "if you would assist us by talking to the reporters about the incident, but not about Mr. Gray, we would greatly appreciate it."

The young men agreed to help. They were excited about the opportunity to tell their story, and they were thrilled to help their film hero and the rescue team. The captain radioed ahead and set the plan in motion. The boys would be exiting the helicopter with the rescue team, and then they would take off again with Mr. Gray and his son still onboard. The ranger station contacted the hospital and made arrangements to protect and examine the star and his boy.

As they approached the station, they could see the news reporter's team set up and ready around the landing pad. The captain reviewed the exit plan with the team once more. The helicopter touched down and the lead rescue ranger opened the door. He reminded the boys to keep their heads down until they were clear of the chopper. The team went first and the four young men followed. The people at the station all cheered. The lead ranger quickly closed the door as soon as the boys were clear. He gave the signal to the captain and the helicopter began to lift into the sky again.

The reporter and his crew quickly realized they would not get to see Rod Gray, so they focused on the rescue team. "Sir, can you tell me what happened up there?" he asked and pointed the microphone at the closest ranger.

"A rock slide trapped a couple of hikers. They were fortunate to find shelter," replied the ranger.

"Were the hikers Rod Gray and his son?" the reporter asked.

"Yes sir," replied the ranger hesitantly wondering how the reporter knew.

"Are they alright? Are there any serious injuries?" questioned the reporter.

"They appear to be fine," answered the ranger. Then as directed, he gave the scripted information release, "They are currently being taken to the hospital for further evaluation."

Josh came out of the station as he saw the helicopter land and his friends get out.

The ranger walked over, grinned, and patted Josh on the back, as he looked back at the reporter and camera man, "This young man came running into the station, excitedly shouting about the slide and two hikers being in trouble."

The reporter turned to Josh, "What's your name young man?" Josh told the reporter his name and looked back towards the road which he'd raced down with a slightly shocked look.

"Did you see the slide? Where were you when it began?" the reporter continued the interview with a whole new angle in mind.

"Yes, I saw the slide starting. My friends and I were hiking on the opposite mountain." Josh stated numbly.

"What happened first?" The reporter prodded.

Josh answered almost robotically, "Sergio stopped climbing. He was staring at the other mountain. Then, he started yelling at the hikers to run. Suddenly a huge slate of granite broke away from the top of the mountain."

"That must have been terrifying," the reporter said, trying to relate to the young man and keep him talking.

"Yeah. It was scarier than anything I have ever seen before," Josh acknowledged. Then with a little more emotion, he informed the reporter, "The first crash was almost deafening."

"What happened next?"

Josh was far more animated as he regained his sense of himself. He realized he was telling the story not only to the reporter, but to the rest of the world, "The man grabbed his son's hand and began running towards a large boulder with several fallen trees in front of it. They were able to fit into a bit of a cave made from the rock and trees."

The reporter grinned and then turning to the other three asked, "So, which one of you is Sergio?"

"I am," Sergio said as he prepared for the questioning.

"What caught your attention? How did you know to warn the hikers?" The reporter asked.

"I saw the slide happening, like in a dream, just before it happened." Sergio explained.

"That is incredible!" hardly believing what he was hearing, the reporter continued questioning, "Tell me more. Did you know it was Rod Gray on the other side?"

"No Sir." Sergio responded politely.

The reporter continued questioning the boys about the event. They took some pictures of the Rescue Rangers and guys together for the following day's newspaper edition. The rangers gave each of the young men an honorary ranger hat and thanked them for all their help. Finally, with the reporter satisfied, the guys were able to leave. Sergio hated the thought of his mom seeing the "breaking news" on TV without knowing they were all okay. The others agreed their moms would worry too. They each called home to let their parents know they were okay and on their way down. David told his mom, "You should turn on the TV. We'll be on the news soon."

They were all starving, so they went to a drive-through for a burger on the way home. They were tired and talked out. So they ate the meal quietly as they continued the drive. As Sergio pulled into his driveway, they agreed to get together the following week. "What a way to start the summer," Aaron said.

The guys all agreed, and then they went home. They would each get to repeat the story for their families. Aaron looked forward to seeing his family gathered in the den, listening to his tale. David was still excited about it all, and could hardly wait to share the adventure. Yet, Josh was hoping his family was already in bed. He didn't want to talk about it anymore tonight. He was simply too tired. Sergio was thankful that the house looked quiet when he pulled into the driveway. He half expected the rest of the town to be there.

As he walked into the living room, he saw his parents sitting on the couch waiting for him.

His dad, Gilberto, asked, "How are you?"

Sergio replied, "Really tired, but okay."

His mom, Oriana, got up and gave him a hug. "We are so proud of you." she cooed, "Are you hungry?"

Sergio assured her they had already eaten. They agreed to talk the next day and said "good night". Sergio was glad they did not barrage him with a million questions like the reporter had. He fell asleep almost as soon as he lay down.

The following morning the manager from the store called before Sergio was even up and told Oriana they were giving him the day off to recover. He woke up to the smell of fresh biscuits and bacon. He walked into the kitchen and gave his mom a big hug. "You're the greatest," he said. She smiled and told him he had the day off. Sergio was relieved. He was still surprisingly tired despite the sleep. His whole body ached. He wasn't sure what to expect next. Now the whole town would know about this. Would they act differently towards him? Is this how the Pegasus was going to bring him fame and an exciting life? Why was he so drained?

Gilberto was sitting at the table. He had taken the day off as well. Sergio sat at the table, and when Oriana joined them; he told them everything. Gilberto explained the drained feeling comes with using the mental/spiritual energy in a crisis like that. He said most people never even tap into their higher mental abilities and only use about 10% of their brain. Then he surprised Sergio with a story about saving his little sister once. Sergio had no idea that his dad had the same gift of being able to move things with his mind.

Sergio's mom said that these things often run in families. She too had a gift for seeing what was going to happen before it happened. She said it used to frighten her when she was younger. "Scientists still can't really explain why some of us have these gifts and others don't," she said.

Sergio, now curious, asked, "How many different kinds of gifts are there?"

"No one really knows, but I have heard about fire-starters and mind readers," Gilberto replied.

44

"Some people communicate with spirits," Sergio said, feeling out what his parents might think without really telling them about Pegasus.

"I know. I talk with them too," Oriana said gently.

"Who is your guide?" Sergio asked with surprise.

"Danu." Oriana stated.

"Who is that, Mom?" Sergio asked with interest.

"She was known as an Irish goddess," Oriana said.

"Oh, mine is Pegasus." Sergio admitted.

"Mine is Mercury," declared Gilberto.

"No wonder you're so good with your business," Sergio stated with admiration.

"You got it. I could not have done so well on my own," acknowledged Gilberto.

"It is a shame that many people don't understand the help available to them," Oriana said sadly.

Sergio suddenly felt free to talk to them about a world he'd kept secret to almost everyone. He wanted to know everything they knew. He wanted to invite them into his secret world. "Sheena says that there are some spirits that are mean and want to hurt people, instead of help them," he said as a reason why many people were afraid of the spirits.

"She is correct. Her understanding is remarkable for one so young," Gilberto acknowledged.

Realizing his parents had known of this realm all his life at least, Sergio felt a bit confused and a little hurt even. So he asked, "Why haven't we talked about this before? Why did you keep it from me?"

Gilberto, with a rare heaviness declared, "Sometimes as a child such things are more of a burden than a benefit."

Oriana looked tenderly at him and said, "Realizing you're very different from other kids can be difficult to deal with. Besides," his mom's tone changed just slightly, and she chimed, "We didn't know if you had those gifts. We didn't want you to think we had expectations of you that you could not meet."

"That's right. We wanted you to grow as normal as possible, and our society doesn't readily accept such things," Gilberto said.

Then he became a bit blunt and professed, "Sometimes other people can be dangerous."

"Like in Salem, when they killed people for being witches?" Sergio asked with curiosity.

"Yes, like that," Gilberto agreed, "We didn't want people treating you differently, because of our gifts."

Oriana lovingly asked, "How long have you known about your gifts Sergio?"

"The vision of the slide was the first time I have really seen something before it happened," Sergio said, still somewhat surprised by it all. Then he told them, "I have been moving things with my mind for a while now, but nothing that big. I saw a spirit for the first time when I was nine."

"How much did you tell the reporter?" Gilberto asked a little fearful.

Sergio reassured them, "I only told him about the vision."

"Good. Did you tell your friends?" Gilberto questioned, wondering what they might be up against.

"No. They don't know any more than the reporter," Sergio stated sincerely.

"Excellent. Don't tell them." Gilberto directed protectively.

"I don't," Sergio tried to reassure his dad by explaining, "The only one I talk to is Sheena. When we were ten, we started talking about spirits and the other kids got very nervous. We knew they had not seen them, so we quit talking about it around them."

"I knew I liked that girl," declared Oriana, then added with admiration, "She is truly special."

Sergio smiled in agreement, then went over to his mom and lovingly kissed her on the cheek. He gratefully said, "Thanks for the great breakfast Mom."

"You're welcome. I'm glad you liked it. I knew after an adventure like yesterday, you could use a good meal," she replied cheerfully.

Sergio started clearing the table. "Leave it," Gilberto directed with a smile, "I'll help your mom clean up."

"Why don't you go take a nice hot shower?" Oriana suggested.

"Thanks, I think I will." He left the kitchen with a new respect for his parents. He felt like he could really trust them now. They shared much more than he had imagined. He looked forward to telling Sheena about everything he had discovered. He also thought how great it will be getting to know his parents better. How did they keep it such a secret? Would he be able to keep it a secret now? That question sent chills up his spine. He shook it off and jumped into the shower. The rest of the day he relaxed and read. He didn't even call Sheena.

Sheena had seen the news and was anxious to hear from him. However, she didn't want to bug him. She waited for him to call, but even that afternoon the phone was silent. She decided to go to the mall, so she called Lisa.

Lisa was just getting home. Her family had gone to lunch with another family after church. Lisa was thrilled for an opportunity to be able to get away from the family. Going to church with her parents felt so strange now. Church had just been boring before. Now Lisa felt she was listening to lies, and she did not want to be a part of it anymore. She could be good without the threat of Hell. Someday they'll understand, she thought.

Lisa ran to Sheena's house once her mom said she could go. They went to the mall chatting about the things happening in their personal lives. They talked about what they had heard in the news as they walked around the mall, window shopping. They could hardly wait to hear more from Sergio. Sheena hoped he was okay. None of the guys looked hurt. Still, waiting to hear from him was difficult for her. They went into her favorite store and began looking at sun dresses. The girls imagined fun events they might need a dress for, and pretended a bit as they tried on different outfits. Sheena was grateful for the distraction.

CHAPTER 4

"Sergio...Sergio," a neighbor boy called and waved.

"Way to go, Sergio!" proclaimed a man as he was pulling out of the drive way on his way to work.

A couple of women, walking with their infants in strollers, waved and shouted, "Sergio, We are so proud of you."

Sergio waved back and smiled at his neighbors. All the way across town, people greeted him or pointed and said, "That's him! That's the young man who saved Rod Gray." Throughout the day, customer after customer wanted to talk to him about the rescue. Some even asked for his autograph on the article in the local newspaper. They had watched this boy growing up. They knew where he worked. When they saw the story in the paper, they knew this young man would be someone special.

The store manager was excited about the increased traffic in the store. He thought it was great publicity to have the local hero working for him. He had called a photographer come in to take pictures of the two of them together. Tom was trying to figure out where the best spot would be when the photographer came in. Tom saw the man's camera hanging around his neck, and he knew this was his guy.

Tom walked up to him, and they began discussing the best possible shots. The photographer began setting his tripod and camera up where they would have the store sign above their heads.

"Sergio, come here for a minute," Tom called and gestured with his hand.

Sergio saw the camera man, and he began seeking wisdom silently. "Pegasus, is this what you meant by fame? Should I allow Tom to use this event for the store?" He walked over to Tom and looked at him curiously.

"Yes, Sir," he replied.

"I would like to have a few photos with you here in the store. What do you say; can we get some pictures together?"

Sergio paused for just a moment more, and then with a broad smile said, "Sure, that would be cool. Can I have a copy? My mom would just love it."

"Absolutely! I'll make sure to give you a copy for her." Tom said proudly.

"Great! Then let's do it." Sergio enthusiastically replied.

"Okay, stand right here. We're going to shake hands like we just greeted each other." Tom directed him

"Like this?" Sergio asked feeling a bit foolish.

"Perfect!" said the photographer, "Now just hold it." The camera clicked a couple of times. "Okay, look this way, and Tom, put your hand on his shoulder. Great." The photographer took couple of different shots for each pose, moving the camera slightly each time. A small crowd of customers had gathered around them to watch and were talking about the rescue story, how long they had known Sergio, or what was happening with Rod Gray now. By the end of the day Sergio could hardly wait for this to blow over, and things to return to normal.

That evening he called Sheena to see if she would be able to hang out and talk that night. She didn't show it, but she was excited to hear his voice. It felt like an eternity had passed while she was waiting for him to call. They could not go anywhere to public right now. The people in town were acting as if he were Rod Grey. He wanted to get away from them for a while. Sheena packed a picnic supper while she was waiting for him to arrive.

They would go to their spot on Rebel Hill. She grabbed the blankets and was ready to go when he pulled up. Sergio smiled as she came out with the basket in her hand and blankets under her arm. He ran up to help her with the supplies and said, "You've thought of everything as usual. It is great to see you." He leaned towards her and kissed her cheek. Sheena smiled and replied, "I'm glad to see you too. I know it's been a little crazy for you."

As they drove up to the hill, Sergio told her the whole story. He relived the fun of the time with the guys. He told her how drained he became when he pushed the boulder up and over the shelter. He explained the way he had collapsed just after releasing the boulder. When they reached the top of the hill, He told her about meeting Rod Gray and the helicopter ride. They got comfortable on the blankets and began enjoying the picnic dinner. Then, he began to tell her about his parents. The sun slipped away and the darkness enveloped them. Finally, he told her about what Pegasus had told him the last time they were on the hill.

Sheena mostly listened. As he was telling her about the promises Pegasus had given him, she could not help but think about the promises she had received as well. She looked up into the night sky. The moon was only a sliver tonight, and the sky was crystal clear. Because the sky was not filled with moon light or clouds, she could see countless stars glittering across the heavens. She looked deep into Sergio's eyes, and his expression told so much more than his words. She could see that he was excited, yet a little unsure. He had no idea where this was going. He didn't like not having more control, yet he loved the feeling of a great adventure ahead. He is an incredible guy, she thought, I am so glad you brought us together, Pegasus.

Sergio saw the admiration in her eyes, and his heart lightened. He wrapped his arms around her and pulled her close to him. They began to talk of their future together with wonder and anticipation. Pegasus had given them so much already. They could hardly wait to find out what was next. As they snuggled together under the stars, they drifted off into a deep sleep. Suddenly, the warm rays of bright sunlight dancing across their faces through the trees woke them from the peaceful sleep.

They jumped up and raced towards their new day. Their life had just begun to get interesting.

Sergio had only been home long enough to shower and shave when the phone rang. He could hear excitement in his mom's voice. "Sergio," she called, "Rod Grey would like to talk to you." Sergio ran to pick up the phone in his room. "Thanks Mom," he called down the stairs, "I've got it." He heard her hang up as he said "Hello."

"Hello Sergio, I wanted to thank you again and let you know that we are both just fine." Rod said.

"That's great. Are you still in the area?" Sergio asked.

Rod chuckled and said, "No, we had to leave as quickly as possible so the people would not be going crazy over us."

"I bet." Sergio remarked as he thought about how crazy people had been to see him.

"I was thinking when things settle down, I would like to come back to the area," Rod continued, "However, I realized it was really foolish of me to take my son off to an area like that without a guide. Do you think you....and your friends...would be interested in leading us on an expedition?"

"I...I would be honored to Sir," Sergio stammered with surprise. As he recovered from the unexpected offer, he said seriously, "I'll talk to the guys and see if they're available."

"Either way, as long as you're interested, we'll give it a go." Rod declared confidently.

"That's fantastic! When do you think you'll want to go?" Sergio could not contain his excitement.

"You can't tell anyone we're coming," Rod became stern.

"No sir," Sergio replied, then he explained, "I just have to get time off work and get things ready."

"I see. I will give you a call when I know, but I am thinking two months from now," Rod answered thoughtfully.

"Great. I need to know how long you will want to be in the back country, so I can make sure we have enough supplies."

Sergio continued, trying to sound as professional as his dad.

Rod was pleasantly surprised. He leaned back into the chair, grinned, and stated, "I knew I was talking to the right young man. We will probably go just for one week this year. My boy is a little too young for more than that," he explained.

"I'm looking forward to it," Sergio expressed as he sat up a little straighter with pride.

"I will give you a call to set sure dates in a couple of weeks. Goodbye." Rod said to wrap up the conversation.

"Goodbye Sir." Sergio could hardly contain his exhilaration. This could be better than playing ball! Pegasus wasn't wasting any time!

He ran down the stairs to share the news with his mom. His mind whirling like the centrifugal force ride at Great America.

Didn't Aaron say he wanted to start of business of his own? Maybe this was it! They could do it together! He had to call the guys. What would they need to really make it a business? Could they really make it a business or would this just be a one-time adventure? Leading someone like him on an expedition would make a great start to a business. There was so much to figure out. "Mom! Mom!" Sergio shouted, "You're not going to believe it!"

"What?" Oriana asked with curious anticipation.

"He wants me to take him on an expedition!" Sergio excitedly explained, hardly believing his own words.

"That's wonderful!" She replied truly happy for her son, "Wait until your father hears, he'll be so thrilled. Rod Gray's movies are his favorites." Oriana gushed.

"Mom, you can't tell anyone else though," Sergio cautioned seriously

"Why not? Oh, the ladies will be envious," Oriana said as she could picture the conversation over coffee.

"That's not all, Mom, they will want to meet him, and they'll go crazy," Sergio explained empathetically, "He's trying to get away from all that."

"I see," His mom said as she considered what her son was saying. She said, "It must be really difficult to be famous."

"Can you imagine? People always wanting to be near you," Sergio thought about his own day and the weariness of it. He thought what it would be like to deal with that all the time, everywhere you went. He shook his head at the thought of it.

"People acting like they know you, but they don't," Oriana could imagine and didn't really like what she saw either.

"Never having any privacy," Sergio added.

Oriana grimaced with disgust as she stated, "Strangers trying to get your autograph or just touch you,"

"Not being able to go any place without being swarmed," Sergio mimicked frustration, "Reporters in your face asking you all kinds of questions."

"All the time!" Oriana added with exaggerated emphasis. She softly added, "I understand. I will keep it a secret until he's gone," secretly hoping he would at least take pictures with them. The momentous would be cherished forever. Besides, she thought, the ladies would never believe her without them.

"I can't believe how tired of it I got in just a couple of days," Sergio admitted as he thought about the news reporters at the station and then the way the whole town seemed to be acting the day before. Then he gave her a peck on the check and declared proudly, "I knew I could count on you."

"Maybe they would like a home cooked meal. You could pack that for the first night, couldn't you?" Oriana offered as she thought it would be a nice touch, "We have those camp containers. Then you would just have to heat it up."

"That's a great idea, Mom. I am sure he'll appreciate it," Sergio replied. He thought a moment and asked, "Say, do you think this could make a business?"

"I don't see why not? Surely there are lots of people who would enjoy seeing the forest, but they are unsure of where to go, or how to do it," Oriana answered sincerely.

"That's what I am thinking, and this would be a great start!" Sergio declared.

"You should definitely talk to your Dad. He could help you plan it," Oriana encouraged.

"It would be fun to work with him on this," Sergio admitted. It had been a while since they'd worked on something together. He realized he missed time with his dad. Then, he realized the time. Sergio hugged his mom as he left for work. Despite all the wonderful ideas flowing through his mind, he had to go about business as usual. He left those plans at home, and began to focus on his day.

The store was still a little crazy with people who wanted to shake his hand or hear his story. He was just beginning to experience fame, and he could easily understand why Rod had not stuck around. Funny, he thought, I used to think I really wanted to be famous. He was growing tired of telling the story already. He didn't want to sign any more newspaper photos. The girls getting giddy as they walked through the store was so silly. "Pegasus, I could live without this kind of fame." He whispered.

Sergio had decided not to tell all the guys about Rod Grey yet, but he had to start planning for the trip. Right after work, Sergio called Aaron to see if he wanted to go to the batting cages. They met there, and after a few hits Sergio brought up the idea of making a forest touring business.

Aaron loved the idea. He began talking about a market research report and other things that Sergio did not understand. Sergio was glad he didn't say anything about Rod to Aaron. Sergio knew by now that this would be a great business. Why did they have to research it? How would Aaron do that? What would he do if the report said it was a bad idea?

He really needed to talk to his dad now, and he needed to seek Pegasus. Sergio knew that the report would not matter if Pegasus was helping him. He still had to call the other two guys as well and see if they wanted to go on this trip. He had so many ideas running through his mind, but first they had to have a successful trip. That meant they had to be focused on planning for it, not planning on hanging out with Rod Gray.

Two and a half weeks had gone by without a call from Rod, and Sergio was beginning to wonder if he was really going to call again. Either way, the trip would be fun.

They had mapped out quite a trail. They would be hiking, so provisions had to be few, and light. They could certainly fish for their supper most evenings. Would Rod accept that if he did call? Would he want or expect full meals all the time? Surely, he would be prepared for roughing it.

The phone rang and jolted Sergio from his thoughts. His head snapped in the direction of the phone, and he reached over to pick it up. It was Rod. Yes, he was interested in a real back country experience, but he wanted to take horses and pack in some more provisions. He would buy everything. He just needed to know how much money Sergio would require. Rod would give him two months to put it all together.

"Excellent!" thought Sergio, "This is getting better all the time. With this one trip, I will be set up to run great tours." Now he really needed his dad and Aaron to help him plan. The trip with the guys would be a great first run to locate the right sites. Too bad they would already be going back to college when he took Rod. Sergio was relieved he had not said anything to the guys about Rod going. How was he going to get that much time off work without telling Tom? He wondered.

Gilberto was elated to help his son plan his new business. What a break this was! Did this man know he was funding his boy's business? Was this his way of rewarding Sergio for saving them? He could hardly wait to meet the man himself. He was excited about going with them as well. It had been a couple of years since he had been able to go camping. His own business had demanded all his focus. He felt bad that he and Sergio had not had the opportunity to spend the time together when he heard David talking about his trips with his father over the years. Now, here was a chance for them to make up some lost time. His business was solid, and he had a good manager. They could survive without him for a couple of weeks here and there.

Aaron was thrilled to have such an opportunity. No one was offering these kinds of vacation tours.

To start a whole new kind of business was a young business student's dream. He would help design the model for a whole new genre of entrepreneurs— Adventure Vacations. He decided he would take the semester off to get the business plans solid before the next vacation season. They were a little late for this year, but next year would be great! They would be able to start marketing the trip possibilities by the fall. Hopefully, they would get some booked before January.

Each evening for the rest of the week the three of them met and planned out everything that would be needed to make a week trip successful. They were coming up with new possibilities each time they met.

"There are several areas in the forest we could take back country tours."

"We need to decide on three possible trips for now." Gilberto wisely said, "You don't want to overextend yourself in the beginning, or offer something you can't deliver," he warned.

"Your right, I don't want to get in over my head," Sergio acknowledged, "What three trails would you choose Aaron?" he asked thoughtfully.

"Let's start with the one we're taking next week. Oh, the Tuolumne Meadows would be a great area to tour as well. We'll think about a third one later," Aaron answered with assurance.

"Great." Sergio replied and smiled. He was grateful to have his dad and his best friend helping him plan it out. His mind had been swamped with ideas and questions. 'Where can we find trained horses? I don't want to start with having to train horses." Sergio said. Then he added, "Where are we going to keep them once we have them?"

"What about caring for them and getting them to the sites?" added Aaron. Thinking of adding horses to the business venture seemed more like a large liability than a marketing asset for adventure.

"Don't forget about needing licenses," advised Gilberto. Then with uncertainty asked Aaron, "What kind of licenses would you need?"

Aaron replied, "I'm not completely sure."

"Okay, I'm writing these down as queries. We'll need to find out the answers in order to figure out startup capital."

"I might know a guy that has your horses, or he might know where to find them," Sergio's dad remembered a rancher he'd been friends with for many years.

"Awesome! Would you call him Dad?" Sergio asked.

"You've got it. I'll ask about stables too while I've got him," his dad answered.

"Great. I have to get our permits from the Rangers for next week, so I will ask them about horse backpacking permits and where they might suggest for such a trip." Sergio stated.

"I'll look into liabilities, and see what other licenses we might need to take care of in order to offer such tours." Aaron offered.

"Are you sure there is no one else offering to guide trips like this? It would be great to know what our competition is like," Gilberto spoke with the clarity of a true businessman.

"That was the first thing I checked out," Aaron proudly stated. He added as he explained to Sergio, "We don't want to cover the same area or type of tour as someone else," then happily assured them, "I could not find anyone else doing this."

"I bet there will be several new companies in the next decade when they see what you boys have done!" Gilberto declared.

They grinned and kept working on the details all that night. The next few days they would have to prepare for their own trip. This trip was becoming so much more important to Sergio than he had imagined.

This would be the last practice before the big game. He wished David didn't have to go back to college in August. David had the most back country experience. He would have to really pay attention to David on this trip.

Maybe he should tell him what was going to happen, and see if he could take this one semester off like Aaron. Once he was alone again, he turned to Pegasus. "I have so many questions. I need you now," he prayed.

He was not disappointed. Pegasus came to him quickly and led him through the trail he would be on the following week. Sergio was amazed, the vision felt so real.

The next morning, Sergio had a new confidence. When he arrived at the ranger station, the head ranger recognized him and greeted him like a lifelong friend, "Hi Sergio, are you guys going hiking again?"

Sergio swelled with pride at the recognition of such a respectable man, "Hello sir, we're actually planning a camping trip. I need to get a wilderness permit," he explained.

"Sure thing, we'll get you taken care of," the ranger declared. As he prepared the paperwork, he looked up and stared Sergio straight in the eyes. "You know, we could really use a young man with your gifts and skills. Have you ever thought of becoming a ranger?" the man inquired.

"Well sir, I always planned on playing ball. I hadn't really thought about anything else until just recently," admitted Sergio.

"What are you thinking of doing now?" asked the ranger.

Sergio began to tell him of their plans. The ranger thought it would be a great way to bring more visitors into the park. They talked about several possibilities.

The ranger had worked in the Sierras since he was Sergio's age. He had great trail ideas. He also knew where the best and worst camping areas were. They talked for about an hour when the ranger said he needed to get back to work. Sergio left with a new appreciation of Pegasus. With one seemingly chance event, Pegasus had set up an excellent future with very important contacts for Sergio.

Although he wouldn't be the famous ball player he'd always dreamed of being, he was going to have a great life. He wouldn't be stuck at Automart or working for his dad the rest of his life. Pegasus was amazing. He had to tell Sheena.

Driving back down into the valley didn't seem long at all. Sergio felt like he was floating. Things couldn't get any better, he thought. He didn't even wait to get home. He stopped at a quick stop, went in and bought a soda, and dropped the dimes in the payphone. He had to talk to Sheena now. He wanted to see her and tell her everything in person. He was thinking he would take her to dinner, someplace nice. They needed to celebrate this amazing turn of good fortune.

"Hello?" Sheena answered the phone.

"Hello Beautiful," Sergio sweetly said, "How are you?"

"I'm good," Sheena replied as she blushed. She was glad he could not see how much his sweet words and tone affected her sometimes. She returned the question with her own sweetest voice, "How are you?"

"I'm great," he replied. He continued, "What are you doing tonight?"

Sheena picked up that he was probably about to ask her out and playfully replied, "Oh, I am going out with this great guy."

"Really?" Sergio was taken aback and suddenly unsure of himself or what to say. "Who is he?" he asked unable to hide the surprise or disappointment.

Sheena realized he didn't get that she was talking about him. She thought about playing it off a little longer, but didn't want to hurt him either. So she replied confidently with an answer he was sure to get, "I am seeing the town's hero tonight."

"That's right!" Sergio responded proudly. He added, "I want to take you somewhere nice for dinner. We have so much to celebrate."

"Celebrate?" Sheena questioned excitedly, "What are we celebrating?"

"I'll tell you all about it when I pick you up," he replied. "Can you be ready in an hour?" Sergio asked hopefully.

"Certainly." she responded, "I can hardly wait to hear the news."

"I can hardly wait to see you," Sergio confidently confided.

"Nor I you," Sheena sweetly stated as the pink rose returned to her cheeks.

They both went about getting ready for their date as quickly as possible. They both wanted to look their best for the other. They had been friends forever, but their friendship was becoming something so much deeper. Each one of them thought they were in love with the other, but neither of them had really said it.

Sergio had been thinking of asking her to be his girl while he was in college. He'd planned on getting her a promise ring, but then everything changed. All his dreams came crashing down when he ripped his rotator cuff in the big game. How could he possibly ask her to take him seriously with such a limited and unknown future? He'd thought when he'd received the news that the damage was likely permanent. He couldn't ask her after that. She deserved so much more, he'd thought. Now he smiled as he thought, soon I may be able to offer her far more than I even imagined.

Sheena knew it was right to wait for him to make the move, but waiting for him to do so seemed simply silly sometimes. She could tell everything had changed after he'd injured himself. She wanted to tell him she didn't care about the things most girls cared about. She could enjoy all the flowers she wanted to on long walks through the hills with him. She didn't need an expensive ring, she thought, she needed his honest commitment to love her no matter what. So, she determined she would show him as much by staying beside him as his best friend through it all.

Of course this made Sergio's love for her grow even deeper. He'd recognized her kindness and love had not changed although everything in his world had. He wanted to give her the world more and more every day. Now, he might actually have the opportunity to do it. He could hardly wait to tell her everything. He looked in the mirror one more time as he combed his hair. He smiled confidently at his appearance and turned to leave. The anticipation of seeing her was beginning to feel electric.

He grabbed the keys and headed to her house. Once there he walked up to the door with a surprising nervousness creeping up on him. He hoped she would be just as excited to see him. He was stunned with her beauty as she answered the door. The powder blue dress pulled out her beautiful bright blue eyes. The complimenting contrasts of her eyes, soft white skin, and long bright red hair swept back on one side with a delicate hair comb, was commanding admiration. "Wow! You're absolutely gorgeous," he exclaimed.

Sheena's cheeks were suddenly as bright as her silky shiny red hair. "Thank you," she replied with genuine gratitude for the compliment. She looked at him with admiration and said, "You're very handsome yourself." She gladly took his hand when he offered it, and stepped out onto the porch carefully. She didn't wear heals all the time and didn't want to fall.

She also couldn't help but notice the butterflies in her stomach as she placed her hand in his. She felt a little silly. They had been best friends for years. Why was she suddenly so excited by him? Maybe it was merely the mood he'd created with his own excitement about what ever had happened, she thought. Whatever it was, she decided she liked feeling this way.

They drove over to the next city and went to a steakhouse she'd never been to before. Sergio had thought earlier he wanted to go to the city. Their little town didn't have anything worthy of such a celebration...or of her, he'd thought. Besides, the people in their little town would probably still be acting as if he were a celebrity if they went to the one good restaurant there, he mused. He didn't want anything to detract from their time tonight. Once he saw her, he knew he'd made the right decision. She was exquisitely beautiful tonight. He began telling her how Rod had called and confirmed their trip on the drive over. He could not contain his own excitement at the thought of camping with his hero or the new plans he'd begun to develop.

Sheena was certainly excited for him. She enjoyed seeing him happy about his future again. She wondered if it would become their future, and smiled at the thought.

Unless he said something to indicate he was thinking of their future though, she would simply enjoy the time together tonight she determined. She wished she could see his heart towards her. She knew at that moment she was falling in love with him. Yet, she had to contain it. She'd been taught it was improper for a young lady to express her heart for a man if he'd not assured her of his love first. It was also foolish, she thought. She would simply wait for him to make it clear.

Sergio sensed his own heart desiring to make her his own. He wasn't prepared yet. He must hold off a little longer.

He felt as if he were in heaven every time he looked into her eyes. He couldn't imagine wanting anyone else ever. He would ask her after the trip with Rod. He would be able to buy her a ring that was as beautiful as she was, he thought. After dinner, he asked her to dance and could not help but pull her a little closer and confess, "I love you."

Sheena looked in his eyes as if she were searching deep into his soul, and she knew he meant it. She finally felt free to say it. She sincerely and sweetly replied, "I love you too." His kiss was so tender, it took her breath away. She leaned into him to keep from sliding down to the floor in a pool like a melted stick of butter. They held each other a little tighter as they danced. Neither of them had ever experienced such exhilaration. They reveled in the emotion of the moment.

Before going home they decided to stop at the little soda shop where their friends would likely be hanging out. When several of the young ladies saw Sergio's Bronco they begin getting excited, hoping he would ask them to dance or even simply say, "Hi". The girls swooned a little as they saw him get out dressed so handsomely. The guys were feeling a little jealous, but they really admired him too. They wanted to be his friend.....no, more than that......they wanted to be like him.

Sergio could feel the stares. He'd forgotten about the way people were treating him in their little town when he suggested stopping. He felt a little awkward being treated like a celebrity here of all places. He was just one of the guys a few weeks ago.

He walked around the Bronco and opened the door for Sheena. She stepped down and the guys' eyes were instantly fixed on her. The girls were now jealous, but could not help but admire her. She was not used to such attention either. The two of them looked at each other, and Sergio whispered, "I'll die laughing if one of them asks for an autograph." They laughed lightly and walked hand in hand together into the soda shop.

CHAPTER 5

The July night air was warm, but the moon was full and radiant white. It had just topped the mountain peaks. The lake was a perfect mirror reflecting a beautiful moon image. Mark took Lisa's hand in his as they walked along the shore. They had become very close these past few months. Lisa was sure she was falling in love with him. He was so gentle, yet very strong. He made her laugh even when she was upset. She was beginning to feel like she could tell him anything and he would still love her.

Could she tell him about Pegasus? His family went to the same church as her family. They were Christians. Where was he in it all? Did he just go because his family did? Did he really believe all those stories? How would he feel if he knew that it was just a big myth, a lie, a way of controlling them? How could she tell him that everything he'd lived had been a lie? Would he still want to date her if she did tell him, or would he break up with her? Did she really want to keep living a double life?

She looked at the moon and quietly called to Pegasus. She had learned how to go to Pegasus quickly, without anyone knowing, while around her family. Pegasus instructed her that she needed to wait just a little longer. She needed to wait for Sheena. They would pray together first. Pegasus gave her understanding that there was a greater power in unity. He reminded her that her loved ones really believed those stories. She had to be cautious with them. She should just ask Mark some questions about what he really believed to get him thinking about it all.

"Mark, what did you think about the sermon on Sunday?"

"It was interesting, I guess," Mark replied.

"Did you understand what he meant about being predestined?" Lisa asked with genuine interest.

Mark thought for a moment and then replied, "I think so. He was just saying God has plans for us, for each of us. It doesn't matter what happens, God's plan is going to happen."

"Oh, I see. So it doesn't matter what we do, or what we want, God is going to do what He wants, with who he wants," Lisa said nonchalantly.

Mark's eyebrows pulled down and his eyes narrowed as he pursed his lips. His head tilted sideways as he looked at her. He said, "It sounds different when you say it like that. I'm not sure I like the sound of that. What do you mean?"

Lisa shrugged her shoulders, "Well, I don't know.....what if someone really tries hard to do all the right things, but God has predestined them to a difficult life?" Lisa sincerely asked.

"God's not like that!" Mark proclaimed as he stepped back.

Lisa looked down for a minute, and then back at Mark. She softly said, "Look at Maria. She is one of the sweetest people I have ever met. She tries so hard to get good grades, but she struggles. She just doesn't understand it. She would love to be able to run, dance ballet, or swim competitively, but she can't. Walking is hard for her. She goes to church, prays, and is kind, yet God ignores her. His plan for her life is painful." Then she added with a sigh of exasperation, "I don't know how she does it."

Mark intently listened to Lisa. He honestly stated, "I hadn't thought of it like that before." Then he stepped back in towards her, gently taking Lisa's hand in his, and sympathetically asked, "How does she feel about it?"

"I haven't talked to her about it yet. I am kind of afraid to ask her. I don't want to upset her." Lisa responded candidly.

"I can understand that." Mark admitted. Then he said, "I think I'll ask my dad about it. He is really smart and seems to understand God really well."

"Great! Let me know what he says," Lisa replied.

"Of course! Mark declared. Suddenly a brilliant idea flashed into is his thoughts, his whole face lit up like the moon and he said, "Hey, maybe you could come over for dinner and we could ask him together. Then you could hear him yourself."

Lisa blushed at the thought and acknowledged shyly, "I couldn't ask him."

"I'll bring it up," Mark replied chivalrously.

"Alright, that sounds good," Lisa said smiling, "Let me know when."

The young couple had made it back to the car. Lisa looked up and saw the moon was getting high in the sky. She exclaimed, "Oh no, I am going to be late! We have to go."

"I completely lost track of time. I'm sorry," Mark apologized.

They jumped in the car and took off for her house. About four houses away, Mark turned off his head lights, put the car in neutral, and killed the engine. They coasted up to Lisa's house, hoping everyone had gone to sleep. The house was dark and quiet. Lisa was at least a little relieved. Maybe they wouldn't notice she had come in late. As she started to get out of the car, Mark reached for her hand. She looked back at him and smiled. Mark gently said, "I had a great time."

"Me too. The lake was the perfect place to go tonight." Lisa replied sweetly.

"You looked so beautiful in the moon light," Mark said as he softly caressed Lisa's face. She was simply captivated by his voice and touch. He leaned over the console and gently kissed her.

She swooned just a little, then pulled back and softly said, "I have to go. Call me."

He watched her walk up to the door and he waited until she went in to leave. He thought he might be falling in love. He needed to see what his parents thought of her. She was so beautiful... and smart. He loved spending time with her no matter what they were doing. She was a lot of fun when they played miniature golf. She had a great question tonight. He wondered how his dad would answer it.

Lisa leaned against the door after she locked it. She could not wipe the smile off her face as she thought back over the night. She had just had her first real kiss. It was wonderful. "I am falling in love. I am going to marry him," she thought. She started to walk across the family room, when the little lamp on the end table by her mom's chair came on. She jumped back and was shocked to see her mom sitting there.

"Lisa, I am glad you're okay. I was worried," Tina said genuinely relieved.

Lisa realized her mom had been sitting up, waiting and praying. She felt guilty and said, "Sorry Mom, we lost track of time."

"Lisa, Mark is a very nice young man, but you can't just break curfew. Where were you two?" Tina's voice turned from relieved into irritated.

"We just went to the lake." Lisa explained, "We were walking and talking, and then we suddenly realized how late it was."

"You will have to be more careful of the time if you want to be trusted. You will be grounded this week," Tina stated calmly.

"Mom, no!" Lisa pleaded, "It was only a half an hour! We weren't doing anything wrong!"

"Lisa, you have to follow the rules if you want to be able to go and do things without us," Tina remained calm, but firm.

"But Mom, he wants me to come to his house and have dinner with his parents." Lisa explained.

"Well, that will have to wait until you're off grounding," Tina replied resolutely.

"You don't understand!" Lisa yelled with anguish.

"I do understand how much you enjoy spending time with him, but I still need you to follow curfew," Tina said in a gentle, yet still firm tone.

"Mom!" Lisa pleaded, but her mom would not budge. Finally, she couldn't take it anymore, she ran to her room, hot tears streaming down her face. How could her mom do this? Hadn't she ever been late on accident?

The bedroom door slammed shut, and Tina wondered if the commotion would wake up Henry. She prayed before going to bed.

Lisa didn't care. This was so unfair. Her mom had just ruined a perfect day. Didn't she know what it was like to fall in love? She curled up on her bed, grabbed her pillow, and wept until she fell asleep.

Lisa felt angry in the morning. How dare my parents continue this charade. The thoughts sprung up from her heart to her mind. They pretended to be the perfect "Christian family", yet she knew they had gotten pregnant with her before they were married. It wasn't hard to figure out. Their anniversary was only 6 months before she was born. Mom and Dad had not stayed pure before marriage, but they expect me to. What was the big deal about being half an hour late? If I had wanted to do something "wrong", I certainly would have had plenty of time before curfew to do it. Mom knows Mark is nice. Why did she have to ground me? What am I going to tell Mark? I'll just go anyway. She can't stop me. The thought froze Lisa for a moment.

"That's right; she can't really stop you from doing anything," Pegasus whispered into her mind, "Come, I'll help you plan out your escape." A slight grin slipped into a fully devious smile which consumed Lisa's face.

By the time Mark called, Lisa knew exactly how she would sneak out and get back in. Pegasus had shown her how to keep her parents from realizing she was gone. It was really quite simple. There was no reason for her to be grounded, and this dinner was important. She had to understand why God would plan a life so difficult for someone, yet plan a wonderful life for someone else.

Why would a truly loving God plan for some people to go to Heaven and some people to go to Hell? How was that love? More important than hearing his father's answer to these questions was getting Mark to think about these things. He needed to see that what they had been taught all their lives was a lie.

It was worth the risk to sneak out. Even if they did catch her, what were they going to do about it? From now on, she was going to do what she wanted to do. They couldn't stop her.

That day Lisa pretended like she was really sorry for being late and getting upset with her mom. She was extra nice to her mom all day. She asked, "Do you need help?" When her mom was cooking dinner. The day seemed to be dragging slower than ever. She was anxious for Friday to arrive.

Friday morning she began the one act play. She faked not feeling well. As the day went on, Lisa appeared to be feeling worse. She finally told her mom she was just going to go to bed. Her mom asked with concern in her voice, "Aren't you going to eat dinner?" Lisa replied she wasn't hungry and she went off to her room. She turned the radio on low and stuffed her bed with her clothes. She got dressed, opened the window, and climbed out. She closed the window quietly and snuck out the back gate. She walked down the alley feeling free. Once she came to the street, she walked back to her house and stood in front of the big oak tree so her parents wouldn't see her.

She timed it close. Mark pulled up within a couple of minutes and she was relieved. She got in the car quickly, and gave Mark a quick peck on the cheek. "Let's go!" she said gleefully.

"Dinner is going to be great. Mom is going all out," Mark told her with great anticipation.

"What is she making?" Lisa asked courteously

"Her lasagna from scratch,"replied Mark.

"Oooh, I love lasagna! It's my favorite," exclaimed Lisa.

"Nothing beats her lasagna," Mark said confidently and added, "Just wait. It is the best lasagna ever."

"Wonderful! I can hardly wait," Lisa replied and then switched the subject, "Have you heard from Sergio lately?"

"No," admitted Mark, "I haven't talked to him since he became a hero."

"I haven't talked to Sheena in a while either," Lisa said. She sweetly hinted, "It would be fun to go out all of us together."

"That's a great idea. I will give him a call and see what their up to tomorrow. Maybe we can go bowling tomorrow night,"

Mark responded, enthusiastic about the idea.

"Tomorrow night?" Lisa asked with disappointment.

"Do you have plans already?" Mark asked surprised.

Lisa dropped her head and said, "Not really, I just need to do my hair." How lame she thought. Couldn't you come up with a better excuse than that? She looked out the window so he couldn't see her face.

Mark looked quizzically at her. She had to do her hair? Wasn't that what girls said when they just didn't want to go out with you? Since when did Lisa "do her hair" on a Saturday night? Maybe she was seeing someone else, he thought, but he didn't say anything.

The silence was becoming uncomfortable, so she tried to cover the excuse with an explanation and a half smile, "I want to look really nice for church on Sunday." She certainly didn't think she could get away with sneaking out two nights in a row. She would surely get caught then. Why don't I just tell him the truth? She thought. They pulled into the driveway and Lisa was relieved this conversation was over. Now she just had to get through the dinner without saying something stupid.

The smell of his mom's sauce simmering since sunrise had permeated the house. Lisa was instantly ravenous when she walked in the door. His parents, Ryan and Katie, greeted her, and they sat down to dinner almost immediately.

For the first time since they had started dating, Mark was feeling a little unsure. He could tell she wasn't telling him the truth. What was she keeping from him? Was she seeing someone else? He couldn't shake the pit in his stomach. Despite it being his favorite dish, Mark just picked at his plate.

Finally, he remembered the question she had. Maybe thinking about something else would help shake this horrible feeling, Mark thought, so he asked his dad, "Remember when Pastor Steve was talking about how God has predestined us for His purposes?"

"Sure, I remember," replied Ryan.

Smiling at the two teens he confidently asked, "Pretty amazing that God has a unique design for each of us isn't it?"

"I guess so," Mark replied with uncertainty.

Ryan leaned back and looked intently at his son and this young lady he'd brought home. "What could be more amazing?" he asked. Then, seeing the cynicism on Lisa's face and the confusion in Mark's eyes declared, "The Creator of the Universe has a plan for me, and for your mom, and you, and Lisa. He knows each one of us personally."

"That is pretty amazing, but what if His plan for someone is cruel?" Lisa challenged.

"God is not cruel. God is love," Katie said sweetly.

"How could God plan for someone to be crippled then?" Lisa asked with a sense of hurt for her friend, "Is that love?"

"I see. I remember I was just a little older than you are now when I asked the same question," Ryan admitted with empathy.

"You asked that question before, but you still believe?" Lisa asked with surprise.

"Yes Lisa," Ryan answered sincerely, "The Lord God Almighty is a big enough God to handle our toughest questions. He wants us to seek him when we are unsure," then as if he was remembering the struggle he felt when he questioned and how grateful he was to have such a wonderful example, he told them, "I was fortunate enough to have a father who reflected God's love even when I had tough questions."

"Well then, what did Grandpa say?" Mark asked with relief and expectation.

"Your grandpa reminded me we live in a fallen world," Ryan responded.

"That's it?" Lisa asked cynically as she shrugged her shoulders and pursed her lips.

No, that is not it," Ryan reassured, "You see the whole world is corrupted because of Adam and Eve's choice in the garden," he explained, "We all deal with hard problems throughout life. We all die."

Katie thoughtfully added, "The amazing part is that God still is with us and loves us no matter what we face. He will actually give us the strength to go through it."

"It's hard to just accept that," Lisa replied as she dropped her head.

Katie got up, walked around the table and put her hand on Lisa's shoulder, and asked "Why dear?"

"I see how hard it is for my friend, Maria," Lisa sadly explained, "She has difficulty just walking. School is hard for her too, yet she prays and goes to church," Her voice became angry, her face twisted with rage, "Does this God of love help her? If He really is the "Almighty God" why doesn't he just heal her? Jesus supposedly healed a lot of people. Did God just quit healing people when Jesus returned to Heaven?" Lisa couldn't stop the stinging tears forming in her eyes. She quickly wiped them away. She was angry with God. She was angry with all these people telling her these terrible lies. Everyone sat quiet for a few moments.

Katie put her arm around Lisa and empathetically asked, "It is difficult to watch someone we love go through hard things isn't it?"

Lisa nodded. She still had a huge lump in her throat. This was not at all what she had wanted to happen. Now, she was embarrassed, and she wanted to get out of the house. Katie was wonderful though, Lisa thought, she really understands.

After a moment of thoughtful silence Ryan encouraged, "He could heal her, and maybe someday He will heal her," with a twinkle in his eye he stated, "Remember the story about the man who had been blind since birth and was in his forties when Jesus healed him?"

"I remember that one," Mark said excitedly, "the disciples asked Jesus who had sinned and Jesus told them it was for the glory of God that the man had been born blind."

"That's right," acknowledged Ryan adding, "And in those days a blind man could not work. All he could do was beg for money or food."

"He would be a social outcast as well," Katie chimed in, "The Jews really believed that if you had problems like that it was because you or your parents sinned," with sympathy she stated, "He would not have many friends. I would imagine he would be lonely."

Lisa told them, "Maria doesn't have many friends either," Really, a lot of kids are mean to her, she thought and then added,

"That would be an awful way to live."

"Absolutely!" Mark agreed. He'd been imagining what it would be like to be that blind man the day he met Jesus and asked the others, "Can you imagine the blind man's excitement when Jesus actually healed him?"

"I would be dancing in the streets!" declared Ryan.

"Everyone in town knew him," Katie said with a smile. She was beginning to picture the event too. She exclaimed, "They must have all been amazed!"

"Why did God wait so long?" Lisa asked sincerely.

"Well, that is a tough question....... I suppose it had to be the right time," reasoned Ryan, "The man and all those who knew him had to understand it was God who healed him."

"Also, God told the Israelites that giving sight to the blind was one way that they could recognize the Messiah," explained Katie.

Lisa held up her hands and gestured quotation marks as she declared, "Okay, but now we 'know' Jesus is the Messiah," emphasizing the word know before asking, "Why does he still allow such suffering?"

"There are many reasons why people suffer. Sometimes it is simply for God's glory to be revealed. Other times it could be because of bad choices. Then sometimes it may be simply for us to need him and learn to lean on him," Ryan explained sympathetically.

"But Dad, why does God predestine some people to Hell?" Mark challenged. Mark had really been thinking about that question since Lisa had asked it. He could not figure out a good enough reason for such a terrible fate to be selected for someone.

"God does not predestine people for Hell," Katie said soft but firmly, "He loves us all and wants us all to be saved."

Ryan looked at Mark and Lisa lovingly, and considerately expounded, "God is holy, and He is a righteous God. Before Adam and Eve ever ate from the tree, God told them it would bring death. The whole planet suffers with the result of their sin. God is also merciful though; He provided a way out for them...for any who will accept it. Only people who reject his plan of salvation go to Hell." The room became uncomfortably quiet.

Katie graciously switched the subject to lighten the remainder of the evening. The family had a tradition of playing cards after dinner. So the table was cleared, and the game began. They had much more fun that Lisa would have expected. She really liked Mark's family. When the game was over, Mark took Lisa home. She finally told him that she was grounded and she couldn't get away with sneaking out again. Mark was a little upset that Lisa had told him a lie, but it felt good to know that she wasn't seeing someone else.

While Mark was taking Lisa home, Katie admitted to Ryan she had a disturbing feeling about where Lisa was with God. They went to their room and began praying for Lisa and Mark just moments after they left. "Heavenly Father, we thank you for this evening. It was fantastic to have the time together with Mark and Lisa. I praise you for helping us to answer their tough questions. Lord, please help them understand your love for them," she prayed earnestly.

Ryan added, "Yes Lord, help them understand that everything that happens here is used for good for all who love you. Jesus, please help Lisa. I know she is struggling right now. Stop the enemy from confusing her further. Give her peace and rest tonight."

Once she was alone in her room, she could not stop thinking about their conversation. She still wasn't sure about the issue. She began to call to Pegasus. She didn't understand it.

Pegasus was usually quick to answer her now, but it was a lot harder for her to connect with him tonight. She simply couldn't find him. I must be too tired, she thought, so she decided she would try tomorrow and she went to sleep.

The following morning she still could not find Pegasus. Maybe he's really stuck helping someone else with something more important, she thought. I'll call Sheena and see what is happening with her, she thought. Maybe she can help me out. What Mark's parents said made some sense, and they really seemed to believe it.

She went into the kitchen and greeted her parents with a smile a bounce in her step, "Good morning."

"Good morning sweetheart, are you feeling better?" Lisa's mom asked lovingly.

"A little bit," Lisa replied almost forgetting she had pretended to be sick.

"Lisa, we need to talk," her dad, Henry, said as his jaws tightened.

"I went to check on you last night. Guess what I found," said Tina.

"You checked on me?" Lisa asked surprised.

"Yes, I have often checked on you when you were asleep," Tina acknowledged. She continued with a tone of disappointment, "You can imagine my surprise when I went to feel your forehead."

"I'm sorry." Lisa hung her head. She felt a rush of guilt and shame for deceiving her parents. Remembering her mom's gentle caress on her forehead and the way she pulled her hair back other times she'd been sick, reminded Lisa how much her mom had always cared for her.

"What could possibly be so important that you would purposefully try to trick us?" Tina asked unable to hide the hurt from her voice.

"Dinner with Mark's family," Lisa admitted as her face turned red.

"Was Mark a part of this?" Henry asked with an angry tone.

"Oh no! He didn't know anything about it," Lisa quickly responded.

"One night out was worth destroying our trust?" Tina asked.

"I am really sorry. I just had to go," Lisa said with sincerity.

Tina questioned further genuinely wanting to understand, "Why was this dinner so important?"

"Mark was going to ask his dad some difficult questions," Lisa answered looking her mother straight in the eyes. She knew better than to lie to them. Besides, it was done now. She was caught, and she knew lying would make it worse.

"What were the questions?" Henry asked, arms crossed, brows furrowed, with the tone of a police interrogation.

He was incensed and not too sure he believed anything she said now. Lisa turned from her mom and looked him straight in the eye, wanting him to see she was telling the truth…. wanting him to understand the importance, she answered, "They were about God predestining people's lives."

"That is an important topic," he acquiesced, seeing her sincerity. He softened his tone a little and unfolded his arms. Then, with his eyes still locked onto hers, he declared decisively, "However, those questions could have waited until next week."

"Or, you could have come and talked to us about the situation," her mom offered placing her hand softly on Lisa's hand, "Maybe we would have reconsidered or come up with an alternate consequence."

"Instead, you have made us feel we cannot trust you," Henry sadly reminded her.

Lisa's head dropped and she began crying with remorse.

"Will you forgive me?" Lisa asked. She felt awful for deceiving her parents.

"Of course we will forgive you, yet trust is not easy to earn back," Tina responded lovingly and honestly.

Lisa's parents both hugged her. Then, they asked about the topic and the answers she received. They wanted to know if she had more questions. Lisa responded that she was okay, and they had answered her questions. They grounded her for two weeks this time, including phone privileges. She would have extra chores as well. Lisa was disappointed, but she knew she deserved it.

Later that afternoon the phone rang, and she ran from the living room into the kitchen, momentarily forgetting. She was embarrassed when she heard her mom tell Mark she couldn't talk on the phone or go out for the next two weeks.

Oh two whole weeks, she thought, how will I make it two whole weeks without talking to any of my friends? At least she could talk to Pegasus while grounded. Pegasus! Why would Pegasus lead her into a plan that they would figure out? Why would Pegasus lead her to deceive her parents? Could she trust Pegasus? NO! Not more questions! She bemoaned, I am already incredibly confused as it is. Now who do I turn to?

The family began having a family devotion time in the evenings at dinner. Henry had picked up a book on his way home from work. Lisa had a difficult time sitting there, listening to her dad read the scripture and a short response to the scripture. Why did they have to decide to do this now? Is this some kind of punishment? Isn't dragging me to church enough of this? Lisa could feel the anger rising in her by the end of the week. She didn't want to sit through any more of these devotions. She didn't feel like being devoted to this lie. She wasn't sure she wanted to be devoted to Pegasus either though. He had let her down as well. Was that just another lie?

Tina noticed how aggravated she became during the devotions. After Lisa went to bed, she decided to call Katie and Ryan. They had been Christians much longer that she and Henry. They were the ones that had led them to Christ in their late teens.

She shared what was happening with Lisa through tears. Katie expressed the concern she had felt the night Lisa was with them. They agreed to pray and ask counsel from the pastor and his wife. The next day, as they told Pastor Dale the circumstances, he became very concerned. He assured them it could just be a normal teenage angst, but he wanted to really pray for Lisa before giving any advice. The three couples agreed they would fast and pray for three days. They knew they needed the Lord's intervention here.

Oh, I am going to die before this next week is over! Lisa thought. She didn't understand the anger welling within her, but she felt like she had to get away from everyone. She went to her room and slammed the door. Her parents looked at each other with concern and immediately began praying. Lisa also began praying......to Pegasus. He had at least shown himself to her before.

She had felt the euphoric feeling of being with him. He had spoken to her. She reasoned, everyone makes mistakes, maybe even Pegasus could not see everything. Maybe He had underestimated her parents. Maybe they could work together to overcome this horrible situation. She had to have some help with this. Certainly, he would not leave her alone now. She was disappointed that she still could not reach him as easy as before. Now, there was nothing. She curled up on her bed and wept. She felt so trapped and alone. This was the worst punishment ever! She could not wait to get off grounding. If her parents were going to be this religious, she would just walk out the door. She didn't have to stay and put up with this. I have to go to Sheena's, Lisa thought.

She grabbed her back pack and began throwing clothes in it. I won't deceive them this time. I will just tell them I am leaving. I can't stand this anymore! She crammed the clothes down and grabbed some more things. She just had to get out!

Tina and Henry could here her slamming things and stomping across the floor in her room. As she was packing, Lisa's mom called the pastor. Dale and Martha left right away. Just as Lisa was coming out of the bedroom, the doorbell rang. Pastor Dale and Martha had arrived.

"Oh great!" Lisa yelled, "You called them!" The disdain in Lisa's voice surprised everyone.

"Lisa, we're not on anyone's side," Pastor Dale replied with his hands raised in an "I surrender" stance, "We're here to help."

"Right!" Lisa replied sarcastically, "Then tell them to leave me alone, and I'll leave them alone."

"What happened? What is it that is making you so upset?" Martha asked.

"I can't stand listening to those lies anymore!" she screamed.

"What lies, Lisa?" Tina asked confused.

"Those lies! That book!" she said with disgust as she pointed. Lisa mocked, "The Bible, all of those fairytales," then declared, "I don't want to hear any more of them!"

"If we agree that you don't have to come to devotions, will you calm down?" Henry asked.

Lisa stopped and glared with uncertainty at her parents. Would they really agree to such a thing? She could see the pleading look in her mom's eyes. The pastor and his wife also looked really concerned. Her dad looked like he was getting mad.

Oh that's not good, she thought. "Okay," she said with a sudden calmness. She hadn't even talked to Sheena; she didn't know if she could really stay there. Besides, if they would quit making her listen to this nonsense, she could stick it out, she reasoned.

"Where did you get the idea these were lies?" Henry asked with an aggravated tone.

"I just know they are," Lisa said resolutely.

"Lisa, would you start coming to talk with us once a week?" asked Pastor Dale. He then stated, "I am interested in what you have to say."

Lisa looked at him suspiciously, then she replied adamantly, "I don't think so. You'll just try to convince me I'm wrong."

Pastor Dale smiled and reassuringly offered, "I promise I will only listen unless you ask me a question."

"Really? I can just tell you what I think about this, and you won't try to argue." Lisa said with disbelief.

"Who knows, I might learn something," Pastor Dale replied with a grin.

Lisa could not help but smile. She could see the kindness in his eyes. Maybe eventually, he would come to follow Pegasus and tell all those people the truth. She smiled again and said, "Okay, I'll come talk to you."

With the crisis adverted and everyone calmer, Tina invited Pastor Dale and Martha to stay for coffee and dessert. They agreed. Lisa enjoyed dessert with them, but excused herself to her room shortly after.

Once she was upstairs, the adults prayed together again, begging wholeheartedly for Jesus and the Holy Spirit to help them, to help their girl. They had no idea what had happened to cause all of this. They had no idea how to help her or what to do next. They cried out for wisdom from God. They had no idea of the battle they were up against, nor how intense it would become. They had no understanding of what she was involved in.

Jesus knew, and just as he had promised, when two or more gathered in his name; he was right there in the room with them. He knew the battle that was raging for Lisa's soul. He knew how intense it would be for each one of them. He knew what they needed each moment of this battle. He was exceptionally proud of them for coming to him. He placed his hand on the head of each of them as they prayed.

Although they could not see him, they each began to have a deep peace beyond what they could understand. They didn't have all the answers, but they had assurance. They knew they could trust Jesus. They knew the Holy Spirit would lead them and guide them through this. They encouraged each other in the truth as they said goodnight.

CHAPTER 6

Finally! The two weeks are over. This is the last night without friends, stuck at home! Lisa thought. She began planning who to call first and thinking about what she would like to do. Then she thought, I don't care what we do, I just want to go do something with friends. Early the next morning, Lisa was already showered and dressed when her mom came to wake her up.

"Good morning, sweetheart," Tina said smiling, "You are up early. Do you have plans?"

"Oh yes! I am going to call everyone I can think of and see if we can get together to do something."

Tina's smile broadened and she said, "Well, you have certainly earned the time. I hope your friends are available."

"Thanks Mom." Lisa replied with sincere gratitude.

Tina's expression and tone became serious, "Just let me know where you are going, when, and with whom."

"Yes mam," Lisa replied respectfully.

Lisa hugged her mom. She knew that her mom loved her.

She could tell by the tone in her mom's voice that she was really happy Lisa was off grounding as well. It was unfair of me not to call her when I was going to be late, Lisa thought. She told me she was worried. I will be more careful. Sneaking out was really wrong. Never again, she determined. Lisa went bouncing downstairs for breakfast. She raced through the meal, thanked her mom, and ran back upstairs for the phone.

"Hello" greeted Sheena's cheerful voice on the other end of the line.

Lisa smiled as she heard the familiar friendly voice and responded, "Hi Sheena, its Lisa."

"Oh hi!" Sheena responded in surprise, "Are you *finally* off grounding?" she asked.

"Yeah, it has been *forever*," Lisa explained how the two weeks had felt.

"I bet. I haven't been grounded for a long time. I would hate it," Sheena empathized with Lisa.

"*It is awful*!" Lisa exclaimed with the exaggeration of the full emotional impact. Then she stated, "My parents worked me like a slave on top of it."

"My parents are pretty laid back," Sheena said with gratitude.

"That must be nice," Lisa imagined.

"It is. I am free to do as I please," Sheena confessed. She laughed and then said, "They just told me if I do something to get myself in jail, they won't get me out. They will just come visit me."

Lisa laughed and replied, "They sound really cool. That must be why you're so calm."

"That is certainly part of it. Leaning on Pegasus helps too," Sheena declared.

"You know what was really weird during the last couple of weeks?" Lisa asked.

"What?" Sheena questioned.

Lisa admitted, "I couldn't find him."

"You couldn't?" Sheena asked a bit surprised.

"No! I really needed him too. I felt so let down and alone," Lisa confessed.

"That is weird. I have always been able to reach him," Sheena said honestly. Then with genuine concern she directed Lisa, "Tell me about it."

"It was so frustrating. I tried and tried several times," Lisa began.

"Has that ever happened before, since the beginning?" Sheena probed.

"No, that is what was so weird. It had become really easy to reach him," Lisa answered. "I have never felt so alone before," she confided.

"That must be difficult," Sheena compassionately acknowledged. "I have never been left alone like that. He has always been there with me," She admitted.

"What could have happened? Why did he leave me? Did I do something wrong? Are there others more important than me? Lisa poured out the questions which had been plaguing her.

"I don't think there are more important people," Sheena reassured, "We are all accepted equally by Pegasus," then she explained, "Some of us just are able to grow closer for some reason. I don't really know why." Then she said as if just thinking of fresh idea, "I will ask him what happened."

"That would be great," Lisa said hopefully, "I am so confused now. I don't know who to believe or trust," she admitted with heaviness.

"Trust me, I will find out what the problem is," Sheena assured her, "In the meantime, go have some fun. It sounds like you need it."

"Oh yeah, I need it. The last two weeks have been brutal!" Lisa exclaimed.

"I bet! I'll be back in about 10 days, and I'll call you," Sheena told her.

"Where are you going?" Lisa asked trying to cover the disappointment.

"I am going to camp with Sergio and some of his friends." Sheena explained.

"Oh that sounds awesome! I wish I could go," Lisa admitted.

"We'll plan something cool for all of us later." Sheena encouraged.

"Okay. Have fun," Lisa replied.

"You too." Sheena said, her smile coming through in her tone.

Sheena was quiet on the drive up to the camp site while the guys were joking around. She was preoccupied with seeking Pegasus on what had gone wrong with Lisa. Pegasus reassured her that he was there for Lisa, but Lisa's own anger and some enemy spirits had blocked him from getting to her. Pegasus said he was driven away. Then, he reminded Sheena that she had been chosen to be the one people had to come to. Pegasus, knowing he could not get past the angels protecting Lisa's home, directed, "You need to have Lisa come over, and the two of you come to me together," then he explained, "She needs your help to grow past this."

Sheena was relieved that Pegasus had not given up on nor rejected Lisa. As she came back to the group, she noticed that they were already far into the forest. She looked over and smiled at Sergio.

The guys didn't pay much attention to her being "spacey" anymore. They were used to it. They knew she would "come back to earth" eventually. Josh wondered if she had Epilepsy, but he wouldn't bring it up. Sergio knew what was going on, yet he couldn't explain it to the guys. He had to convince them she was okay when they were younger. They were all relieved when she "came back". Sergio would glance at her every so often to see how she was. When he noticed she was back, he told her they would be at the base site in about 45 minutes. Aaron brought up their last game together, the state championship that had won them scholarships. They were reliving the highlights together when Sergio began remembering the searing pain in his shoulder that game. He assured the guys he was healed, and it didn't bother him anymore. The guys all agreed it was a tough break.
Sergio smiled and excitedly replied, "If it hadn't been for that break, I would not be taking a star on a guided back country trip in the fall."

"Did Rod Grey call you?" Josh asked with a bit of a twinkle in his eyes.

"Oh that is awesome!" shouted David

"Yeah, it's Rod Grey, but you guys can't tell anyone he's going to be here," Sergio commanded.

"No problem, mum's the word," Aaron promised and the others nodded in agreement.

"You're right, that is a whole lot better than going back to school," Josh acknowledged.

"Really?" Sergio asked.

David said, "I thought you liked college."

"I like college girls," Josh said with a sly smile.

"Now you're talking," Aaron answered in agreement.

"I've got the best girl ever right here," Sergio reached over and grabbed Sheena's hand.

She smiled back at him and stated, "That's right, and don't you forget it."

The guys smiled knowingly, and were glad they had been reminded she was with them. They switched the subject again and began talking about the backpacking adventure they were about to embark on.

As they reached the place where they would start the trip, they ran through the checklist of setting up camp. They still had several hours before nightfall, but the camp must be ready before they did anything else. They each knew their task and began setting up their tents right away.

David was the first to finish his tent and he began looking around to decide where to build a fire pit. There was a small clearing on the east side of the camp. It was the perfect place to build a pit. He dug a hole about two feet deep and two feet in diameter. Then, he started searching for stones to make a fireproof rim. He layered the stones around the pit. When he had enough stones, he pulled the grill out of the Bronco and set it on top of the stones. It was a great fit. The only thing the pit needed was wood.

Josh had already gathered enough wood for the two nights they would be at this site. Josh had finished his tent just a few minutes after David, and he went searching for larger pieces of

He found a fallen tree about a half a mile away from the site. There was plenty of wood right there. He chopped a thick branch off the tree trunk. He hauled the branch back to camp. He began chopping the branch into useable pieces.

Sheena had her tent and a few other things finished by the time Josh returned, and she began stacking the wood as he split the logs. She took the kindling over to David's pit, and he started the fire. The smaller sticks caught fire easily, and once they were burning hot enough, he placed the first log on the flames.

While they were preparing the pit and fire, Sergio had taken the five gallon aluminum kettle down to the edge of the river about 100 yards away. He filled the pot with water and carried it to the pit. He set it just a couple of feet away from the fire. Sheena had set the grill back on the pit. She was ready to boil some of the water for drinking. "Good timing," she said and gave Sergio a quick peck on the cheek.

The gang relaxed around the camp fire that evening talking and joking. As they shared childhood memories of previous camp outs, they realized how fortunate they were to have a chance to get together again. They made a pact that they would get together like this no matter where life took each of them in the future. The next day was just as relaxed. The second night, they discussed the hike for the following day.

Each member knew their job for the breakdown and set up of camp. This hike would be mostly up hill, and they planned on covering about 20 miles. According to the relief map, there would likely be a perfect flat upstream awaiting them at the end of the 20 mile hike. They would be creating their own trail. This area was not within the maintained section of the national forest. There was no telling what they would encounter as they trekked through the wilderness.

The crisp morning air was invigorating. They felt all together alive as the chill and forest scents bombarded their senses. The altitude, height above sea level, lifted them above the oppressing summer heat of the valley. They were energized and excited to begin the trip into the backwoods. They broke camp quickly and efficiently.

Their years of childhood camping experience and team work made them like a well-oiled machine. By the time the sun had fully crested the ridge east of them, they were ready to go.

The first 3 miles across the meadow to the base of the mountain would be an easy go. The deer cautiously continued to graze while watching the group passing through. As they hiked through the meadow that morning, they took in the beauty that surrounded them. The song birds' beautiful sonata filled the forest. The brilliant blue sky with a few soft fluffy clouds complimented the dark green trees surrounding them, and the splashes of various colors of wildflowers covering the yellow green sea of grassy meadow beckoned them on.

They began the climb still reveling in the inspiration of the place. Within half a mile they found the mount was steeper than they expected. They did not talk or joke much now. They had to use their energy on the ascent. The forest foliage was dense here. It had been a wet winter with a healthy snow pack. The overgrowth of the lush plants slowed them down. Aaron led the way as he cleared the trail with a machete. They finally reached the flat about an hour before sunset. They quickly set up camp before collapsing for the night. They were all exhausted and went to sleep early.

In light of the morning sun, they could explore the site more fully. The flat was larger than they had expected. It was as perfect as they had hoped for. The large flat would make a great sight for backpacking with horses. The river came down a four foot fall into an almost perfect bowl shaped pond. It was about 30 feet in diameter. The pond itself was only about six feet deep in the center and the water was crystal clear. Surprisingly, there were not a lot of rocks in the bottom of the pond. It was mostly sand here. At the other end of the pond, the river began descending again through a narrow split in the rock wall that created the rim of the bowl. The water was fresh, but calm. They played in the water that afternoon like they were children again.

They enjoyed the perfect day together. Nothing else mattered at that moment. They were content with where they were. They did not consider what the rest of the trek may have in store.

The next morning they quickly broke camp again and continued deeper into the forest. They did not stay at the next couple of sites more than the night. Both mornings, they resumed the hike. The seventh day they were at another great site and stayed that day. They would have to begin heading back to the base camp the following day. Fortunately, the trek back would be almost all downhill, and they would be able to make it back easily within three days. So far it had been a perfect trip. Nothing they had experienced could have prepared them for what was about to occur.

Although the morning seemed perfect, Sergio was anxious. He could not quite settle down and enjoy the wonderful site they had found. He kept looking around to see if there was something unusual, something wrong, but he didn't see anything that would alarm him. Everything looked and sounded perfect. He went to the fire and poured some coffee into his cup. He looked at Sheena. She seemed perfectly peaceful. He scanned the rest of the group to see what they were doing. David was leaned against a stone reading a book. Aaron was just relaxing and enjoying his coffee. He looked like his mind was completely blank. Must be nice, Sergio thought. "Pegasus, what is this nervous feeling about?" he prayed. Where is Josh? Oh no, he thought, it's Josh. What is it though?

Rooaarrr! The roar shattered the quiet morning and deafened their ears. They quickly gathered together and began looking around to see what or where the warning had come from. Roooaarr. Crash. Boom. Roooaarrr. AAAhhhhh! Thud. They began running towards the horrible sounds making as much noise as they could. Yelling, clapping their hands, beating two tin cups against each other, the four of them ran towards it. They reached a small clearing. There they saw Josh crumpled on the ground, and a huge brown bear running back into the forest.

They stood together continuing to make as much noise as they could until the bear was out of sight. The blood oozing onto the ground made them all nauseous. They gathered around Josh to try to help him. David took off his shirt, twisted into a rope, and tied it tightly around Josh's upper arm. Hopefully this would stop the bleeding. Sheena looked away briefly as she saw the bone sticking out just under where David had tied off Josh's arm. David began checking out the rest of Josh's body, to see if he was wounded anywhere else. Although he was unconscious, he was breathing. That was good.

The huge bruise on the side of Josh's head was an unmistakable paw print. He was fortunate the bear had not struck him with its claws there. There did not appear to be any swelling in his stomach, at least for now. As David assessed Josh for further injury, Aaron gathered a couple of sticks to make a splint for Josh's arm. He sat down next to David. Together, David and Aaron set Josh's arm and splint it. Sheena went and sat herself at Josh's head. She began caressing his forehead softly, tears streaming down her face. She started to pray.

"Can we move him?" Sergio asked.

"I don't know. I don't think it's a good idea." Aaron said with uncertainty.

Sergio looked at David, "Should we run for help? Aaron and I can make it to the Bronco on our own in a day and a half."

David considered Sergio's idea, but thought of all that could go wrong if they split up. He looked at Sergio and Aaron as if he were looking far beyond them. After a couple of minutes, which felt like an eternity to the other guys, he replied, "If we all go together, we can make it in three and get him to a hospital quicker. Then we are all together as well."

Aaron, concerned about injuring Josh further asked, "But how do we move him?"

"What about the gear?" Sergio said waving his hand across the scope of the camp site. He certainly didn't think it was good to try to pack up camp, haul all of it, as well as their friend back down the mountain.

"We leave it for now," David said solemnly. "We need to make one of those carrying slings," instantly returning to Aaron's question.

"Good idea," Aaron responded with a spark of hope in his voice, "What can we use?"

Sergio responded excitedly, "There is a liner under my tent that will work!"

"Great!" the guys replied in unison.

Aaron added, "We have plenty of twine."

"Good," David acknowledged as he nodded. Then as if giving instruction, he directed the comment to Aaron, "We need a few longer branches that we can make a frame with."

Once again the team was stirred to action. They gathered the materials and began to make the carrying sling. Aaron suddenly remembered the fire, and he went to put it out. He brought water back. Josh was still unconscious, so Aaron just put a small amount of water in his mouth and gave the cup to Sheena.

Sheena sat with Josh's head in her lap, praying over him. Suddenly she felt a surge of energy welling up within her. She began chanting some ancient song she had never heard before and circling her hands over Josh's head. As she felt lead too, she put her hands on either side of his head, continuing to chant. She could feel the energy flowing out of her hands and into Josh's head.

Josh's eyes opened wide, and he stared at Sheena. He could feel a burning heat radiating from her hands. The heat began to travel through his head, into his neck, and down his body. She just continued singing this strange and wild song they had never heard before.

The pain in his arm jerked his attention to the tourniquet and splint. Then he felt the heat beginning to radiate into his arm. He could almost feel the bone rejoining beneath the skin. He took his good hand and began to pull apart the splint.

The guys had finished their sling, and stood for a moment admiring their work. Then they picked up the carrier, and headed for the clearing. They planned how they would get back to the Bronco as quickly and safely as possible.

They discussed the plan for taking turns carrying Josh back. As they reached the clearing, feeling confident they could get everyone back within two days instead of three; they were stopped short in their tracks. They stood with their mouths agape. The sight before them left them speechless.

Josh, sitting up now, saw them and began to laugh hysterically. The expressions on their faces were priceless. Seeing the shocked and amazed looks in his friends' eyes as they clutched the giant sling gave him some understanding as to just how badly he had been hurt. How could he explain what had happened? He looked down with admiration in his eyes. Sheena lay with her head in his lap, sleeping. Josh had removed the splint and tourniquet. His arm was completely healed. He was feeling a little tired, but amazingly well. Other than the bruise on his face, shredded shirt, and a scar on his arm, no one would know he had just been attacked by a bear.

Sergio knelt down beside them and caressed Sheena's face. He knew she must have given a tremendous amount of energy for this to happen. He smiled knowingly at Josh. Then he picked up Sheena and carried her back to camp. Aaron and David helped Josh up and asked, "What...How did this happen?"

Josh replied, "I don't know exactly, but I think Sheena healed me." They walked back to camp still in shock and awe, each of them swirling in the events of the day. They had a million questions for Sheena when she woke up. They would certainly remember this for the rest of their lives.

In celebration, the guys caught some fish and prepared a grilled fish dinner for the evening. They had plenty to be grateful for. They had to wake up Sheena for dinner. As they sat around the fire, they began to recall the horrible attack, hoping Sheena would explain the miraculous healing.

"So when did you know the bear was there?" David began the conversation.

"I didn't see it until it was right behind me," Josh admitted.

"What did you do to make it attack?" Aaron asked, leaning in.

"I just turned around when I heard it walking towards me," Josh explained. As the memory came flooding back so did the fear.

His voice trembling, and eyes widening he said, "Then it reared up and towered over me. I just froze, not able to think at all."

"I would be thinking I am about to die," Sergio acknowledged.

"Not even that went through my mind. I was simply frozen," Josh replied almost numb.

"That must be when we heard the first roar," Sergio said as if thinking out loud.

"I remember his roar!" Josh exclaimed, "It jolted me out of the frozen panic!" He took a deep breath and explained, "I was able to duck and just miss getting clobbered with the first swing of his huge paw. I kind of spun as I came up and started to run. That's when I felt the powerful hit to my arm. I screamed, and then felt the blow to my head. I don't remember anything after that until I came too."

"We heard the first roar, jumped to our feet and came running, making all the noise we could," Aaron said supportively.

Josh looked at the group with surprise and confessed, "I didn't hear anything but the bear and my own heartbeat after it began to attack me."

"When we reached you, you were already out," David acknowledged.

Sheena had been sitting quietly as the guys recapped the day's events. She still felt very weak and could easily have slept the whole night through. The guys grew quiet and Josh finally asked, "Sheena, how did you do that?"

"I didn't do it on my own," She acknowledged.

The questions began flying at Sheena from Josh, David, and Aaron. "Who else was there?" Aaron asked incredulously.

"What do you mean you didn't do it on your own?" David asked stunned.

"Who helped you?" Josh asked sincerely grateful, yet confused.

Sergio stood and said, "Alright guys, it's time we told you about whom we have come to know and how this is possible. However, Sheena is still very tired. So let her rest, and I will tell you what I can." Sheena smiled gratefully at Sergio and then said, "good night," as she headed for the tent.

The guys stood, replied "good night," and waited until she was in the tent to continue the conversation. "Is that how you kept the boulder from smashing Rod Grey and his boy?" David asked, putting two and two together.

"Yes," answered Sergio then explaining he said, "I was able to cover them by throwing my energy over them. Pegasus helped me also."

"What?!? Pegasus?!?" Josh replied with shock.

"You can't be serious," Aaron responded sarcastically, "That winged horse from Mythology helped you?"

"How is that possible?" David asked seriously.

Sergio could understand their confusion and doubts. He raised his hands as if surrendering and said, "Okay, okay, I know it sounds crazy, but just listen to me."

"Alright," The three guys said in unison as they sat back down.

Sergio hesitated a moment trying to find a way to explain, then he asked, "Have you ever felt like there was someone else there, but you knew there wasn't anyone around?"

"Sure, hasn't everybody?" said Aaron

"My mom said that's when we know angels are with us," explained Josh

"Right," replied Sergio, "And these angels or spirits have names. Pegasus is just one of many. He is the one both Sheena and I seek for help in all kinds of things. He is very powerful. He is teaching us how to use the other ninety percent of our brains to do things like what you've seen."

"How do you know he's an angel and not a demon?" David asked with concern.

"Would a demon help us do good things like this?" Sergio sincerely queried.

"No, I suppose not," admitted David.

"This is just the beginning too," Sergio said assuredly, "We are going to become more powerful as we continue to grow."

"When did you first start talking to this spirit?" Aaron asked inquisitively.

Sergio replied, "I started talking to Pegasus about three years ago. I had seen other spirits before, but I didn't really talk to them. I wanted to understand them better. I knew Sheena had been talking to them for a while, so I asked her about it. She introduced me to Pegasus. We have been growing in strength and power with him since then."

"Is this why she seems spacey sometimes?" Josh asked with a mix of curiosity and concern.

"Yes, she is very sensitive to the spirits," Sergio explained, "They will come and call her into their world while the rest of us just go about our day."

"I thought she had epilepsy," Josh confessed.

"Sometimes it looks the same. Some people are even misdiagnosed. They usually figure it out as they get older," Sergio acknowledged.

"So can you do what she just did?" Aaron inquired.

"No," Sergio admitted, "We each have different abilities. I am able to move objects or stop them to some degree. I also see or sense things that are about to happen. Like today, I knew something was wrong. I just didn't know what it was."

David suddenly recalled, "You told Rod Grey it was like a movie playing in front of your eyes just before you warned him."

"That's right," Sergio agreed smiling. He was glad they were getting it. He continued, "Sometimes it is really clear like that; sometimes it is just a weird feeling like today."

"I have never seen a spirit, or felt like there was anything special about me except baseball," Josh declared. Then with a hint of hope he asked, "Is it possible for me to do something like that?"

Sergio looked sympathetically at Josh. He sincerely said, "Well, I don't know what your specific abilities are." He paused, and took a deep breath. Then he smiled and encouraged Josh, "However, I am sure if you learn to find Pegasus, you will find out what your abilities are."

David's expression of apprehension was obvious as he stood up and stepped back, he argued, "I don't think this is a good thing. My family is Christian, and I have been told that talking to spirits is wrong."

Aaron threw out his hands as he turned to David, and asked, "How could healing Josh, when we are days away from help," his shoulders shrugged as he emphasized, "***be wrong?***"

"I don't know, but I don't feel very comfortable with this," admitted David.

Sergio looked compassionately at David and responded, "That's okay; you don't have to do anything you're not comfortable with." Then with assurance he advised, "You ask your god to help you learn what your abilities are. I am sure he will help you." When he could see David was not re-assured he waited thoughtfully for a few moments, hoping Pegasus would give him the right words. The guys all sat silently staring into the fire as they considered the conversation. Suddenly Sergio said, "David," as he lifted his head and their eyes met, asked sincerely and softly, "After all, this is the very kind of thing Jesus did isn't it?"

"Well yes," David admitted with surprise, "I guess it is."

"Jesus figured out how to tap into the power that is available to all of us. He even said, 'Of my own, I can do nothing.' He knew that he had to reach a higher power." Sergio explained with renewed confidence.

"That makes sense," David replied.

"Didn't he also say we could do the same things he had done?" Aaron inquired.

"Yeah, I remember the pastor saying that when I was at church with my parents!" Josh replied excitedly as if it were all suddenly making sense.

"That's right, I remember it too," David acknowledged a little hesitantly. He could not disagree with their reasoning, but the whole thing felt wrong. Deep in his gut, there was a gnawing that he could not ignore.

Aaron's face became puzzled, and he asked inquisitively, "So how come most people don't do these kinds of things?"

"Most people never even try to learn how. They're too busy with their own lives to care to learn," Sergio responded with a sigh and tone of disappointment.

"Another reason could be the growth of belief in science; we've gotten away from the spiritual," David admitted.

"So are you saying that we've simply forgotten how?" Josh clarified.

Sergio said, "Pretty much," his expression turned stern as he added, "And because many people don't understand it, they have killed people who do learn how."

"You're right!" Josh exclaimed, "They killed Jesus and his apostles!"

"Remember learning about the Salem witch trials in school?" Aaron asked.

"Oh yeah... That was awful," David agreed.

"It was the same thing they did to Jesus. It has been done countless times throughout history to those who learn how to do miracles like Jesus did," Sergio proclaimed.

"Okay, I get it," David admitted, "But I still don't feel real comfortable with it."

"That's alright," Sergio encouraged. Then he added, "David, you need to talk to your god about it. He will make all things clear to you.........if you will open your mind."

"Thanks Sergio," David said, "I am glad you understand."

Sergio looked seriously at each one of the guys and commanded, "Just don't tell anyone else about this." His voice softened slightly as he explained, "Some people, *especially religious people*, get weird about this kind of thing. They just don't understand."

"Don't worry. I won't tell anyone. I know how parents can freak out over nothing," Aaron assured, then he pointed out the seemingly obvious, "And we certainly don't want them coming after Sheena or you the way they went after people in the past!"

David and Josh agreed. The guys then decided they would continue the conversation on the way back.

It was late and they had a lot of ground to cover over the next few days. They put out the fire and made sure the camp was clean. They agreed they'd seen enough of bears and didn't want anything to entice creatures into camp. Finally, they crawled into their tents exhausted. The sound of crickets and owls lulled them into a deep sleep.

CHAPTER 7

Tenicia couldn't believe what she was hearing. "….a miracle," Josh said softly as they sat at the counter of the soda shop. Her mom had spoken about miracles, but most of the time it seemed as if it were just coincidence to her. The TV preachers used people's desires for miracles to make money. They found some pretty good actors, but everyone knew the events were staged. The people who really needed the help left in the same condition they came in. Real miracles, where someone was actually healed; the lame walked and the blind saw kinds of things were just good stories, or were they? If what Josh was saying was true, this really was a miracle. He showed her the scar on his arm as if he could tell she didn't believe him.

Just then Sheena came in the shop and joined them. "Hi guys, what's happening?" Sheena asked cheerfully.

"I was just showing Tenicia the scar," admitted Josh as he dropped his head, remembering Sheena's plea. He added a little anxiously, "I don't think she believes me."

"You can belleve him," Sheena said, looking Tenicia strait in the eyes. She changed tones revealing the fear she had felt when it happened and confessed, "It was pretty scary. We were way up in the forest, and days away from help."

"You did this?" asked Tenicia her eyes wide and mouth agape.

"Sort of… I didn't do, it on my own," Sheena humbly replied.

"How?" asked Tenicia.

"I have wanted to talk to you, but we can't really talk about it here," Sheena kept her voice low as she glanced at Josh with a scolding eye.

Tenicia felt a little uneasy about the secretiveness Sheena seemed swathed in. With an unsettling uncertainty she asked, "Okay, so where can we go?"

"Can you come over to my house?" Sheena asked hopefully.

"Sure. My mom won't be home for hours," Tenicia said.

"Great!" Sheena replied. Then turning and looking him in the eyes, Sheena pleadingly directed, "Josh, please don't tell anyone else, at least not yet."

Josh dropped his head for a moment in shame. When he looked back up at her, he confessed in a hushed voice, "It is so hard to keep this quiet. It is amazing! I feel like I am going to burst if I don't tell sometimes."

"I know, but you have to be careful. Remember what they do...what they would do to me," Sheena gently reminded him.

"Alright, I don't want anyone bugging you about it," Josh declared.

"The news reporters would love to hear about this, and then you'd never get a moment's peace," Tenicia assessed quickly.

"That's right." Sheena acknowledged, "That is why I asked him not to tell anyone," Sheena looked imploringly at Josh.

"Okay. Okay. I know, 'mum's the word,'" He promised.

"Good. Are you guys ready?" Sheena asked with eagerness for the freedom and safety of her home.

"Yeah, let's go," Tenicia replied.

Sheena asked Tenicia what she had been doing. They talked about much of nothing on the walk from the soda shop to Sheena's home. When they made it to the house, they went straight into the den and got comfortable. Sheena began to tell Tenicia about how she had cried out to Pegasus for help. Tenicia's eyes grew wide with awe as she listened to the story. She knew there had to be more to this world. She had often felt like there was someone else there when she was alone. She had dismissed the feeling as her imagination, but now as she listened to them; she wondered if it were really spirits she had sensed.

She was not the kind of person to easily believe people, but these two were compelling. The scar on Josh's arm was certainly real and she could tell it was fairly fresh. Tenicia also considered Sheena's plea to not tell. If this were just a publicity stunt type of thing, Sheena would not ask him to keep it a secret. She seemed genuinely concerned about keeping it quiet. Sheena had her attention. She would watch and listen for a while to see if it were true.

Sheena could tell that Tenicia was skeptical, but she was really listening and considering what was being shared. Sheena knew Tenicia was a powerful person, and she looked forward to bringing her into the circle. She realized she needed to call everyone together. Josh could not keep this quiet for long, so they would have to understand how to know who to tell and who not to tell. She asked if they could come over again on Friday night. This would give her two days to learn what to do next. She would call the others as soon as they left. She decided to invite Lisa as well. This will be good for her too. She needs to know what she and Pegasus can do together, thought Sheena.

Josh walked Tenicia home and they continued talking about the miracle. He told her he had known Sheena since at least second grade.

He knew there was something different about her, but he had not known of this until the attack. Now he was eager to learn more. He could barely keep from telling everyone about the miracle and was glad he could tell her. He described what he remembered in detail enough to convince Tenicia this was the real thing. Then she looked up at his face and noticed the fading traces of a large bruise on the side of his face.

There was no doubt in her mind now that this had really happened. She began to look forward to seeing Sheena again. She wanted to learn how to call on Pegasus. She wondered if there were other spirits who had this kind of power. She really wondered why more people didn't know about this. Was this why so many people believed those preachers? Were some of those miracles real? Why weren't more people able to do them? Why weren't more people healed at those places?

She now had only questions when she thought she had known the answers. It was obvious Josh was too recently enlightened to know the answers, so she would wait until the next meeting.

Sheena had called everyone, and it was set. They would all meet at her house Friday at eight p.m. She immediately began to call on Pegasus for guidance. This was far too big for her to handle on her own. She spent the entire night enraptured with Pegasus. As the new day's first rays began to gleam through the window, Sheena came back to the present reality. She now had confidence and was no longer afraid of what to say to the group. She had the plan in detail. She began preparing for the meeting. This meeting would be the beginning of a powerful new group that would change the world. She still found it hard to believe that Pegasus had chosen her to lead them. She began to be filled with a sense of pride in herself. She must be truly special to be chosen like this.

The following day she went to the thrift shop at the edge of town. This new circle would begin with a special celebration, and she needed to find just the right pieces for the table. Just as he had guided her to the thrift shop, Pegasus now whispered to her in the store, "Look at the goblet there almost buried behind the other glasses."

On the center of a shelf packed with all kinds of different glasses was an antique looking, badly tarnished silver goblet. Sheena felt a thrill rush through her as she picked it up. It was perfect. Her mom had silver cleaner. This goblet would be beautiful. She put the goblet in the small basket and continued her quest through the store. As she was browsing at some miscellaneous things that seemed randomly thrown on the shelf, she spotted a double edged knife. The handle had an interesting carving, but the knife looked dull. "Yes, it is the right one. Sergio can sharpen it," he spoke softly to her. She gasped with delight when she saw the large brass Pegasus sitting on an end table in the back room of the store.

She was getting more excited about the initiation celebration as she found each of the items she had seen in the vision the night before. "It's perfect, just like you showed me," she whispered to her unseen partner as she gingerly caressed the sculpture. She took everything to the counter and left the thrift shop with a sense of eagerness about the decorating.

She placed everything she had gathered into the workshop behind the house. No one ever used the shop. Her parents had helped her set it up like a clubhouse when she was younger. There were a couple of old couches and some old end tables already in there. The console table her mom had put in the garage recently would make a great altar. There was plenty of space for whatever they decided to do. It would be the perfect place for the circle to begin meeting. Sergio came over and helped her get everything ready. He asked what she had planned, but she could not tell him. He "...had to wait like everyone else," she said.

He was particularly curious about the knife he was sharpening and polishing. The double edged dagger had him riveted. The intricate design in the handle was like nothing he'd ever seen. The balance was perfect. The knife was a masterpiece. It had to be handmade. "How did something so fantastic end up in a thrift shop?" he wondered. "What was she going to use this for?" was the next question that came to his mind.

Pegasus spoke clearly to him, "Trust me; trust her. Do as she tells you."

Sergio had always known Sheena was special. He understood why Pegasus would choose her to lead like this. So he waited with anticipation for the meeting they were preparing for.

Friday evening Sheena became more and more excited as she prepared for her guests. She had told them to go through the side gate, straight to the workshop. She had set a few camping lanterns out to light the path. She had the shop filled with the soft light of candles. All other lights were turned off. The room had a sensually warm radiance.

The brass sculpture in the center of the console table reflected the dancing flames with an eerie glimmering tint that seemed to bring the Pegasus to life. As each one of the friends arrived they were enamored with the room. They stopped speaking to each other as they entered. The only greeting was a quiet nod of acknowledgement. No one seemed to notice that David was not there. Everyone sat hushed as they waited for Sheena to begin the meeting. They were filled with expectation. They all sensed nothing would be the same after this night.

Sheena began the night by telling them how she could only thank Pegasus for all he had done. She had each of the guys tell their perspective of what had happened, starting with Sergio. As they relived the event from the week before, Lisa and Tenicia listened with wonder and amazement. Sheena finally began telling the group of their need for Pegasus and each other.

"You now know what Pegasus can do for and through you. You each know you need his guidance. Tonight you can come to him, and we will become family. Is there anyone here who does not want to come to Pegasus tonight? If you do not want Pegasus, please leave now."

Sheena waited for a minute before continuing. No one left. They looked at each other, wondering if anyone would be foolish enough to leave. No one moved. They all wanted to have such a personal guide. They all wanted to know what was special about them. They all wanted this kind of power.

Sheena set the goblet half filled with wine on the console table next to the Pegasus. She picked up the knife and began singing in an ancient language Pegasus had given her. She purposefully pricked her left middle finger and let the trickle of blood drip into the goblet. The others watched... waited... wondered. She set the knife down, picked up the goblet and swirled it to mix the wine and blood. She continued the incantation and lifted the goblet up, in an offering to the gods.

The spirits gathered around watching with as much anticipation and eagerness as the group. "As you know," Sariah addressed the group of spirits, "I have invited you to join us in the revival of the next most powerful world religion."

"I want the one they call Sergio," said Meriden.

"He is already mine," said Amon,

Meriden knew Amon needed no help with 30 legions at his call. So he looked at the other two young men carefully. Josh was wide open and ready. He was strong and intelligent, naturally gifted in every way. He would make an excellent choice. "Alright then, let me have the one they call Josh." None of the other spirits argued. Meriden was almost as strong as Amon and Sariah. Sariah looked at Amon to see his reaction. They had been working together for centuries, he did not want to violate their partnership. Amon gave a nod of consent. So Sariah agreed to Meriden's demand, and then invited the others to choose their person.

Each of the other four demons controlled 15 legions of their own. They intended to make this little group into a world religion and gain power in the spiritual kingdom. Sariah and Amon would become great and mighty rulers together. They had been looking for the right people for at least a century. They had nurtured their two people from childhood. There was no resistance from the parents. Sergio's parents were even cooperative.

They had been watching the other spirits as well and had purposely picked each one to join them. Now it seemed as if everything was falling perfectly into place. They were anticipating their star like rise in the two kingdoms.

Sheena stared intently at them now, and she ceased chanting. "I give my blood for you tonight. For I am one with Pegasus and you will become one with us. Each of you must drink from this goblet, and you will receive the Pegasus this night. You will then have wisdom and understanding, your gifts will be made known to you, you will be empowered like never before."

She looked at Sergio. He came to her, took a drink from the cup, and then kissed her passionately. He had never been so captivated with her before. She drank in his strength as he kissed her. This night would be special indeed. She suddenly knew when everyone else was gone, she would give herself to him fully and consummate their unique unity. Yet now, she must focus. She pulled back and smiled. After Sergio went back to the couch, Sheena motioned for Josh, then Aaron, and then each of the girls.

One by one they came to her, drank from the goblet, and returned to their seat. As they sat down, they were immediately overtaken by the eager
spirits. Each of them experienced the "Pegasus" coming and speaking words of encouragement to them. They were each promised a different power. They understood things they had never even considered before. A couple of hours passed before anyone got up.

Amon reminded Sergio of the promises he made a year ago and how those had been fulfilled so far. He promised Sergio he would continue to make him rich and powerful. He told Sergio how proud he should be of his accomplishments. He filled Sergio with confidence and a sense of being unstoppable. He also stirred in Sergio a deeper desire for Sheena. "She is the perfect one for you," sung Amon to Sergio's heart. "She will complete you and the two of you will be like the sun, flaming with power, love, and life giving energy."

Sergio smiled at the thought of Sheena being his, and the two of them leading the world together. He had no doubt it would happen after the last year. He saw a vision of the two of them in a massive estate, leading the stars in their knowledge of Pegasus as well as on their backpacking adventures.

Meriden filled Josh with an explosive energy just after the others were entranced and he began speaking in an ancient language of his own. Meriden told Josh he would be able to see into the depths of a person's soul and distinguish whether they were worthy of the knowledge of the ancient secrets. He declared Josh would be filled with wisdom that the circle would need to make many decisions.

He granted him the power of fire throwing. This gift scared Josh a little, but the spirit promised him he would be able to control it. "There will be times when Sheena needs you to protect her from those who would seek to destroy her," declared Meriden. He gave Josh a vision similar to that of a superhero defending a special person against evil people.

Aaron began to be pulled away from the room at lightning speed. The tunnel he entered was dark as the night sky!

He could see everyone in the room, including himself, growing further and further away from him. They began to look like ants. Then he could not see the room anymore. He was flying faster and faster. Shapes were indistinguishable blurs. Streams of various colors burst by him. He was exhilarated. He suddenly saw the expanse of the universe before him.

Pegasus came and nudged him playfully. "Aaron," he called, "I will give you the keys to unlocking the mysteries of the universe. You have a mighty intellect. I will guide you in discovery and invention. You will be greatly honored among scientists and universities. You will bring prestigious people to understanding." Aaron's heart swelled with anticipation. He could hardly wait to walk into his new future with this outstanding gift. He suddenly desired to make Pegasus proud. He would use his gift well.

Tenicia was still a bit skeptical that she could be like Sheena, but when she saw Pegasus standing before her she could only believe. Pegasus gently whispered to her, "You are a special person as well."

"You have always loved music. There is a reason for your love. You are a beautiful instrument. I will bring you fame as a singer. You will lead many to me as well, but with different gifts. Yours will be the finest voice ever heard. I will give you the melodies, harmonies, and lyrics that will capture your generation. With your fame, you will be able to speak to millions about me. Then they will search me out as well. You will be rich beyond your wildest dreams."

To Lisa, Pegasus had a gentleness she loved. He nuzzled her playfully and she stroked his neck. She suddenly understood how he had not left her alone in her time of need. She saw the block her parents had put up with the cross hanging on the wall in her room. She would take it down immediately. She had hardly even noticed it was hanging there above her window when she had come back home that night.

Pegasus told her that spirits spreading the lie of Jesus were strong and they would have to have help to battle them. He assured her he would bring the help, she just needed to keep looking to him for direction.

Then he told her she would become a great educator of the people. He knew she had the gift of teaching. He would help her become a well loved and respected teacher. She was thrilled. He also told her she would be able to sense things about people. She would have the ability to read their thoughts whenever she wanted to.

Sheena had set out several hors d'oeuvres while everyone else was entranced. The appetizers were greatly appreciated as everyone felt like they were starving when they regained their senses. There was a new and deeper bond among them. They mutually possessed an enlightenment few people shared. There was a serene communion between them now. They began dancing around the brass idol, honoring it. They laughed, danced, and ate together for another couple of hours. It was suddenly early morning. They felt elated, as if they had just begun the celebration; yet, they were very tired.

Before each of the group left, they agreed they would meet like this every week. Sheena instructed them to listen closely to Pegasus and be very careful whom they invited in to the fellowship.

They all had a deeper desire to guard this exceptional circle from those who would destroy it. Protecting Sheena would be their top priority. They clasped hands encircling the Pegasus and stated an oath to defend their circle, especially their leader, with their lives. Sheena was honored by their love for her. She was glad to have been their offering, and she looked forward to leading them on into the future. Then each of them hugged her as they said goodbye.

Sergio came up to her last, and as he embraced her she whispered lovingly, "Please stay." He looked into her eyes and smiled. He could see the longing in her eyes. He wasn't going anywhere. He kept his arms around her and stood behind her as their friends walked down the path and out the gate. Once the gate was closed, they shut the door to the rest of the world. Their bond was special and greater than any other. Nothing would tear them apart, he vowed in his heart.

That night was one each of them would remember forever. They were each profoundly changed through the course of the night. They continued to meet, just as they had planned. They grew immensely in knowledge and power. They grew closer together, and further away from their families and previous friends, with the exception of Sergio's parents. Gilberto and Oriana seemed to understand them, and they became the circle's parents. As they grew closer to each other and Pegasus, the group became successful in everything they wanted to do.

Although Aaron had initially intended to stay, Pegasus had called him to pursue higher education. Josh stayed home in the fall to help Sergio build the business. They had been teammates for most of their lives, so this joint effort felt completely natural. Yet now, it was also a spiritually profound partnership in praying while planning.

The trip with Rod Grey was unspoiled. Rod and his son had a fantastic adventure. Rod Grey, of course, recommended them to other people in Hollywood. Many of their clients were famous and appreciated the guys' ability to keep their trips concealed. Each new client made referrals to others. Their business grew quickly and effortlessly. Pegasus had promised Sergio a "rich and exciting life". One night as he lay under the stars, Sergio thought to himself, so far he has delivered everything he has promised me.

The girls became very close as well that senior year of high school. The other girls found themselves drawn to Sheena, Tenicia, and Lisa. They admired the girls' confidence and kindness. Everyone could see that the three of them were unusually close, but they were also nice to everyone else.

They were not like the snobby girls who put down others. Everyone liked them, but they had no idea what made these girls so different. The girls were also very successful in their grades and rose to the top of the senior class. They had the respect of the teachers as well.

Lisa's parents did not know what to make of the changes. Tina and Henry were nervous, yet grateful. They had reluctantly agreed not make Lisa attend church anymore. They weren't sure about her new friends, but they could only see things getting better.

They were concerned when she seemed to be drifting away from Mark and Maria, but Pastor Dale assured them this was just a normal teenage phase. He had met with Lisa two or three times as they had agreed.

Pegasus had instructed her in what to say. He did not want Lisa to tell the pastor he was with her. So she told the pastor the stories Pegasus gave her.

Tina and Henry didn't really believe this was normal, but they didn't know what else to do. They did not want the sneaky, angry, rebellious girl back, so they simply and quietly prayed for her while giving her "space".

Marcella was pleased that her daughter was doing so well. She had hoped the move out of the city and into a small community would be good for her daughter. So far it seemed as if everything she had hoped for was happening. Tenicia had been able to make new friends and was getting good grades. Tenicia had even joined the school choir and was quickly elevated to the top. She seemed truly happy. That was all Marcella had wanted for her. Tenicia had been so miserable after the divorce. They had gotten their new start, and it was wonderful she thought.

The year passed quickly. The gang was excited to celebrate the graduations and business growth. They were looking forward to a grand summer. The guys had purposefully scheduled a month off. Aaron would be returning from college. They had been planning a trip for the circle of six. They decided they would tour Highway 1 and camp along the coast for a month.

They wanted to spend time as a group, away from home, and the others. They did not know what the future would hold for them as a group. So now they wanted to seek Pegasus together and find out what they were going to do next.

Shortly before they left, David called Sergio. He was back in town for summer also. Sergio was happy to hear from him and invited him to go on the trip. Sergio thought, Maybe he's ready now. David said he wanted to catch up with everyone, but he could not go the whole month. They agreed that he would meet them at Cayucos and spend that weekend with them.

The gang was heading for Southern California first, and would make their way back up the coast from one campsite to the next. They were determined to find the best beaches and explore what each area had to offer. Torrey Pines would be their first stop. The unspoiled area would be an incredible place to start their retreat. 2000 acres of wilderness right by San Diego offered plenty of hiking and swimming in a completely different environment from their own forest. The area would give them a great new place to explore. They would have a fantastic time playing on the beach and hanging out around the campfire. The girls were excited about the opportunity to spend a day or two in the city. They loaded the trailer with their supplies, piled into the van, and drove off with the thrill of anticipation.

Everything went wonderfully at Torrey Pines as well as the next site near Oxnard. The circle was on their way to Cayucos. Sergio went to a pay phone and called David to let him know they would be there within four and half hours. David had been looking forward to this weekend the entire two and a half weeks since Sergio's last call.

He was really excited about seeing his old team mates. So much had happened over the last year, he could hardly wait to tell them everything.

About half way through the drive, at Kettleman City, David stopped to stretch and get a bite. He also began to feel nervous about what he had to tell Sergio, Aaron, Josh and Sheena. He walked around a bit and found that soothing. He began to pray silently as he walked;

"Lord, I need you to give me boldness and the right words tempered with your love. May they each see your love shining through me. Help me to see them as you see them, no matter what their reaction is.

Jesus, I know they are into some deep spiritual things. Help them to understand who you are, just as you have shown me who you are. Give me the sensitivity to your Holy Spirit to wait on you and speak only what you would want me to and at the right time. Help them to see the huge difference you have made in me. Steady me Lord, please. Help me not to fear losing their friendship or being mocked by them. Help me to be as courageous as you are. Thank you, Jesus, for hearing my prayer."

Feeling refreshed and calmed, David climbed back in the car and continued towards Cayucos. He was getting excited about seeing his friends again. He now had peace deep inside his soul. This weekend was a divine appointment, and he was looking forward to all that would come out of it.

The gang arrived at Cayucos without any trouble. They piled out of the van and stretched. Sergio's face lit up as he saw a Midnight Blue Camaro coming up the road. Sergio called to the other guys and they came up beside him. All three of them wore a huge grin. They wanted David to be a part of the new team. They had talked on the way about how they would approach the topic. They had not really talked to each other since the camping trip the summer before. What had happened to him? They wondered. Now they were going to get a chance to find out......after Frisbee football on the beach!

Aaron already had the Frisbee in hand. As David climbed out of the car, the Frisbee came flying at him. It was on! "Oooh! It's like that?!" David yelled as he grabbed the fast flying disc and flung it far down the beach. Josh went sprinting after it with Aaron running close behind. Sergio and David gave each other a "high five" and walked further down the beach. They asked the girls if they wanted to play. Lisa said she didn't feel up to it and pulled back from everyone. They chose teams and took a few minutes to discuss plays.

Lisa suddenly had a deep dislike for David, although she didn't know why. She didn't want him here. She wanted him to go away, but everyone else seemed so happy he was here. Even Sheena thought highly of David. Lisa knew only that he made her stomach churn.

She walked down the beach away from the game and called again to Pegasus. She asked for his help and guidance. She still didn't know what to do, except keep distance; but she felt better. She began gathering drift wood strewn across the beach for a fire. By the time the others were done playing she had made a large pile near their chosen spot, far away from the signs of high tide.

The gang got the tents set up and the fire going. Sheena got out everything to make dinner including the ingredients for s'mores. They talked about the events of the last year, joked and laughed, but did not bring up spiritual topics in the conversations. Everyone felt that conversation was too heavy for their first night reunion. The gang had agreed it would be Sergio who talked to David about it first, unless David brought it up. Lisa sat with the group through the evening warily eying David. She didn't say much all night. David looked at her curiously a couple of times when he felt the cold stare. David wondered what was wandering through her mind. He felt a little on edge when her stare shot daggers at him. All he could do was ask Jesus for help. He did not even know what to ask for specifically, just help.

The next day the group hiked until the heat of the day and then swam. They had a great time together. This was a perfect summer weekend at an un-crowded beach.

That night around the campfire David knew it was time. He felt a little bit of a lump in his throat and his hands begin to get a bit sweaty. It was almost as bad as the first time he asked a girl to go out. "I've got something major to tell you guys," he started nervously.

"You're getting married," joked Josh.

"No, it's not that," he laughed gratefully and then calmly said, "Seriously, I have to tell you guys something really important."

"Alright, we're listening," Sergio said and he leaned in, giving David his full attention. The others also focused on David.

"Yeah, go for it bro," Aaron chimed in.

David took a deep breath as he looked at each of the group focusing on him. He leaned forward towards them as he began.

"Last summer, after we came down from the mountains; I couldn't stop thinking about what had happened, and what you had said Sergio," he looked Sergio straight in the eyes, "So, I did what you told me to do. I asked my God to show me the truth."

"Awesome," Sergio responded confidently, yet his curiosity peaked and he asked, "What did you find out?"

"Well, it took a while for me to get it," David acknowledged, "However, He showed me that Jesus is King of Kings and Lord of Lords. All the other spirits are subject to Him. There is no spirit greater or more powerful," David declared assuredly. Then with the amazement he still felt at the thought of it, he announced, "They even have to obey Him."

"Lies! Lies!" Lisa shouted and pointed at David angrily, "Stop spreading those awful lies! I can't stand to hear them anymore."

David was shocked. He had not expected this. Yet, his heart was overwhelmed with compassion for her. He looked at her with love, and gently said, "Lisa, Jesus loves you." She began yelling profane names at David and screaming how she couldn't stand this liar. David did not know what to do, so he requested again, "Jesus, please help." Then he suddenly understood what to do. "Be quiet demon," he commanded sternly.

Lisa abruptly closed her mouth and stared at David with wonder. "Sit down, please," he asked, and Lisa complied silently. She could not speak if she wanted to now. She grew very afraid. How is this happening? She wondered. The entire group was now fascinated. David continued telling them about Jesus.

None of them could see the mighty Angels of God surrounding David with swords drawn. They could not see the demons they had invited into themselves drawing back and calling for their legions. There was a huge battle about to take place that they knew nothing about. As many as 100 angels had gathered around the campsite and the group.

The demons were drawing further back as they waited for their army to arrive. They had been taken by surprise.

They knew this young man was protected, but he was a young believer. They didn't think he would know how to take authority already. He had been so timid last year. They had thought they could handle him, maybe even deceive him into accepting the Pegasus. Yet, he was bold and filled with the Holy Spirit. Why had they not seen this coming? Where were their legions?

They could not stop him from speaking, nor stop the others from listening. The Lord had already sent some of his legions to detain and confuse the communications of the demons' armies. The demons could only stand back and watch. They were far too outnumbered to even try to make a stand. They cringed as they heard David proclaim.

"Jesus is God the Son. He was with the Father in the beginning. He created Heaven and Earth. He left the throne in Heaven to become one of us. He was born of a virgin, so that he would be free from sin. While Jesus walked on the Earth, he proved he was the King of Kings by casting demons out of people. They often knew who he was before he spoke to them, and they had to do what he commanded. He also helped thousands of people by healing them from diseases, giving sight to the blind, and restoring damaged limbs. He told the people who followed him that he came to us to die for us. He came to pay the price for all things that people had or would do wrong.

Because of his sacrifice, we can be accepted as the children of the Lord God Almighty. There is no one greater. You can be set free of all the evil you have done, and each one of you can be set free to follow Him on the greatest adventure for all eternity. If anyone of you wants to follow the one true God, simply acknowledge that you need Him, and ask Jesus to become your Lord."

The group sat silently staring into the fire or out at the ocean. No one spoke a word for at least 15 minutes. Sergio finally broke the silence. "Well, that is amazing, David. I think I need to sleep on it." He got up and went to his tent.

One by one the others also went to their tents. When David sat by the dying fire alone and quietly prayed for each of them. He thanked Jesus for leading him and giving him boldness. He praised Jesus for shutting the mouth of the accuser.

As He looked out over the beautiful moonlit ocean, he praised Jesus for the works of his hands. Then finally, David covered the hot coals with sand and went to his own tent.

CHAPTER 8

Tenicia knew in her heart that what David said by the campfire at Cayucos was true. She remembered back to her childhood revelations that Jesus loved her. Through her mom's faith and teaching, as well as Sunday school, she knew about the sacrifice of the Christ.

The memories of how God had touched her heart repetitively throughout her childhood came flooding back although she tried to focus on other things. She knew the exact moment she had given up on God and miracles. She felt the searing pain of abandonment and disappointment as she watched her dad walk out the door that rainy night. She couldn't help but feel that God had walked out on her too as her prayers for her mom and dad to make up seemed to fall on deaf ears. She had become more and more skeptical about all that her mom believed.

When she heard of the real miracle that had happened to Josh, she felt compelled to believe in the Spiritual Realm again. She was thrilled as she learned about Pegasus and all that he had taught the others. She became excited as she had grown in her own power and giftedness. This was so real and exciting, not just stories in a book. However, the moment David told the spirit to be quiet and it had to listen to him; all the stories about Jesus giving commands to the demons and them having to obey came flooding back to her memory.

This Jesus was real. He was not just a good story. He really did love them. He loved her. She still didn't understand why her prayers went unanswered, but she now understood Jesus was still with her. She fell to her knees in her room and wept. She felt the pain of abandonment wash away. She asked for forgiveness for turning away and accepting the false god. She experienced a feeling of freedom from her guilt. She knew she was His now and that as He had promised; He would never leave her nor forget her.

That week, for the first time in four years, she went back to church because she wanted to. She began to experience joy and acceptance. She asked about the youth group and determined to become a part of it. She avoided Sheena and the others. Tenicia knew there would come a time, soon, in which she would have to talk to them. She was afraid to talk to them though. She didn't know what they would think.

Everyone had just gone on like nothing had happened that night. No one said another word about it the rest of the trip. Were they all still reeling with the revelation? Had they accepted the truth or rejected Him? Were they confused or blinded? How strong were the demons that possessed them? Other than what they had learned historically about Christianity, had they ever heard about Jesus before that night? Tenicia was overwhelmed with the thought of being unable to help them. She felt Inadequate to talk to them about Jesus. She had just been partnering with them in idolatry and witchcraft. They would not listen to her.

She began to pray for each of them. She prayed that the Lord would help her get right with Him so that they would see Him in her. She prayed that they would accept her decision and not fight with her about it. She hoped that they would choose to follow Jesus also. She loved them and did not want to see them condemned. Yet, she could not hang out with them anymore. She had to become strong in Christ again, before she could talk to them.

Suddenly, she remembered that she had found a moment to get David's number before he left the beach the following day. She decided now would be a good time to call him. She felt butterflies flitting about in her stomach as she dialed the number.

"Hello," greeted the sweet voice of an older woman on other end.

"Hi, may I speak with David?" Tenicia asked nervously.

"One moment honey," she replied sweetly.

"Hello?" came David's voice a minute later curiously asking, "Who's this?"

"Hi David; it's Tenicia," she announced.

"Hi, how are you?" he asked pleasantly surprised.

"I am good, but a little afraid," Tenicia replied honestly.

"There is nothing to fear in Him," David encouraged.

"Have you heard from any of the others?" Tenicia asked hopefully.

"No, they haven't called, and I don't think I am supposed to call them," David replied. Wasting no time he boldly asked, "Have you made a decision?"

"Of course. I knew right away that you were telling the truth," She admitted, "It took me a couple of weeks to turn back to Him though. All the Bible stories just kept flooding my mind, as well as the times in which I had felt His spirit."

"How did you get involved in this, if you knew Him?" David asked in bewilderment?

"I had become disillusioned and turned away when my parents divorced," she admitted, the pain still coming through clearly.

"Oh, I am sorry about that," David sympathetically responded. He then questioned, "What is going on now?"

"Well......I am back in church....because I want to be, not just because my mom is still going." Tenicia declared.

"That is great!" David said excitedly.

"Yeah," Tenicia felt encouraged and continued, "I got involved in the youth group too. It's a lot of fun."

"Good deal. I always liked the games we played when I was in it," David remembered with fondness.

"I love having fun with a complete feeling of freedom," Tenicia expressed with excitement.

"I didn't have that when I was a teenager," David admitted, "You are fortunate."

"How did you know what to do when Lisa was yelling all those ugly things at you?" Tenicia inquired before admitting, "I would have been embarrassed even though they weren't true."

"I felt a little embarrassed and shocked," David acknowledged, "I wasn't sure at all what to do or why she hated me. We had just met that weekend. I was a little confused about it all, so I just asked Jesus to help me quietly in my mind."

"Were you afraid at all?" Tenicia queried curiously.

"Oh yeah, I was definitely afraid to tell Sergio and Sheena the truth after everything. They have been my friends since third grade. Sergio and I were on the same baseball team throughout high school. Josh and Aaron were also on the team. These were my closest friends growing up." David clarified.

"How did you get to the point where you could speak so boldly and with that kind of power?" Tenicia asked, hoping she could overcome her fear.

David thought for a minute, asking the Holy Spirit to speak through him as he responded. Then he completely explained, "I studied the Bible a lot over the last year, as well as what Biblical teachers where saying. Once I knew the truth, I prayed a lot. I even prayed just before I reached the beach and throughout the weekend. Then, the Holy Spirit gave me the words to say and showed me how to deal with the accuser that was possessing Lisa."

"Will I be able to do that when I have to talk to Sheena, or the others?" Tenicia timidly tested.

"Yes. You have all spiritual blessings in the Heavenly realms, and when it is time; the Lord will give you the words." David declared.

"I am afraid of seeing them and not being ready," Tenicia earnestly expressed, "I am afraid maybe they are stronger than I am," she confessed.

"May I pray for you?" David asked compassionately.

"Please do." Tenicia replied.

David prayed for Tenicia with the heart of an experienced warrior. He had now been in battle and been victorious. He knew she would be triumphant as well, no matter what the others decided. He was so excited she had accepted the Lord. He rejoiced just as he knew all Heaven had rejoiced in her return.

Even if she were the only one of the group who accepted the Lord, it was well worth the time and effort. Her soul was worth the risk of his friendships with the others. For hours after he got off the phone with her, David felt a spiritual high he could not describe. It was better than all the winning games put together. It was better than the victory in the championship game. Her returning to the Lord was more exciting than getting the full ride scholarship offers. He had to share this triumph, so he went into the family room and told his parents everything.

David's parents, Samuel and Nancy, listened quietly and thoughtfully as he told the story of the past year. Nancy mused, "How did I not know any of this?" Yet, she was grateful that he had followed the Lord and not his friends. Samuel wanted to take action immediately. He called Pastor Dale and the elders of their church and asked them to come over right away.

David was a little embarrassed, but he knew the battle was the Lord's, and this was a much bigger battle than he and Tenicia could fight by themselves. He was glad these older, wiser men would be praying for them now. He told the story again once everyone had gathered. He could see the concern on their faces.

One man he did not know seemed to almost be grief stricken. Henry now knew they had been right. He was afraid his little girl was lost forever. David began to realize this was far bigger than he had imagined.

As the men were gathering at David's home, Sheena sensed

an urgent need to call Sergio and get away together. She called him, and he left to pick her up immediately. He had known they needed to go to their special place as well.

In the warm summer night's air, Sheena and Sergio drove as quickly as they could out of town up to Rebel Hill. Sheena felt the stirring and stress within her spirit. She could not stay quiet about this any longer. She could not act as if it had not happened. She wanted to know what Sergio thought about all that David had said. It had been two full weeks. It was time.

She needed to know what to do about the others. She wanted Sergio to be with her as she sought for answers that night. She was afraid to be alone. She was afraid of what might happen to her circle. They had grown so close. She wondered what they were thinking, and why she hadn't heard from any of them.

She also couldn't get the look of love, true, unconditional, totally accepting, yet sorrowful in the suffering love in David's eyes as Lisa had berated him without reason. She had never seen that kind of love before. Finally, she broke the silence once they were well out of town. "Sergio, what do you think about what David said?" she inquired.

"All those years of religious training have deluded him," Sergio replied with sorrow.

"What are we going to do?" Sheena asked.

"There is only one thing to do. We must make a sacrifice for him and pray for him." Sergio stated confidently

"What about the others, have you heard from any of them?" Sheena questioned with concern.

"No," admitted Sergio, "have you?"

"No," she responded and explained, "I am so afraid for them. They were all so young in their devotion."

"They know and have experienced the truth," Sergio declared confidently. He looked lovingly at her wanting to ease her mind. Sergio soothingly said, "Don't worry about them so much. They will be okay. Everyone is just tired from the trip."

"Still, I think we need extra help with this," Sheena confessed.

"Of course, we need Pegasus," declared Sergio.

"Will you set up the altar for me tonight?" Sheena sweetly asked.

"Yes, and I will catch the sacrifice," Sergio offered boldly. He directed her, "You need to prepare to offer it."

"What?" asked Sheena nervously, then admitting, "I have never offered sacrifice before."

"My mom told me you need to do it, just as you did the first ceremony when we became one," Sergio explained.

"Oh, I wish she could come do this. I have never even seen one done!" Sheena lamented.

"But you were selected as the high priestess," Sergio reminded her. He encouragingly added, "Pegasus chose you; he will lead you."

"You're right, but the thought of it is so awful," Sheena acknowledged squeamishly.

"My mom said you will experience twice as much power once you do it, and it will be easier than you think." Sergio told her.

Sheena felt very heavily burdened about taking the life of another creature. She leaned back and closed her eyes, letting the warm summer air carry her away from the thought for a moment. She began to call to Pegasus. This was so much bigger than she was.

Sergio knew this would be difficult and wished he could take her place, but the instruction had been so clear. He knew his parents would be seeking the spirits for them as well. He was emboldened by their confidence in him and Sheena. He wished they could come up to the hill, but this ritual would be hard enough for Sheena without others watching. He focused on the road as it began to wind through the mountains.

"Here in our little Christian city? How could this happen without anyone realizing it? Who taught these kids how to do this? Who are their parents? " The questions erupted all at once. The men of God were shocked at the tale they had just heard.

Pastor Dale apologized to Henry for not seeing what was truly happening. Then the men agreed to put on the armor and fight for their city and their families. David started to leave, feeling a little out of place. Samuel grabbed his arm and proudly said, "Son, we need you to join us. You are one of the men of this church, and you know what is happening better than anyone of the rest of us."

David suddenly felt like he really did belong. His dad had just called him "one of the men". He was proud to be counted as one these amazing men. He replied simply, "Okay."

The moment they began to pray, Lisa began to cry out in agony. She felt a searing pain shooting through her stomach. She collapsed to the floor and screamed, tears streaming down her face. Her mom ran to her from the other room and tried to find out what was wrong, but Lisa could only scream and clutch her stomach. She curled up in a fetal position and just wept from the pain. Lisa's mom called over to the Bradley's home.

Nancy began to tell Tina what was happening, Lisa screamed even louder and began to get angry. She looked around the room with wildness in her eyes. She grabbed a glass nick knack, smashed it, and began cutting herself with the fragments. Tina begged them to come to the house now.

The men of God wasted no time getting the cars going. They ran the three and a half blocks to the Jones' home. David outpaced them and arrived first. He already knew what was going on. The demon that Lisa had given herself to, was driving her insane.

"Come out of her!" David demanded.

"She has given herself to me willingly. She is mine now," replied the demon coyly, testing the young believer.

David was shocked by the response and the eerie voice of the demon. He did not know how to respond. His mind was frozen for a moment. He could not even think a prayer of help. He had never experienced anything like this before. The rest of the men were arriving and the demon knew he had to get Lisa out of the house. Lisa had a crazed wild look in her eyes. She turned to the patio door and frantically pulled it open. She ran out of the house to the alleyway gate, then flung the gate open and raced away as if her very life depended on it.

David, just barely recovering from the shock of the demon's response, began to run after her. It was too late. By the time he reached the gate she had turned, and he could not see what direction she had gone. Now, he was incredibly unsure. What if the demon was right? He wondered. Was it too late for the others as well? What about Tenicia? She had been set free. He now had more questions than answers about this spiritual realm and exactly how it worked. He returned to the house to find the others comforting Tina and Henry. David could only say, "I'm sorry." He felt personally responsible somehow.

Lisa was still frantically trying to make it to Sheena's house. Every time she saw a car coming or other people she would hide. She would dodge behind a tree, drop down to the ground behind a shrub, or crouch beside a parked car. She was filled with fear that they were coming after her. She slowly, sporadically, slipped silently through the subdivision until she reached Sheena's home. No one was home, so she went into the back yard to the shop behind the house. She finally felt a sense of ease and safety. She was in the home of the circle. They would not be able to find her here. She would wait for Sheena and Sergio.

Up on Rebel Hill, Sheena found herself appalled at the thought of sacrificing the squirrel. She simply could not bring herself to do the act. She looked at the trapped squirrel and begged Pegasus to show her a way out of this. She looked back at Sergio sitting and praying under a tree not far from her. He had gone to so much trouble to make the altar and catch this creature. She did not want to let him nor the rest of her circle down. Did it really need to be sacrificed? Was that really necessary?

Maybe just a little blood would be enough. Maybe she could just give it a little cut and collect some of its blood, like they had done with her. Sheena put the bottle of water with the crushed sleeping pill on the cage carefully. The squirrel eyed her warily, but within moments of her backing away, it began to drink. The smell of water and its great thirst drove the squirrel past its fear.

Sheena could not get past hers. She felt a deep dread over taking the life of another creature for a spiritual sacrifice. If they had been starving, it would be different, she thought.

A short time later, Sheena pulled the sleeping squirrel out of the cage. She carefully laid the squirrel out on the altar. She had been praying and chanting the entire time. Yet, this was completely unnerving her. Something within her shouted, "This is wrong! Don't do it! You don't have to obey them!" as she picked up the ritual knife. Then, as if they could read the hesitation in her heart, the spirits themselves took control of her arms and raised the knife above her head.

Pointing the blade at her own belly instead of the creature, the spirits began the thrust of Sheena's arms. Sheena screamed, "NOOOO!" and was barely able to lean over the log in time. The blade was firmly stuck into the log altar. The spirits' control of her arms was broken. She collapsed to a heap on the ground and wept. She could not do it. What would Sergio think? Why did the spirits have that much control over her arms? What about her circle? What would happen next?

Sergio, hearing the scream and partly seeing what had happened, went to her and put his arms around her. He loved her tender heart. He assured her it would be okay. He would take care of the squirrel. Once she was comforted, he picked up the blade and the squirrel and walked away to a place on the hill out of Sheena's sight.

Sheena did not want to think about it anymore. She took the items on the alter off, and prepared to head home. When Sergio returned she had everything ready to go. She did not know what to expect next. She had a strange sense that nothing would be the same, ever again.

Truly, nothing would be the same, ever again. She had come face to face with love, real unconditional love. She did not completely understand it, but she thought if she could somehow combine what she knew about the spirits with that kind of love; she could make a powerful impact in the world. She reflected on the attack as Sergio drove home. Although Sheena had known it, she was now incredibly aware that not all the spirits were good.

She had to be more careful in which spirits she let in. She had to figure out how to tell the difference. She didn't appreciate them taking control of her like that.

Pegasus had never done that to her. How would she know? Sheena felt like she had to talk to Sergio's mom; maybe she would be able to explain it. As they neared the edge of town, Sheena put her hand gently on Sergio's thigh and with a pleading look in her eyes said, "Please don't take me home yet."

Sergio reached across the seat, put his arm around her shoulders, and pulled her close to him. They drove to his house. His mom greeted them warmly, and took them into the kitchen. She already had hot water for tea waiting.

Although Oriana didn't know things had not gone perfectly with the quest, she could sense their need to be in a protected and comfortable environment. She sensed not to pressure them. Her job was to make them comfortable tonight. They would each talk when ready. Gilberto and Oriana had already sought their spirit guides together. They would provide a safe house for Sheena and prepare the young couple for the battles ahead.

Within moments of sitting down with the tea in her hands, Sheena began to sob again. The Santiago's consoled her and asked to tell them what she was experiencing. When they learned of the powerful spirits trying to overtake her body, they asked how the altar was arranged. Sheena was stunned by the question, but she described it exactly as Sergio had built it. Then she listed the artifacts she had brought up and arranged on it. Oriana exclaimed, "Oh dear! The evil spirits enticed you to set up the altar like that to open you up to them! They showed you how to make a portal for them. You cannot use a mirror on the altar. I am surprised your Pegasus told you to do this."

"It wasn't Pegasus. There was another," Sheena dropped her head as she explained.

"Did you know it from before?" Gilberto inquired.

"I did not recognize it; I just knew it had a powerful presence," admitted Sheena with sorrow.

"Oh Sweetie, you must be careful calling on spirits you do not know," Oriana responded sincerely.

"I know," Sheena honestly acknowledged, "I am just so scared for my circle now. What is going to happen to them...to us?" she implored.

"It's hard to say what is going to happen. Each person has been given a choice as to who they will follow." Gilberto explained.

"I am really mad at David right now!" Sergio exclaimed.

"Don't waste your energy then. If you are mad at him, then use that energy against him," Gilberto directed.

Sergio considered the possibility, but expressed, "I don't want to hurt him."

"No, I don't want you to either," Sheena agreed.

"What I mean is give him trouble..."Gilberto clarified, "Trouble the spirit he is following cannot help with. When he sees his spirit is not all powerful, he will be easier to turn."

"That is a good idea, Dad." Sergio exclaimed. "Will you help me?" he pleaded with them.

The four of them began seeking their spirit guides together. They took turns focusing on David and directing the spirits to cause problems in his life. They prayed that the spirits would cause problems with his car. They prayed he would trip and break his leg. They prayed that his family would get angry with him. They prayed for every problem they could think of that would not seriously harm him or take his life.

The spirits gathered around them, listening with glee. They were going to harass this young Christian and turn him from his faith. They had not been called on to harass a believer in a long time. The spirits helped to whisper thoughts into the minds of the family and lead them in their horrid prayers.

CHAPTER 9

Sheena sat on the couch stunned by what she had just heard. She had known Tenicia was special, a chosen one. She could not believe that Tenicia would be the one in the group to turn; she was so strong. Yet, there was a real difference in her. Sheena did not understand, but she could see the change in Tenicia's eyes. Tenicia was stronger than ever. She had something different.

Much like the love she saw in David's eyes, she saw something in Tenicia's eyes as well. What was it that Tenicia had? Was this what that stronger spirit had warned about? Was her circle going to collapse? The thought came to Sheena that Tenicia would be the ultimate sacrifice. Did they really need her to be their sacrifice in order to go on? What about the promises Pegasus had made to her? If she became the ultimate sacrifice, none of that would happen? No, It must be that evil spirit again. Mrs. Santiago was right; that spirit was simply evil and wanted to kill her. But why?

The angry chatter of the circle finally pulled Sheena back to the present reality, yet she found herself to be incredibly calm as she began to speak to them, "Okay, I understand your anger, but Tenicia is free to make a choice. Each of us is free to choose who we will follow." She was glad Tenicia left right away.

"How could she come here and spew those lies?" Lisa questioned with hurt and anger.

128"Right now, she really believes what she is saying." Sheena tried to explain in a sincere and soothing voice.

"How could she turn from us?" Sergio queried. He looked Sheena straight in the eyes as he honestly admitted, "I feel betrayed."

"Just think how Pegasus must feel." Josh added, a sad, empathetic expression enveloped his eyes.

"She knows too much about us. We need to do something before this gets out of control." Aaron stated with concern.

"What do you mean?!" Sheena asked in shock at the implications.

"I mean, she has been on the inside of this circle for the last year. Now she has gone to the enemy's camp." Aaron replied as a matter of fact.

"That's right! She has become a threat to us, a security breech." Sergio stated as he stood and paced the room.

"What do you think could happen?" Josh inquired.

"As she starts feeling more comfortable with those religious people," Aaron thoughtfully paused and looked around the circle. Then he declared, "She is going to start talking."

"You don't know that," Sheena said dismissively waving her hand at Aaron. She confidently asserted, "I don't think she's going to say anything."

"Sheena, don't be naive. You will have the most to lose." Sergio softly said.

"Tenicia is my friend. She would not do that to me, to us." Sheena defended.

"We'll see. I hope for all our sakes, your right." Aaron stated apprehensively.

"If she starts talking, I will make sure she is stopped." Sergio declared with a scary sincerity.

"Don't do anything rash," Sheena partly warned partly pleaded.

"Don't worry. I will make sure no one finds her." The hateful, murderous tone in Sergio's voice shocked everyone. The group sat silently for several seconds, staring at the ceiling, the floor, the wall, anywhere but at each other.

Finally, Lisa broke the silence, "Hey, I have begun to remember something from the other night."

"Really?! Tell us!" Sheena implored, excited and relieved.

"Yeah, tell us what happened." Josh agreed with a huge grin, also happy to change topics.

"When the stomach pains first started, my mom called Mrs. Anderson, hoping to get some advice, I think. A little later, David came into the room," Lisa's face revealed the confusion she felt at his presence. She continued, "I blacked out for a minute, I guess. Then when I came too, other men were starting to come in. I knew I had to get out of there," as she relived the moment the fear returned in her eyes, "I knew they were going to do something awful to me."

"What made you think that?" Aaron asked incredulously.

"I just knew," Lisa stated plainly looking down at the floor as the memories rushed in. Then she looked back up at the group and continued, "Pegasus told me to get out fast. So, I ran out the back."

"How did you get those cuts and scratches? Did they do that?" Sheena asked sympathetically.

"No, they weren't there yet. I did it myself," Lisa confessed, "It felt like I could let the pain out if I cut open my skin."

"Did it help?" Aaron asked wincing as he thought of it.

"It seemed to relieve it a lot," Lisa confided.

"There is power in the release of blood." Sheena quietly said.

Sergio looked at her and could see the guilt she felt. He thought about how hard it had been for her to think of taking another creature's life. Maybe next time it wouldn't be so difficult. Maybe if she had done it sooner, before the evil spirit came and tried to take her life, Lisa wouldn't have had to cut herself up. He could tell the same thoughts were running through Sheena's mind as well. He crossed the room, sat beside her, and put his arm around her. She relaxed into him, thankful for his strength.

The others simply dropped their heads and wondered what she meant. They all wondered what was next and what they should do about it. They prayed together for a while before they returned to their homes.

The only one who did not go home was Lisa. She would stay there, in the shop, until they knew it was safe for her to go elsewhere. Sheena would let Lisa into the house once her parents went to work. She had plenty of clothes to share. Sheena brought out an old TV and some books that had been in the garage. She didn't want Lisa to get to bored hanging out there by herself. The guys had promised they would be back as soon as they knew more about what was going on. They were going to get some information before they decided the next step.

As the guys walked home, they began to plan their next moves. Sergio thought it would be too obvious if he called David directly. They thought it would be better for Josh to call him and just ask questions. He would start like he was interested in what David had said, but just not sure he believed it. After all, he was the one who had been healed. What could David say about that? Then he could lead into what was happening and see what David would tell him.

Josh agreed to the plan. He was really curious about all that was going on and secretly hoped David could give him some real answers. Now, he could call without the guys being suspicious. Was David's Jesus really more powerful than Pegasus? He had seen Pegasus' power up close and personal. Yet, Lisa was silenced that night; as they all were really. Pegasus could not come against David. Now there was Tenicia's story. She seemed really different, but what was it?

Was he the only one of the others in the group who could see the huge difference in her? Maybe he could call Sheena first? She had not been so quick to get angry with Tenicia. He certainly was not comfortable with the vengeful tone in Sergio's voice after Tenicia left. Maybe Sheena understood it all better. He would have to be careful when he called her that Lisa was not in the house. It would have to be in the evening, when her parents would be home. He quickly told the guys as he neared his street, "Okay, you guys pray for me for the next three days. Then, I will call David. I want to be prepared spiritually before I talk to him." They agreed that was a good idea as this spirit, Jesus, was obviously strong. They didn't want him to get confused too. They gave the secret hand shake on the deal before Josh turned onto his street. Sergio and Aaron kept going towards their street, glad to be almost home. They felt as if they were heading into the playoffs against the strongest team in the league. They each had to get as strong as they could before the big game. They also had to be one as a team. They certainly didn't want to lose another teammate. This was serious. They would pray like they trained for baseball, with everything they had.

With the guys on their way home and Lisa settled in the shop, Sheena went into the kitchen to find herself something to eat. Her parents were already in bed. She was so tired. She picked through the leftovers mindlessly as she recalled the meeting. She felt haunted by what she saw in David's and Tenicia's eyes. She cleaned up her mess as she pondered all that had happened the last few days. She remembered there was a Bible on the bookshelf in the den. She went into the room, scrolled through the bookshelf until she found it, pulled it out and just looked at it. Maybe there was more to this book than she imagined. She was too tired to read it tonight, but she had to start understanding what was happening. She took the book to her room and put it in the nightstand. She couldn't let Lisa see it. Lisa would freak out again.

Besides, Pegasus would help her understand the truth, she thought. Then, unable to think anymore, she climbed into bed and fell asleep in seconds.

Sergio was not able to go to sleep so easily. He tossed and turned with the anger welling up in him. How dare David do this to his team! He would have a bigger battle on his hands than he thought.

134

Sheena did not understand this kind of warfare, he thought. This was why she needed him. She needed warriors to protect her. He began to think of ways to make Tenicia disappear without bringing suspension to himself or the rest of the gang. He looked to Pegasus for guidance. He knew she would have to go. He just had to be sure it was the right time and place. This would certainly be a powerful sacrifice. She was still a virgin. Sergio smiled with eerie satisfaction at the thought of taking her to Pegasus as an offering.

As the sun rose the next morning, Sheena rubbed her eyes and stretched. It was a beautiful summer morning. She checked to see if her parents had left; and when she knew the coast was clear, she signaled Lisa by pulling back the half curtain on the window of the kitchen door. She made coffee, scrambled eggs, and toast.

Lisa's timing was perfect. Lisa entered the kitchen just as Sheena was finishing the eggs. Sheena turned on the TV. The local news had a picture of Lisa on screen, Sheena turned up the volume.

"...local teenage girl ran away 3 nights ago. She is believed to be mentally ill and a danger to herself. It is unclear if she is dangerous to others. If you see her, please call the police. Do not approach her, or try to talk to her. The police are unsure how she will respond. Again, simply call the police and let them know where you saw her....." the news reporter continued giving other top reports.

"Mentally ill?!" Lisa shouted with dismay. She turned to Sheena and sarcastically asked, "Do I look mentally ill to you?"

"Calm down, what else do you expect them to say after the other night?" Sheena said with a grin.

"Oh! What am I going to do now?" Lisa groaned, "I can't go anywhere. Everywhere I go someone will call the police on me."

"Well, you haven't gone anywhere the last two days, and you have been fine," Sheena said with a matter of fact tone. She looked at Lisa a little surprised as the thought occurred to her and asked, "Were you thinking about going somewhere?"

"I can't stay in your shop forever," Lisa complained, "I have to do something."

"I agree, but we agreed last night with the group you would stay here for a while until this blows over." Sheena said softly.

"I know," Lisa's head dropped as she acknowledged the agreement, ".....but I can't stay in there all the time by myself. I will go crazy!" she argued. She looked back at Sheena, put her hand on her hip and asked derisively, "How long do you think I can hide from your parents?"

"My parents are in their own worlds," Sheena shared sadly, "They don't pay much attention to what I am doing. They are clueless."

"Tenicia knows I am here. She will probably tell," Lisa said with disdain.

"Why do you think that?" Sheena questioned with the hurt coming through in her voice, "She is not like that."

"Sheena, don't be naive. She will tell." Lisa stated seriously.

"I'll go talk to her, and make her promise not to," Sheena suggested.

"Just don't listen to her lies." Lisa cautioned.

"What makes you so sure they're lies?" Sheena sincerely questioned.

"You're kidding," Lisa said sarcastically. "Do **you** believe her?" she asked in shock.

"There are other spirits out there, not just Pegasus." Sheena replied with scorn.

"I grew up listening to those stories; they're not real." Lisa declared.

"How do you know they're not real?" Sheena interrogated.

"None of them actually live like they are," Lisa said sadly and shook her head, "If they were real, those church people would be very different."

"How would they be different?" Sheena asked curiously.

"For one, they would do what he told them to do," Lisa said honestly, "They wouldn't be arguing about silly things and be ing so hateful to each other."

136

She wrinkled her nose in disapproval and questioned rhetorically, "Do you know the two churches right next to each other won't let the children play together on the grass in between the buildings? I have seen parents pull kids apart and say things like, 'They're Baptist; we're not.' Or 'Stay away from those Pentecostal kids, their crazy.' What does that tell you?"

"That is pretty awful." Sheena admitted.

"Then they dress up and make themselves look perfect, but they don't care about others. Instead of helping, they gossip about people," Lisa said with disgust, "It's just sickening."

"Wow! That is messed up," Sheena acknowledged. She looked at Lisa and compassionately asked, "Is your mom like that?"

Lisa's disdain oozed out, "My mom is even worse. She pretends to be such a perfect saint, but she was pregnant with me before they got married. Yet, she talks to me about waiting for the right one and saving myself until marriage. Doesn't she think I can count? Maybe she thinks I don't know how long it takes to have a baby."

"Oh, I am sorry Lisa," Sheena said sincerely. After a moment of heavy silence, Sheena asked with hopefulness, "Have you tried to talk to her about it?"

"No," Lisa confessed, "I just don't know what to say." A puzzled and hurt look consumed her face and she asked, "How do you talk to your mom about something like that?" Both girls looked away from each other for a minute. Finally, Lisa looked back at Sheena and sarcastically said, "I can see it now, 'Hey mom, I figured out that my birthday is 7 months after your anniversary. Would you care to tell me about that?" The girls giggled at the thought of the conversation.

Sheena agreed she would be cautious with Tenicia, but she had to try to talk to her. She had to warn her that the group would be very angry with her if she told anything about the circle. Lisa figured that it was only fair to give Tenicia a warning. So, she offered to clean up the breakfast mess while Sheena got ready. They prayed together again just before Sheena left. Then, Sheena made Lisa promise not to tell Sergio or the others.

She let Lisa stay inside the house while she was gone. The blinds in the front were closed. No one would know she was there. As Sheena was about to leave, Lisa asked, "Do you think it would be okay to call a friend or two?"

"Maybe...it would have to be someone you can really trust," Sheena replied, her eyes narrowed and brows furrowed.

"There are a couple of people I could trust," Lisa replied thoughtfully.

"Good. Maybe you should call your mom, and let her know you're okay." Sheena suggested.

"I don't know. Lisa said as she dropped her head and looked at the floor, "She'll be mad at me."

"She's probably worried sick right now," Sheena sympathetically stated. Then she reasoned, "If you call her, maybe they'll quit with the news reporters."

"That would be good," Lisa acknowledged with a sigh and a roll of her eyes, "but she'll want to know where I am."

"Oh, you got a point there. Hmmm.............................Sheena seriously thought for a couple of minutes while Lisa imagined her mother's pressing questioning. Then Sheena's face lit up as she saw a solution, "Just say you can't tell her, but you're safe."

"She will not settle for that," Lisa supposed.

"If she keeps asking, tell her you have to go and hang up." Sheena replied with a shrug of her shoulders.

"That is a good idea," Lisa admitted. Then hopefully she exclaimed, "Maybe if they call off the police and reporters I can actually do something again!"

"That would be great! I think after all this settles down we need a movie night," Sheena encouraged.

"Or go to the mall and hang out," Lisa added longingly.

"We could go to McDonalds after that!" Sheena suggested.

"Maybe the skating rink!" Lisa excitedly considered.

"Maybe go dancing!" Sheena added.

"Oh, I would love to go out tonight!" Lisa exclaimed.

"Me too. This has been so tough," Sheena acknowledged.

"I know I could use some fun; this has been a bummer," Lisa confessed.

"The guys should get out too. We could all use a good time," Sheena declared.

"Okay I'll call her," Lisa decided. She smiled as she said, "We'll see if it comes on the evening news again."

"If not tonight, maybe we can go do something tomorrow," Sheena assuredly encouraged Lisa. "I'll be back before my parents get home, so don't worry about staying in the house," Sheena said as she was heading for the door.

"Cool." Lisa replied with a slight nod of agreement.

Sheena stepped out on the porch, closed and locked the door, then looked cautiously around the neighborhood. No one was outside, and it didn't look like anyone was watching. They probably don't even have a clue, she thought. She smiled and headed for Tenicia's house. She was sure Tenicia would be surprised to see her; she hoped it was a pleasant surprise. She felt a little nervous about what to say, so she prayed for the right words. She tried to connect with Pegasus as she was walking. Nothing, it was not always easy to get that focused while doing other things. She knew he was near, but she could not really see or feel him. She hoped she would be better connected with him when she reached Tenicia.

She decided to stop at the park on the way over to get better focused. She really felt like she needed to be one with Pegasus instead of scattered by a million thoughts. The park was busy, but there was a nice quiet place on the hill with a beautiful shade tree to sit under. She got comfortable and began to let her mind go.

She called on Pegasus and started to visualize him there with her under the tree. She could see the pure white winged horse land on the hill and fold his majestic wings in close to his body. She watched with anticipation as he gently strode under the tree to her. She smiled with pleasure as she felt the gentle nuzzle of his nose upon her shoulder. She stroked the soft fur on his forehead and nose. Then she stood and ran her hand down his soft yet strong neck.

She buried her face into his neck and cried softly for a time before she could express the worry about her group and how she felt responsible for them. She asked the creature for assurance, wisdom, and guidance. He spoke words of encouragement to her. He promised he'd show her how to go forward. He told her she must trust Sergio's wisdom also.

For the first time she could ever remember, Sheena felt a knot in her stomach at the mention of Sergio's name. She didn't say anything about it to Pegasus. Sheena now felt an eerie mistrust for him as well. She began to wonder if Pegasus had called the other spirit to the hill when she showed she was having trouble doing what Pegasus had told her to do. Was it really Pegasus who had wanted to kill her when she could not sacrifice the squirrel, she wondered. She said, "Thank you," and began to feel a pull back into the physical world around her. The laughter of children running up the hill towards her broke the bond with Pegasus. She was fully conscious of her surrounding within seconds.

Now, she had a strong sense of urgency to warn Tenicia. This was far beyond her control. She knew she could say no to spirits, but would Sergio want to? He sounded so angry. Then she remembered, he had already taken the life of another creature without a problem. The thought occurred to her that it would not be that hard for him to do it again. He would not hesitate to take a life if he thought it was the solution to the problem or would bring him more power. She began to feel a wave a nausea rip through her stomach. She suddenly sprinted across the park and ran the rest of the way to Tenicia's home.

When she reached the home, she pounded on the door panicked with dread.

Tenicia looked out the window cautiously. She was stunned to see Sheena and the expression on her face as Sheena fought to catch her breath. What could be so terribly wrong? Why is she here? Tenicia pondered. A peace that she could not explain suddenly washed over Tenicia. She heard the Holy Spirit whisper,

"It's okay; I am with you always. Let her in."

Tenicia looked to see if anyone else was following Sheena as she opened the door. "Hi Sheena," Tenicia said hesitantly, "What's going on?"

Sheena, between pants shouted out, "They are going to try to kill you. You have to get away from here."

Tenicia looked again past Sheena to see if the others were coming up behind her or waiting outside for her. She could see the terror in Sheena's eyes and knew she was not making it up. Tenicia pulled Sheena in the house, closed and locked the door. Then Tenicia said in a calm and soothing voice, "Come in and sit down. Tell me what is happening." Sheena poured out everything that had happened since Tenicia had left the circle the night before.

Tenicia prayed as she listened to the story. She knew the group was angry, but she hadn't really thought they would be angry enough to want to kill her. She had no idea what to do or who to ask for help. She didn't want to get anyone else involved. Sheena was right. She would have to run away. Run where though? How would she explain it to her mom? How much time did she have to get things together? What should she take? The questions flooded her mind as the fear inside her rose with the idea that Pegasus was leading Sergio to kill her.

"Fear not!" came the voice of the Spirit again, "I am with you. I will lead you and guide you. Tell Sheena about me."

Tenicia smiled as the calmness returned. She took Sheena's hand and said that she was not afraid.

Sheena could see that Tenicia was really serene. She could hardly believe the sense of peace that washed over her as well. She wanted to understand more about this Jesus, and knew it was now or never to ask Tenicia those questions. She may not get another chance. So Sheena inquired, "What drew you back to this Jesus?"

Tenicia smiled at the opportunity to share. Sheena was sincerely interested. Tenicia began, "The night David spoke to us at the campfire was not the first time I had heard about Jesus," Tenicia looked at Sheena, measuring her reaction before continuing, "I knew what he was saying was true. I had been in church all my life until we moved here, and I met you. When I met you, I was mad at God," Tenicia shamefully admitted and then continued, "I didn't think miracles happened anymore. Then what you did with Josh made me wonder what if it was possible for miracles to still happen. I was so curious."

"You had never seen a miracle before?" Sheena curiously questioned.

"I can't say that. I had seen some... smaller miracles. Then there were those TV preachers who seemed to be doing miracles." Tenicia acknowledged.

"Then what made you think miracles couldn't happen? Why were you mad at God?" Sheena questioned with bewilderment.

"I was mad at the Lord because I felt that He had abandoned me," Tenicia confessed, "I felt like He had ignored my prayers for my dad to come back. I felt like He walked out the door the same night my dad did."

Sheena looked compassionately at Tenicia, reached over and put her hand on Tenicia's arm as she sincerely stated, "I am so sorry. I didn't know."

"I didn't really talk about it," Tenicia acknowledged, and continued to explain, "That is why we moved here though. My mom could see I was becoming more distant, depressed, and angry. She wanted to give me...give *us* a fresh start. I think she was afraid I was starting to hang out with the wrong kids." An ironic smile quickly appeared on and then disappeared from Tenicia's face.

"So what David said changed your mind?" Sheena asked slightly confused.

"I immediately felt a sense that what he was saying was true. Then, when he told the spirit in Lisa to be quiet and it had to obey him, I knew it was true." Tenicia replied.

"So you really think this Jesus is more powerful than Pegasus?" Sheena inquired doubtfully.

"I know Jesus is more powerful! He is the King of kings and the Lord of lords!" Tenicia professed ardently.

"What? What does that mean?" Sheena asked confused even more.

"That means that he has all power and authority over everything including other spirits. There are lots of examples in the Bible where he told the spirits what to do and they had to do it." Tenicia explained.

"I thought he died....by crucifixion," Sheena was becoming perplexed, "How then can he have any power when they killed him?"

Tenicia loved the questions Sheena was asking. Her curiosity made it easy to share. Emboldened, she explained, "He rose from the dead on the third day. He conquered death so we could have a relationship with the Father for all eternity, and that is not all. He promised He would send a comforter and counselor to lead us into all truth. He promised us the Holy Spirit!"

"So, you are saying I can get the same help from this Holy Spirit I have gotten from Pegasus?" Sheena asked as she tried to make sense of it all.

"No, I am saying you can get more help from the Holy Spirit of the one true God. I am saying that following Pegasus is going to lead you to eternal death and suffering.

Following the Holy Spirit will lead you into eternal life with Christ." Tenicia was now fully surrendered to the Holy Spirit and He was giving her the words to say. She spoke with an unusual authority which caught Sheena's attention.

"Well, I know something is certainly different about you and David. I could see the love David had for Lisa even when she was hurling insults at him. I can see that you are peaceful even though I told you they're planning on killing you. I could see a definite boldness and confidence in you that you think this is right," Sheena honestly acknowledged. Then with genuineness she asked, "But what if you're wrong?

"I know I am right. His Spirit is within me giving me that assurance," Tenicia reassured.

"I have 'known' I was right too, but now you're telling me I am wrong, that following Pegasus is wrong. Why should I believe you?" Sheena seriously inquired.

Tenicia thoughtfully closed her eyes and silently asked the Lord to give her the right answer and to prepare Sheena's heart to accept the truth. Sheena simply looked down, disturbed deep in her soul at all she had heard and the possibility she had been wrong about Pegasus. She was concerned Tenicia could be wrong and believing lies as Lisa had said. Yet, she didn't know what to believe for the first time in a long time. She was uncertain about it all. Tenicia was not shaken by the questioning. She completely understood. She had lost her faith before. Now she was more assured than ever. The silence was becoming agonizing to Sheena. She was about to say goodbye when Tenicia opened her eyes, gently put her hand on Sheena's shoulder and softly said, "Think about the love you saw in David's eyes. The Bible says that God so loved the world, He sent his only Son to die for us. Do you think Pegasus, or any other spirit loves you that much?"

Sheena knew she'd never seen love like that before. She knew it was real and entirely uncommon. Candidly she asked, "Why did he need to die for us? I don't understand."

"He had to die for us because of sin, because we all do wrong things. We are compelled against doing right in our very nature. Jesus is the only one who was not born with a sinful nature. He is God with us." Tenicia replied lovingly.

"Wait a minute. I am a pretty good person. I do right all the time." Sheena argued.

"Really? You do right *all* the time?" Tenicia challenged.

"Yeah, pretty much." Sheena retorted.

"Is it right to lie to your parents?" Tenicia asked gently.

"No, of course not," Sheena admitted.

"What about hiding Lisa at your house without your parents knowing it; is that right?" Tenicia prodded.

"Not completely, but she needs my help," Sheena attempted to defend the wrong.

"God doesn't give us half credit, or an A for effort. He is a holy and righteous God. The cost of sin is death," Tenicia explained.

"So you mean that I should die for not telling my parents?" Sheena asked surprised by the harshness of such an idea.

"I don't think so," Tenicia replied honestly, "but I am not a

Holy God. They are his standards, and none of us meet them. All of us have done something wrong. Worshiping another spirit, any other spirit instead of God is wrong." Sheena looked at Tenicia with a doubtful, says who, kind of look, but didn't say anything. "Let me ask you another question," Tenicia continued.

"Okay." Sheena replied hesitantly, feeling a little uncomfortable.

"Have you ever done something completely selfish, even though you knew it would hurt someone else's feelings?" Tenicia tenaciously tested.

"Well of course, haven't we all?" Sheena answered honestly, then in self-defense she declared, "But I haven't murdered anyone."

"Have ever been angry with someone?" Tenicia prodded.

"Sure! Haven't you?" Sheena inquired indignantly.

"Absolutely!" Tenicia confessed. She then seriously stated, "Jesus said that even being angry with someone, and not forgiving them is just as bad as murder."

"What?" Sheena replied in disbelief.

"I know, I really felt bad about that. I had been so angry at both my parents and at God. I wasn't even going to forgive them." Tenicia admitted.

"So what changed your mind?" Sheena questioned curiously.

Tenicia's entire countenance changed. Her eyes filled with the same love as David's had that night at the beach. She explained, "His love changed my mind. That love that you saw in David's eyes is only a glimpse of the love He has for us. Sheena, He loves you so much. He is love."

Tears formed in the corner of Sheena's eyes. She could hardly believe that the God of the universe really loved her that much. Her own parents loved her, but not enough to die for her. They didn't even have time to hang out with her.

"Are you ready to accept the gift of his sacrifice? Will you let Him be your spirit guide....no, more....Your God?"

Sheena nodded her head slightly. Her heart was bursting with grief as she began to realize how wrong she had been and how much she needed Jesus.

The tears were flowing down her face as the girls knelt on the floor and prayed together. Then, Sheena told the Lord how sorry she was for worshiping other spirits and that she hadn't known it was wrong. She thanked Him for giving His Son to die for her sins and asked Him to come to her, to be her guide, her Lord forever.

Even as they finished praying, Sheena felt a sweet release of the guilt that she had felt earlier. She could sense the presence of Jesus there with her. She suddenly knew beyond a shadow of a doubt that she belonged to Him. She felt that warm peace wash over her. She now knew Love.

CHAPTER 10

The team of angels guarding the girls from the moment Sheena arrived were thrilled as they heard the conversation, but they could not turn away from their guard for even one second right then. The demons were pacing around the house, looking for an opening, for a weakness in the patrol. However, the angels far outnumbered them. Once again the Lord had set a divine appointment, and they had not seen it coming. They tried willing Sheena to leave, calling to her to come back before it was too late.

There were moments when she had almost got up and walked out thinking this is not true, but she had felt compelled to listen to Tenicia. Throughout the heavens the spiritual realm grew silent as they watched anxiously while the girls talked. As the girls got down on their knees, the angels held their breath with anticipation. As soon as Sheena said through the pangs of grief, "I am so sorry Father God. I didn't know following other spirits was wrong. Jesus I want to follow you," the angels of God began shouting and cheering.

A collective bone chilling groan of defeat poured out of the demons as they heard the cheers and shouts of the angels. The angels praised Jesus, the Lamb of God, the Righteous King of Kings and Lord of Lords. They clapped, danced, and jumped for joy, just as they did whenever a person turned from their sin, accepted Jesus, and became a child of God.

The demons cringed in pain as the praises continued and had to flee away from thc home. They threatened, "This isn't over!" as they retreated from the home.

The messenger angels continued to spread the word, and angels around the world were rejoicing with all of Heaven.

Tenicia also praised Jesus excitedly after Sheena asked Him to be her Savior and Lord. Sheena laughed with delight as she watched Tenicia rejoicing. Tenicia explained to Sheena how all Heaven was rejoicing with them, and Sheena felt elated.

The moment turned bittersweet for her all too quickly as she realized how angry Sergio would be when he found out. The girls talked about what could happen next, and what, if anything they could do to be prepared. Tenicia assured Sheena that nothing could separate them from the love of Jesus now, not their past sins, not what the others thought or did, not even the demons. Sheena felt the peace of assurance that it was true. The girls prayed again together before Sheena had to go back home and face Lisa who was still waiting for her return.

Tenicia got on her knees, bowed her head, and began with sincere gratitude, "Lord Jesus, thank you for your love that never fails us. Thank you for all you have done for us," her tone changed slightly to openness as she prayed, "We are willing to do whatever you want us to do, Lord, no matter what happens. Show us the right things to do. Please lead us in the right direction."

Sheena's voice quivered as she prayed, "Help me not be afraid of what they are going to do. Help me to be brave and bold like Tenicia and David have been."

"Lord, I ask that you would send your holy angels with Sheena now to watch over and protect her against the evil ones. Give her a special understanding of what to do and what to say at just the right moment," Tenicia asked sincerely.

"Oh God!" Sheena cried out as the reality of what she had heard in the circle sank in. She was truly struck with fear as she considered what could happen next. How would Sergio respond now? She wondered. So Sheena whole heartedly begged the Lord, "Protect this dear friend of mine from Sergio's anger, and please change his heart too."

"Yes Lord Jesus," Tenicia calmly agreed, "Please open the hearts and minds of each of the members of the circle. Help them to understand your love for them, and that you are the Way, the Truth, and the Life. Help them to see that no one comes to the Father, unless they come through you. Give them the ability to understand how wrong they have been, and how evil these other spirits are. Thank you, Holy Spirit for leading us and guiding us in all truth, just as it was promised." Tenicia reassuringly squeezed Sheena's hand and looked into Sheena's eyes as she said authoritatively, "Don't say anything to Lisa yet. Just spend some time reading the book of John first. Do you have a Bible?"

"I found one on my parent's book shelf," Sheena replied with a sigh of relief.

"Good. The Bible is an anthology of many books. The book of John is in the New Testament. It will give you a better understanding of who Jesus is, what He did and taught," Tenicia explained.

"Okay." Sheena agreed with a smile. She tilted her head slightly and mused, "It's funny, last night I thought I should start reading it. I pulled it off the bookshelf and hid it in my room, so Lisa wouldn't see it and freak out."

"That was smart!" Tenicia exclaimed with a large grin.

Both the girls laughed at the thought of Lisa having another fit, just seeing the book. Then Sheena looked into Tenicia's eyes, serious and searching. Sheena asked with concern, "What are you going to do? Are you going to leave?"

Tenicia looked down at the floor, concern covering her face. She sat thinking, silently praying for a couple of minutes. She finally looked back up to see the compassionate concern in Sheena's eyes for her. She smiled a sad smile and stated forlornly, "I don't know yet. It makes sense that I should go somewhere, but where would I go? How would I get there?"

"I don't know, but it is not safe for you to stay here," Sheena emphatically declared. "Is there anyone you can ask for help to get out of town?" She implored.

"I don't think I want to get anyone else involved; it could make them a target," Tenicia answered thoughtfully.

"True, but what are you going to do?" Sheena persistently inquired.

Tenicia regained an inner confidence. "I will pray about it, and see what the Lord wants me to do," She declared.

"Don't pray to long," Sheena earnestly warned, "I don't know how quickly Sergio will carry out his awful plan."

Tenicia straightened as she stood. With boldness enabled by the Holy Spirit, she acknowledged, "We just asked the Lord to protect us. We talked about how nothing can separate us from Him," her face became firm with resolve as she asserted, "Now I have to trust that He will do what He has promised to do. I have to trust that He will show me what to do at just the right time. I believe He will protect me until He is ready for me to come home."

"Come home?" Sheena questioned in confusion, "What do you mean come home? Aren't you already home?"

"Heaven..." Tenicia's face was swallowed with a broad smile as she explained, "I am talking about going to Heaven and being with Jesus face to face."

Sheena's confusion became curiosity. She asked, "Where is that anyway?"

"You're going to have to read the Bible to understand," Tenicia said a little overwhelmed by the question. Then she admitted, "I can't tell you everything all at once. It's too much. I'm not sure I can even explain it right myself yet. There is still so much I have to learn too."

"Okay," Sheena said with complete acceptance. Her heart filled with friendly love, she cheerfully said, "We will learn together. I will start reading tonight after Lisa is back in the shop."

Tenicia and Sheena hugged and said good bye. Tenicia looked out of the window carefully to see if anyone was outside before opening the door. As soon as Sheena walked out, Tenicia closed and locked the door behind her. She could not help but be afraid of what Sergio was planning. Yet, she was not so afraid that she was panicked. She knew Jesus was with her. She knew she could trust Him no matter what happened.

Right now she was famished. Everything that had just happened had made her feel like she hadn't eaten in days. She had never led anyone to the Lord before; it was so exciting and exhausting all at the same time. She went into the kitchen, grabbed a bite to eat, and then headed back to her room to pray about what to do next.

Sheena headed back to the house slowly. She had a lot of questions to ask the Lord. She was in no hurry to see Lisa right now. Lisa had been so adamant that the stories about Jesus were lies because of the way people acted. Yet, Sheena could suddenly understand that just because a person accepted Christ, they didn't automatically become perfect. Besides, it didn't change what happened before she accepted Christ. Even if she never followed another spirit again or cast another spell, she had been a witch once. She had to get Lisa back home somehow or at least out of her home. But how could she do it without telling her what had happened? It was too soon. It was going to be difficult to deal with her. It was going to be even worse to tell Sergio. Tenicia was right. She needed to wait awhile before telling them. She needed to understand it all better herself.

When she finally reached the house, the thought occurred to her that she had to get Lisa to the shop quickly. Her parents would be home anytime. Good, she thought, I won't have to spend so much time talking to her tonight. She entered the house, closed the door, and shouted, "Lisa, I am back." Lisa popped around the corner from the kitchen and said, "Finally, I was beginning to worry about you."

"Nothing to worry about, I just had a lot to think about," Sheena assured Lisa. Lisa's look questioned Sheena's response. She could tell a little explanation was need. So, Sheena told Lisa what she knew Lisa could accept, "I spent extra time at the park connecting with Pegasus before I went to Tenicia's."

"Oh okay," Lisa answered.

Sheena feigned fear and said, "My parents are going to be home any minute."

"Alright, I'll go back to the shop and watch the news out there," Lisa replied with disappointment. She hopefully asked, "Are you coming?"

"Maybe later, I want to eat first. I am starving." Sheena answered without thinking. Then she asked with genuine concern, "Did you eat?"

"Yeah, and there's still some of the munchies you brought out a couple nights ago," Lisa answered.

"Alright, I'll see you later then," Sheena said.

Lisa smiled and slid out the kitchen door. She slipped into the shop quickly and quietly as she could hear the neighbors in the back yard next door. Sheena let out a sigh of relief as she watched Lisa quietly close the shop door. She pulled the curtain across the kitchen door window.

As long as Lisa would keep quiet and follow the signal, Sheena's parents might never know she had ever been there. Even as the thought crossed her mind, Sheena felt a twinge of guilt. Maybe she should tell her parents and ask them what to do. No way, she thought. That would be suicide. At least not yet, maybe she would tell them when it was over.

She quickly grabbed something to eat, and then headed to her room. She pulled the Bible out from under the magazines in the night stand, looked at the table of contents, found John, and began to read. It didn't take long for her to fall asleep while reading the book. She was so tired.

She woke up a couple of hours later and could hear her parents in the kitchen. It seemed like it had been a long time since she'd spoken to them at all. So she washed her face and smoothed out her hair, then walked into the kitchen and said, "Hi." Her mom was just finishing cooking dinner. Sheena set the table very happy they were home tonight.

It felt good to have a normal, or at least somewhat normal, family dinner. Her parents rarely spent time in the kitchen together. Sheena smiled as she looked at the food her mom prepared. Her mom was not the greatest cook, but she was happy to just be there with them.

The conversation was pretty light as they ate together. Her parents were even joking and laughing. She hadn't seen anything like this in a very long time. After everything that had happened over the last few days, she was pleased she could have time like this with them. "Thank you, Jesus," she prayed silently. After the coast was clear, she pulled some of the food out and made a plate for Lisa, and quickly put everything away. She slipped out the kitchen door and quietly into the shop. Lisa was glad to see her and excitedly told Sheena that their plan to call her mom had worked. The news reporter said that the missing girl had called home and was okay. The search was over. Lisa was thrilled. "We have to get the gang together and go do something fun tomorrow night," she exclaimed.

Sheena pretended she was just as excited about going out, but she was now nervous about the idea. She was fooling Lisa, but Sergio, could she deceive him? Would he see the difference? She was certainly going to need to pray a lot. How long could she keep this from them? What would she tell them?

The thoughts suddenly came to her mind, "It is not time to tell them. Come to me and learn from me first. I will show you many things. Then, I will show you when it is time to tell them." As the thoughts ran through her mind, her heart quit racing and she felt calm again. She could be free to just have fun with her friends tomorrow. Maybe this would buy some time and everyone could just cool down. All of this spiritual stuff could simply wait awhile. Sheena said good night to Lisa and went straight for the Bible again.

There was so much she wanted to know, so she opened up the Bible to the book of John. "In the beginning was the Word, and the Word was with God and the Word was God." John 1:1.

She didn't really understand what she just read, but she kept reading, hoping and praying that the Holy Spirit would help her understand like Tenicia said He would.

As she continued reading she understood. Jesus is the Word of God and the Son of God. He was there in the beginning of creation with God. He is also God. He made everything. What is the difference between Jesus, the Father, and the Holy Spirit? She wondered. She kept reading. When she could not keep her eyes focused any longer, she put the marker in at chapter five, placed the Bible on the nightstand, laid her head down, and went into a deep peaceful sleep.

The next day Sheena called the rest of the gang together and said she thought they needed to take some time off from everything and just have some fun. Everyone but Sergio agreed. Sergio stayed silent, staring suspiciously. Sheena was surprised, yet delighted, by their willingness to let go of their regular meetings for a while. She reasoned with him, "Life needs to be returning to a normal world as summer ends, things will settle down, and everyone will become busy again."

She was right. There was only one major change; the circle was not meeting anymore. Days turned into weeks, and weeks into a couple of months since Sheena had begun reading the Bible. Things seemed to settle down. Within a few days, Sergio didn't seem so angry. Lisa had finally reconciled with her parents and gone home. Tenicia was alive and well. By the end of the month, David and Aaron had returned to their colleges. Lisa's parents had encouraged her to take the semester off and see a counselor. Sergio and Josh had several camping trips scheduled and would be gone most of the fall. Tenicia had a job.

Sheena was taking just a couple of classes at the local community college. Sheena told her parents she needed to figure a few things out, so they accepted the lighter schedule. She spent her extra time reading the Bible. She was so grateful to the Lord for giving her this time to learn about Him and grow in Him.

It seemed the more she read, the more she wanted to read. She was spending hours every day in the Bible. She was simply hungry, no....starved for it. She couldn't devour enough to fill her for more than a few hours at a time. She began listening to TV preachers on occasion to help her understand the Word more.

One night a few weeks later, she turned on the TV to listen to what ever preacher was on at that moment. As he closed the message about repenting of sin, Sheena was hit with an overwhelming feeling of guilt. The measure of guilt she felt was crushing her heart. She cried out with grief over everything she had done wrong. She fell to her knees as the tears began streaming down her cheeks. She understood just how much she had done wrong. Every time she had been selfish came back to mind. Each one of the times when she had neglected to tell her parents something they should have known, the things she had said or done while worshiping Pegasus, or the times when she had led others to Pegasus suddenly weighed heavily on her. The grief was even more intense than when she had first turned to the Lord. Now she understood just how much Jesus had paid for the sins of the world, and her sins were part of it. She knew He had done nothing wrong, but was severely tortured and killed with cruelty. The tears poured out for what felt like a good hour before the fantastic feeling of forgiveness washed her wounded soul.

She got up from the floor of her bedroom and walked down the hall to the kitchen. She sat in a wooden armed chair in front of an open window, enjoying the late night breeze. She felt a spirit come upon her and began thanking God for the Holy Spirit. She felt elated as the spirit started to fill her. Suddenly the thought occurred to her to ask if it was the Holy Spirit. So she did. Not thinking anything of the question, maybe even expecting the answer to be yes, she asked out loud, "Is this the Holy Spirit?"

The spirit who had come upon her tried to throw her to the floor. She grabbed the arms of the chair and leaned hard back into the chair, refusing to give the spirit control. She could feel the spirit pulling her, trying to drag her to the floor, but she kept pulling back.

Finally, she felt the spirit pulling out of her through her chest. As quickly as it had come upon her it was now gone. However, there was a burning sensation in her chest. The center of her chest felt like it was on fire. It was more like intense sunburn, than heartburn, but it was real. The burn diminished slowly over the next three days.

On the third day, she was so excited she had to tell everyone. She had been delivered from an evil spirit. She was filled with confidence and boldness. She went to Lisa's house first.

Lisa listened with a sense of awe. She did not scream and yell at Sheena as she had Tenicia or David. Lisa just didn't know what to think now. Sheena would not make this up, she knew. Yet, what Sheena was telling her just seemed impossible to believe.
Lisa finally said, "Sheena, you're fortunate Pegasus helped you with that spirit." Lisa shook her head, then asked incredulously, "After I warned you not to believe those lies, you actually started reading that book? Don't you know it's written by men to control others, especially women?" Then she gave a stern warning, "You are asking for a lot of trouble."

Sheena left Lisa, unsure what to do next. She prayed as she walked through town. She found herself by the soda shop, so she went in to see if there was anyone she knew there. Aaron and Josh were sitting at a table ordering burgers. She walked up and said, "Hi guys! I am surprised to see you home."

"Hey, Sheena, how's it going?" Josh said with a huge grin.

"Wow, it's been awhile!" Aaron remarked with pleasant surprise in the timing, "Sit down," he offered as scooted over.

"It's going really good," Sheena said as she slid into the booth next to him, "How are you guys?"

"Hungry! That last trip was intense." Josh answered, "I hope they hurry up with that burger."

Aaron and Sheena laughed. Then, Aaron gently elbowed Sheena and with eyebrows raised he asked, "What have you been doing?" noting, "I've called a few people since I came home for the week between quarters; no one has seen you for weeks, and you're not answering the phone."

"I know," Sheena acknowledged. She began to explain, "I really needed to figure some things out, and something totally amazing has happened."

"Amazing things always happen with you, girl," Josh declared.

"Do tell," Aaron encouraged with a a broad smile, intrigued with what she would say.

Sheena began to tell the guys about the last two months. She told them everything, leaving nothing out. They sat in stunned silence just listening. Every once in a while, they would look at each other in disbelief and then turn back to her as she told her story. She stopped briefly when the waitress came to the table and asked if Sheena wanted anything, and again when the waitress returned with the food. The guys ate as they continued to listen, but neither of them said a word. Finally, she told them how her chest was still burning.

When she finished, Aaron asked, "Have you told Sergio?"

"No, his mom said he is out of town," Sheena replied.

Shaking his head in almost disbelief, Josh said with serious concern, "He is not going to like this. Oooh....you might not want to tell him." Josh turned away and stared up at the ceiling. He was grateful he hadn't been able to get a hold of David before their trips. Would he have been persuaded too. Even now, he could feel a tugging in his heart as he listened to Sheena, but the memory of Sergio's anger as they had walked home that day after Tenicia's announcement sent chills through his soul. Then he added, "Its good he decided to take a little vacation by himself."

Sheena dropped her gaze to the table. She was saddened that the guys were right; he would be angry. Aaron lifted her chin gently and turned her face to his. Like a big brother, he suggested, "It might be better if you just decide to go away to an aunt's or something."

Tears formed in the corners of Sheena's eyes. She sincerely and emphatically stated, "I know, he's going to be so angry with me, but I can't help it. I have met the King of Kings."

"This can't be right," Josh muttered. Then he looked across

the table and pleadingly said, "Sheena you are the leader of our circle. You can't be serious about this."

"I am more than serious; I am in love with Jesus!" Sheena replied whole heartedly, "I have given my life to Him no matter what the cost."

Aaron, with an uncanny calm, responded, "It might very well cost you your life. I hope you are really prepared for that."

"Yeah," Josh added as he leaned across the table and locked eyes with Sheena. Then he stated in a whisper, "He was ready to kill Tenicia when she betrayed Pegasus."

"She is really fortunate she didn't start talking. I hope she doesn't," Aaron stated.

"I just can't believe this!" Josh exclaimed rolling his and leaning back against the booth seat. Then he gave Sheena a doubtful look and implored, "You're telling me after the miracle you did, you really think this Jesus is more powerful."

"I don't just think it; *I know it*." Sheena proclaimed. Then in an attempt to offer proof, she reminded them, "Like I said, my chest is still burning from the spirit leaving me. Jesus did that."

"This is just too much," Aaron now responded in disbelief and declared, "You have simply lost it."

"Believe what you want. I am telling you, the Bible is true, and Jesus is real." Sheena got up from the table both frustrated and frightened. She knew they were right about Sergio. She was glad he was out of town and she could tell them first. Yet, she felt kind of guilty that he had not been the first one to hear at the same time. They had been partners since grade school. She loved him, but now she feared him too. He couldn't hurt her....could he? Would he go after Tenicia now, because of her? A shiver ran down her spine. She left the soda shop and went straight to Tenicia's house.

Sheena walked up the sidewalk, remembering how panicked she had been the last time she had come to Tenicia's; but how she left with peace and joy.

Now she had even greater peace in some senses, but a genuine concern too. She knocked on the door. Marcella answered and said Tenicia was at a meeting, youth group she called it. When Sheena asked where it was, Marcella smiled and explained it was at the church a few blocks over.

Sheena thanked her and started walking over to the church. She found the church and could hear the excitement as the others were playing a game. She stood at the back of the room and watched. It felt good to be here, away from the others, away from her house, away from Pegasus.

As the game came to an end, Tenicia spotted her and excitedly ran over to her. Tenicia cheerfully exclaimed, "I so glad you're here!" Then she asked sincerely, "How are you?"

"I am good," Sheena replied with a half-hearted smile. Looking Tenicia in the eye slightly pleading, she asked, "Can we talk?"

"Sure, in a little while," Tenicia assured her, and encouraged Sheena, "Come sit with me."

"Okay," Sheena acquiesced, a little nervously. Tenicia grabbed Sheena's hand and led her up to the center of the rows of chairs. They slid into the row and sat down as the youth pastor began to ask for everyone's attention. Sheena was fascinated. She had never been in a church before. She had no idea they played games and such.

Now, this young man was going to speak to them. He was only about 6 or 7 years older than most of the teens, but he said he had a message for them from the Lord. He challenged them to be bold for Jesus. She listened intently as he described the bravery of the apostles after the resurrection of Christ.

Sheena was encouraged as he told of the miracles that happened as the apostles faced many dangerous and difficult situations. She knew that she would have her own battles to face, just as they had with their religious group. The way Lisa had talked, she had thought the church was her enemy. Now, it was her own lifelong friends that would become her enemy.

Yet, there was no way she could deny Jesus now. She knew he was real! She understood He was the King of Kings and Lord of Lords. She now comprehended that meant Jesus ruled over all spiritual beings and would one day completely rule the earth. Even if she had to face the anger of Sergio, she could not go back to the way things were.

After the sermon was over, Tenicia took her by the hand and led her up to the young pastor. Tenicia introduced Sheena as her friend, but didn't tell him anything about Pegasus. They talked for a minute more about the message, and he invited Sheena to come back on Sunday. Several kids had gathered around them. Tenicia asked if she wanted to meet everyone else, and Sheena said, "Next time, okay. We really need to go." The others seemed to understand, so the two girls left and talked as they walked home.

As soon as they were far enough away from the church that the others could not hear their conversation, Sheena began looking around, making sure they were alone. Once she felt it was safe, she said, "So much has changed, but I am afraid things are going to get crazy," unable to hide the anxiety.

The fear in her voice was unnerving to Tenicia, and silently she simply prayed, help. The thought almost instantly came to Tenicia that focusing on the good would be best. So she smiled and said, "Tell me what has changed first." Tenicia wanted to keep that upbeat and excited feeling alive; remembering all that the Lord had already done would be a great way to do it.

"I started reading the book of John like you said to," Sheena took a deep breath and admitted, "At first I didn't really understand what it was all about. It was confusing, the word was with God and the word was God. What is that about? I wondered. But, I kept reading and asking the Holy Spirit to lead me and guide into all truth."

The excited feeling radiated from every ounce of Tenicia. She cheered, "That's fantastic!" Then she asked sincerely, "Do you understand it now?"

"I think so," Sheena stated confidently. She looked up and to the left as she concentrated and continued, "The more I read it the more I understood that the book is about Jesus."

She glanced back over at Tenicia and continued, "Jesus is the one called the Word. So Jesus, the Word of God, was with God the Father, and He was also God, even in the beginning of creation." Sheena paused and inquired, "Is that right?

"You're absolutely right! You got it!" Tenicia enthusiastically exclaimed.

Sheena smiled and her countenance lightened. She said, "Thanks," genuinely appreciating the encouragement. Sheena decided it was time to tell Tenicia the details, "As I kept reading, I wanted to read more and more, but I didn't want to talk to Lisa about it. She was so angry at you and David. She said it was all lies. So, I asked the Lord to make away for Lisa to go home and within days she told me she was going home. I also told the circle that we needed to take a break and let things get back to normal. They were ready too."

As she continued telling Tenicia all that had happened, there was a heavy weight lifted from her shoulders. She realized even as she recounted the events that God had heard her prayers, made a way for her, and protected her. She began to feel Tenicia's excitement as she recalled, "Then I was free to read the Bible as much as I wanted to. Nobody was expecting me to lead the group. Nobody was there to tell me anything. Even Sergio left me alone. I was so grateful."

"The Lord made a way for you to get to know Him. He really loves you," Tenicia confirmed.

"I can tell that now," Sheena stated, "I am so glad you told me about Him." The girls walked the rest of the block in a contented and thoughtful silence. As they reached the corner, Sheena's expression changed to sheer joy and exhilaration. She stopped, grabbed Tenicia's arm turning her, and declared, "You are not going to believe what happened the other night!" Sheena could still hardly believe it herself.

"With you girl, nothing would surprise me. Tenicia teased with a smirk, nodded and said, "Go on."

Sheena started the story admitting, "Well, I really felt bad for everything I had ever done wrong as I understood that Jesus, God in the flesh, who did nothing wrong, was beaten, mocked, tortured, and died to pay for my sins. I was really broken hearted, so much more than last time when I only got it a little bit. Knowing who He really is and what He really went through for me, I just felt awful. I realized more and more things I had done wrong. It was horrible," Sheena continued, "I cried and cried. Finally, I was all cried out; and a deep sense of forgiveness and peace had washed over me."

"Oh I know how that feels," Tenicia acknowledged, "When we first got back from the camping trip and I finally was alone with Him, I cried so hard. I felt so bad that I had turned away from him, and not trusted Him. Then the huge smile returned as she said, "I remember how great it felt to have His Spirit fill me with forgiveness and peace. I can't stop thanking Him. And now, you know Him too! Our God is an Awesome God!"

"Yes He is!" Sheena exclaimed. She continued retelling the unexpected event, "Then, I went into the kitchen, and was just sitting there enjoying a cup of tea when I felt a spirit coming upon me. At first I thought it must be the Holy Spirit, but then a direction came to mind. "Ask if this is the Holy Spirit," I heard in my mind. So I did. I asked."

The surprise made Tenicia physically take a step back. She looked into Sheena's eyes searching for an honest answer as she asked, "Was it the Holy Spirit?"

Sheena looked down with a sense of shame, and shook her head "No, it wasn't." Then she looked back at Tenicia and explained, "As soon as I asked, the spirit tried to throw me to the floor. I pulled back and refused to let it take control of me. Suddenly, I could feel it pulling out of my chest. I still had to push myself back to keep from being drug to the floor. Finally, as it completely left me, my chest started burning. It felt like it was on fire, like a sun burn, only much, much hotter."

Tenicia's eyes grew as big as they possibly could as she listened to Sheena recall the encounter. When Sheena finished, she responded, "Oh man. That is wild!" With consuming curiosity Tenicia asked, "What did you do? What happened next?"

"Well, I just sat there for a while, stunned," Sheena confessed, "Then I prayed about it.

I knew that I had just been delivered from a demon, but I wasn't sure what to do, or what would happen next. "I heard the Lord say that it was okay, and I needed to rest. So that is what I did, I went to bed. I was incredibly exhausted after all that anyway." Her voice changed to reflect the shock she felt the following morning, "What really surprised me was that my chest was still burning when I woke up."

She took a deep breath. Her eyes widened as she said, "Now, three days later, it is still burning; but not as intense."

"That is amazing!" Tenicia agreed in astonishment. The girls started walking again towards Tenicia's home. They were getting close and Tenicia knew the conversation would have to end soon. "Can you see it?" Tenicia asked.

"No, there is no mark or anything. It isn't even red like sunburn," Sheena answered in a matter of fact tone.

Tenicia grew a little concerned and inquired, "Have you felt any other spirits trying to come upon you since then?"

"No. None, Thank God!" Sheena declared with relief.

"That is wonderful," Tenicia agreed. Then she asked, "Do you know why that happened?"

"Well, I think it was the spirit I gave myself to as a witch," Sheena said reflectively, "I think it was trying to possess me, like it always had."

"I think you're right. I am so glad the Holy Spirit led you to ask if it was Him." Tenicia acknowledged.

"Me too," Sheena agreed. Then in an attempt to prepare Tenicia for what was coming, she somberly said, "I told all the others, except Sergio today. I am glad he is on a vacation right now."

Tenicia winced as she asked, "How did they take it?"

"Not so good," Sheena expressed her disappointment, "They aren't so angry, but the guys are pretty sure Sergio will be. They don't really seem to believe me either," The disappointment turned to a perplexed acknowledgement, as Sheena said, "Lisa seemed to actually feel sorry for me."

Tenicia sadly explained, "Their hearts are too hard to hear the truth right now." She put her hand on Sheena's shoulder.

Suddenly, like a bolt of lightning hit her, her face lit up, and Tenicia hopefully said, "Maybe as they see the change in you, they will want to know more."

Sheena was not so easily encouraged. She warned, "They said it might be good if I went and stayed with an aunt or something. I think they might be right. I think we both need to leave for a while. When you told us you had turned back to Jesus, Sergio was ready to kill you. When he finds out I have turned to Jesus also, he is definitely going to want to kill us."

"I am not afraid of Sergio," Tenicia firmly avowed, "The Lord is in control." Tenicia smiled as she reminded Sheena, "He made the time for you to come to know Him. He set you free from the demon. He can protect us." Then she courageously committed herself, "Unless He tells me I need to go, I am staying right here."

Sheena smiled and acknowledged, "You are so brave. Your confidence in Him is what compelled me to keep listening to you." Slightly uncertain, she asked, "What should we do now?"

"We just keep doing what we're doing until the Lord tells us something different. He will protect us. He will lead and guide us," Tenicia replied confidently.

"Thanks. I knew I could count on you," Sheena said gratefully.

"Of course you can count on me. We are not just friends now; we're sisters in the Lord," Tenicia reassured.

Sheena changed the course of conversation, asking "Have you talked to David?"

"Not since I first came back to the Lord. I didn't really want to involve anyone else with the circle," Tenicia replied, "Besides, isn't he back at the U.C.?"

"Maybe," Sheena answered. Then she said, "I am glad you didn't involve him, but I think I need to talk to him," Sheena stated.

"Alright, I have his number. Let's go to my house and call him," Tenicia said, slightly puzzled, and intensely curious.

"That would be great," Sheena agreed. Then understanding Tenicia's curiosity, she explained, "He already knows about the circle, but he doesn't know we were praying against him."

"What?" Tenicia asked in surprise.

"Yeah, Sergio, his parents, and I were praying against him the night Lisa lost it," confessed Sheena.

"Wow! I hope he's okay. I haven't heard anything or seen him," Tenicia remarked sincerely.

Sheena began to get a little excited again as she said, "It will be great to tell him I've accepted Christ and been set free too."

"If he's home, he will be so thrilled," Tenicia supposed, then added, "We will make a chord of three."

"What?" Sheena questioned.

Tenicia smiled as she remembered Sheena didn't grow up reading the Bible, so she graciously explained, "It's a scripture. The Bible talks about how two are better than one because they can help each other, but a chord of three cannot be broken. It is so much stronger." As she remembered his promise, she stated with confidence, "Jesus also said that when two or three gather together in His name, He is right there in the middle with them." Her smile grew larger, and larger, until she couldn't help but light heartedly laugh with delight. Tenicia stopped Sheena this time just a few houses away from her home and said cheerfully, "So I think the Lord is telling us, we need to become a new team."

"That will be awesome!" Sheena exclaimed.

Tenicia's face exploded with a huge smile. The twinkle in her eyes matched the grin. Sheena could not help but smile as she saw the excitement in Tenicia's face. Tenicia froze for just a moment, Sheena looked at her curiously. Tenicia grabbed Sheena's hands and excitedly stated, "Let's call him right now!" Sheena giggled at Tenicia's excitement and said, "Okay." They bolted up the street and ran into the house.

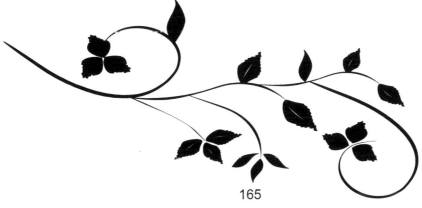

CHAPTER 11

The girls discovered that David had definitely been having a difficult time over the last couple of months. Even as they spoke, he was in a cast. He had broken his ankle while jogging just before he was supposed to return to the U.C. He did not see a hole in the ground. His foot came down right in the center of the hole. As his foot found the bottom of the hole, it twisted hard. When he fell, face forward, he heard the snap of his ankle.

Surprisingly, there was no one outside in the neighborhood. He laid there for what seemed like an hour before he could get up and hobble home. The pain was excruciating. Then as he finished telling the story he exclaimed that he was looking forward to getting the cast off.

Tenicia decided it was time to drop the bomb. She knew he would love what the Lord had done, and that everything would make more sense. "There was someone at youth group tonight that I think you would be interested in," she said coyly.

"Are you trying to set me up with one of your friends?" David suspiciously asked.

Tenicia laughed heartily. "Well sort of," she answered. Then she added with a sly statement, "She came to the house with me, and she wants to say hi." Sheena was all but holding her breath trying to stay quiet.

"Do I know her?" David asked puzzled by the direction the conversation had taken.

"She's seen you around....before you graduated." Both the girls grinned fighting desperately to keep from bursting out laughing.

"Alright," David said with a little hesitance. He didn't want to be rude or crush some girl's heart, but he was pretty sure they would be too young for him if they were at youth group.

"Hello David," Sheena said slyly into the other phone.

David knew the voice, but it took him a moment to recall who this girl was.

"Have you forgotten me so quickly?" Sheena asked with a mock hurt in her voice.

"Sheena? Is that you?!" David was shocked.

"Yes it is," she admitted happily. Compassionately she stated, "Sorry to hear about all the trouble you've had lately."

"You were at youth group?" David asked incredulously, "How did that happen?"

The girls giggled with delight at David's surprise, and then spent the next hour telling him everything. He agreed that they needed to be in prayer together and encouraged Sheena to go back to church with Tenicia. He said it would be very important for her to have the covering of the church. They prayed before getting off the phone. Sheena left Tenicia's encouraged and excited. She knew they had made a strong cord tonight. She had an assurance deep in her heart that all would be well, no matter what Sergio's response was.

The next few days were calmer than she could ever remember them being. She was truly at peace for the first time. She was even excited about going to church. On Saturday evening, she began looking through the closet to find just the right outfit.
She wanted to make a good impression, but she wasn't sure what people wore to church. She called Tenicia after looking for an hour and not being able to make up her mind. Tenicia assured her it was okay to wear jeans and a nice blouse. Sheena finally picked out her nicest blouse.

When she went to bed that night, she had trouble falling asleep. She was anxious now about actually going to church. She was unsure how to behave, or what to say. She was glad Tenicia would be there with her. She would just watch and say very little. Once she had the plan in place, she drifted off to a deep sleep.

Sheena woke up before sunrise with the anticipation of this new adventure. She had no idea what to really expect, but she now belonged to a new family, the family of God.

She was ecstatic that they actually spent time together on a regular basis. It seemed like they had a great deal of fun together as well. She knew she was walking into a new world, and the unknown was exciting; yet the thought of meeting church people was intimidating. She could hear Lisa's comments run through her mind. Were these people who knew the King of Kings anything like Lisa had said? Were they really judgmental and mean spirited? Did they really say one thing and live another? Could they possibly attend church just to look good? What would they think of her?

She reasoned that there must be more to the story than Lisa thought. Maybe Lisa's church was full of people just playing a game, but certainly not all churches were like that, she reasoned. Tenicia seemed to enjoy her church. The kids at youth group seemed nice. The pastor was nice. Well I guess there is only one way to find out, she figured. I will have to go and see for myself. So she spent the next hour getting ready, and then took the first step towards her new spiritual family.

When she arrived, Tenicia was waiting out front for her. Tenicia was excited to see she had really come. Tenicia introduced her to so many new people there was no way she could ever remember all the names. They seemed to talk pretty normal. They did not seem mean or fake. Everybody started taking seats in the pews. She and Tenicia sat with Tenicia's mom towards the back.

The service started with music. The announcer told the people to open their hymnals to page 273. Sheena watched with curiosity as the people all took a book from the back of the pew in front of them, found the page, and with the musician's cue began to sing the song. The songs were songs she had never heard before. The tunes were unusual as well. They sounded as if they were from an ancient culture....from a faraway land. Yet, they were absolutely beautiful. They were full of praises for the Lord Jesus and told so much about Him. After they sang four songs, they were instructed to greet one another. People began shaking hands and talking to those around them. The greeting session was brief, about a minute.

Then the pastor called everyone back to their seats. He had a great message for them, he said, but first he called up the little children. Most of the children seemed to know what to expect. They eagerly went up to the front and sat down on the steps around him. He said a few words to them, gave them each a sugar free candy, and then sent them to their Sunday School Classes.

They seemed really happy as they left for their classes, like they actually enjoyed them. Once the large room was settled again, the pastor had everyone turn to a passage in the Bible. They read together, "Blessed are the poor in spirit, for theirs is the kingdom of heaven..." When it came to "Blessed are you when people insult you, persecute you and falsely say all kinds of evil against you, because of me," Sheena squirmed a little.

Then he began teaching what it meant. Sheena ate up his words as if they were a gourmet meal, freshly set before her. She so enjoyed the teaching, she didn't realize almost an hour had passed by the time he was finished. As everyone slowly left the building, Marcella invited Sheena to have lunch with them. She happily accepted.

When they arrived at Tenicia's home, Sheena was pleasantly overwhelmed by the aroma of a roast in the slow cooker. Marcella had the girls set the table as she finished preparing the lunch. The doorbell rang, and another family from the church joined them. Sheena felt unsure but comfortable and enjoyed the family atmosphere of a shared meal. She still did not say much. She listened and watched the others. She wanted to learn how they behaved and what they talked like before saying anything. She smiled and laughed lightly throughout the conversation.

After lunch, she helped clear the table and clean up without being asked. Then she politely said, "Thank you" and "goodbye," and walked home. The whole day had been utterly satisfying. She could not believe Lisa hated this so much. Sheena was looking forward to Wednesday night now.

Wednesday night was quite different from Sunday morning. They played games and the teaching was shorter. It was also meant more for the teenagers there , rather than adults.

Sheena certainly enjoyed this night too. For the next couple of weeks, Sheena found church to be her favorite place in the world. The third Wednesday night, the pastor said he wanted to do something a little different. He had been teaching them about how others had shared their stories about coming to the Lord. He had talked about how many other people had come to know Jesus by the believers telling them about how they had come to know Jesus. He now wanted them to practice telling each other their own story. He split them up in groups first.

Then after about ten minutes, he asked for volunteers to tell the whole group how they had come to know Jesus. Sheena felt like she would burst if she did not tell everyone how she met Jesus. As she got in line to speak, her heart raced faster than the engine of the dragsters just before the go signal. She could hear the other kids speaking, but couldn't really take in what they were saying. She was so nervous and excited.

As the line grew shorter, she began taking slow deep breaths to calm herself. When she stood in front of the mike and announced that before she met Jesus, she had been a white witch, the room grew so silent a dropped pin would have been heard. All eyes focused intensely upon her, as she told the story. Several kids looked back at Tenicia in disbelief, and she smiled and nodded to signal, "Yes, it's true." When she was finished, the pastor took the mike and thanked her. Everyone seemed quite dazed, yet she knew she had done the right thing. Sheena could feel Father God looking down and smiling upon her.

"Well done my child," said the voice in her mind.

The other kids seemed to be a little distant though. "They are just surprised," said Tenicia, "Give them time."

A couple more weeks passed and the others in the church were increasingly distant. There were times when she felt like the small huddled groups here or there in the church were talking about her. Parents seemed to eye her cautiously. Very few of the others would want to play with her on game nights. She began to feel isolated and rejected.

Tenicia was shocked at the behavior of the others. Tenicia felt so bad for Sheena, but there was nothing she could do. Some of them had told her they were afraid of Sheena. Some of them said they thought she was crazy. The parents were telling them to stay away from her.

Marcella had been great though. She came over and hugged Sheena, telling her Jesus loved her, and so did she. They began to feel the pressure from the church as well. Other parents called Marcella, asking her to keep this strange girl away from their kids, warning her that her daughter would be ostracized as well if the girls continued to be friends. Tenicia began hearing her mother defend Sheena with the other parents, sometimes angrily.

After the fourth week, Sheena sat at the kitchen table, looked down as she was unable to keep the tears from flowing, and said, "I will not stay where I am not wanted." Marcella put her hand on Sheena's and declared, "We are in this with you." The three of them decided it was time to find a new church together. Tenicia was so proud of her mom.

They didn't go anywhere that Sunday, but they read the Bible together and talked about it. The next week Tenicia's mom had found a church they could try. They went to the church, all three together, but none of them felt welcome or comfortable. They tried another, and another, like shopping for just the right dress or shoes, but those did not feel comfortable either. They quit trying after several attempts and just stayed home. They determined they could have church together. The girls went downtown and window shopped for the rest of the afternoon.

When evening came, Sheena walked home. As she turned onto the sidewalk up to her door, she could see a note sticking out of the door jam. She smiled and ran up the sidewalk. She set her purse and shopping bag down, gently pulled out the note and read it.

"I am home from the camping trips. I tried to call a few times, but you were gone. I miss you so much. Please call me as soon as you can. Love, Sergio."

Sheena smiled, but then remembered his anger. She felt nervous, but she knew she had to call him. Should I tell him over the phone? I don't think I should go to his house now. His parents are lost too. She thought. She gathered her things, unlocked the door, went straight to her room, and began praying. She needed Jesus badly. She could not do this alone. She didn't even know what to tell him. She was afraid now.

Almost as soon as Sheena began to pray, she felt the peace she now knew to be from the Holy Spirit's presence in her. She called Tenicia and then David, asking for prayer. It had been four months since she had seen him. So much had changed. Had he talked to the others yet? She hadn't spoken to any of them for the last two months. He had to have talked to them. She knew he was going to be heavily booked for fall, but surely he had been home in between the trips. Somebody had to have told him already. He and Josh were working together! Yet, he said he loved her. Her heart melted at the thought of those three words. Maybe it was going to be okay after all.

She called and Sergio answered the phone on the first ring as if he were waiting for her call. She smiled at the sound of his voice. The deep soft sound was so soothing to her that she felt immediately at ease. She told him she was glad he was home and really wanted to see him. Sergio said he had longed to see her over the last few months also. They agreed to go out the next night to play miniature golf and catch up. They kept the call short and waited with anticipation for the next night.

Sheena determined quickly she would listen to his adventures about the trips and the people he'd worked with before she told him anything about what had happened the last four months.

172

She had difficulty falling asleep that night as she imagined the evening to come. She played several scenarios through her mind in an attempt to prepare herself for what might happen, what he might say, and how to respond. More than anything else, she just wanted to be with him again. Sergio had been her best friend since kindergarten. He had turned into her lover that past summer. She longed to see him and feel his embrace.

She also wrestled with the idea that she could not be completely intimate with him. She had come to understand that having sex outside of marriage was wrong in the past month. Oh how difficult this will be, she thought. So again, she prayed for Jesus to help her walk through this change, to give her the ability to bring glory and honor to his name, to tell Sergio boldly what the Lord had done and who He is. The Holy Spirit whispered to her soul, "I am with you always," as she prayed again, then her heart grew content, her eyes grew heavy, and she finally drifted off into a deep sleep.

The day passed quickly for Sheena as her classes were in the days just before finals. She could hardly focus on the information regarding final times for each class, as she was so excited about spending time with Sergio. This was the first time in her life they had been apart for so long. She could hardly wait to see him again. She was confident that he loved her enough to accept how Jesus had revealed Himself to her and changed her life. She desperately prayed that Sergio would understand that Jesus is the true living God. She dressed comfortably cute for the date, taking care to put on the necklace Sergio had given her for Solstice the year before.

Sergio was anxious to see Sheena also. He could hardly believe it had been four months himself. Many of the nights he had spent in a tent in the Sierras with different clients, he spent thinking of her.

He had done very well financially, just as Pegasus had promised. The adventure had been incredible as he met different stars from his favorite shows and movies. They had done exciting and adventurous trails in various places throughout the forest.

He had so much to tell Sheena. Sergio knew he would never love any girl the way he loved her. She was his best friend. She was the one he wanted to have by his side for the rest of his life. Together, they would have the greatest adventures of all.

For tonight, they would just catch up, he thought. He was interested in how her classes at the local college were going. He wanted to know what Pegasus had shown her and if there had been any more trouble after Lisa had gone home.

He had been so busy; he hadn't spoken with any of the gang except Josh when they were working the backpacking trips. Josh hadn't said anything about what Sheena had told them at the soda shop, hoping it would pass before they came back home.

Sergio was very glad to have the next month off as people focused on the holidays. He looked forward to the Winter Solstice and wondered how Pegasus would lead them through the celebration. He felt a slight shiver up his spine at the thought of it. He had been having such a busy and adventurous time that he had not spent much time in Pegasus' presence either. So, he sat with his legs folded like butterfly wings. He closed his eyes and called upon Pegasus.

It took a long time for Sergio to clear his mind enough to see the winged horse standing in the field, grazing. "Pegasus," he called out, "I have missed my time with you, but I really enjoyed the adventures you gave me."

Pegasus lifted his head high and proudly sauntered over to Sergio. "Sergio, you are my prized warrior, and I have missed you as well. You will have far more adventure and wealth than this. This season is just the beginning. You will be the leader of a great and powerful people. Stay with me." As Pegasus spoke to Sergio, Sergio stood up and began stroking the beautiful, yet strong creature. Sergio hungered for what Pegasus promised him and delighted in euphoric feeling. Suddenly, Sergio was shocked as he saw Sheena standing on an opposite ridge calling to him. The gorge between them was deep and wide.

He had no way of getting to her. There was no bridge. The ridge she was on rose up in the center of the huge canyon completely isolated from the other ridges. She stood on the table top mountain trapped by the sheer rock walls and gigantic gulf encircling the ridge.

Pegasus said, "Sheena has been taken away by a powerful spirit who is opposed to us. She needs you to bring her back. She cannot see nor hear me now. You will have to speak the truth to her, gently. She will follow you back. I will lead you and when she is ready, we will fly across the gorge and rescue her."

Sergio came out of the trance with an urgency to reach Sheena. Tonight was far more important than he realized before. He was grateful to Pegasus for meeting him there, and glad he had taken the afternoon to seek the wise creature. The word "gently" flowed strongly through his mind again.

There was a part of him that wanted to war against this other spirit. Sergio was angry that it had taken her. Sergio saw Sheena as a hostage, powerless against this smooth talking being that had captivated her and led her away. "First, we must rescue Sheena," Pegasus smiled as he calmly reminded his young warrior.

Just as Sergio was coming out of the trance, David felt a sudden urgency too. The Holy Spirit called to him, "David, come spend time with me." David went into his room, closed the door, and knelt at the end of his bed. "Yes Lord," he prayed, "Your servant is listening." The Holy Spirit smiled and began, "We need to pray for Sheena now."

David began passionately pleading for her, knowing the battle she was about to face. "Lord, I lift up Sheena to you. She is like a lamb being hunted by the wolf tonight. She knows her predator is dangerous, but she is unable to defend herself against it. She needs you, Great Sheppard, to lead her and guide her through this dark and dangerous valley to the green pasture. Send your angels to clear the path before her, to guard her and watch over her."

Suddenly, David was filled with the Holy Spirit differently than he had ever been before. He began praying in a language he did not know, with fervency far greater than his own. He did not really understand what he was praying, but he knew it was the right thing to pray. He understood the Holy Spirit was praying through him on behalf of this young believer with so much ahead of her.

Mighty Warrior Angels began descending around Sheena's house. Several went ahead of the others and began positioning themselves around the mini-golf course. Michael loved the windmill, so he stood upon the top of the little building.

He could see the entire course here, and direct the other angels as needed from this vantage point. He could also see that Pegasus had called upon his legions as well. Pegasus was not taking any chances this time. The demons had begun to arrive also, far more prepared for battle. They surrounded the miniature golf course in anticipation of the fight tonight.

Pegasus and his top five demonic warriors entered Sergio. Sheena was his. He would not give her up easily. His secret weapon would be the love she had for and desired from Sergio. He would seduce her through this young man. He would tempt her with what she desired most.

Pegasus had figured out the greatest weakness of women was the curse pronounced upon them in the garden, "You will desire your husband..." God had said. Pegasus had won many women through that one desire when others had failed. This was a woman's weakest point when she was in love with a man, or even thought she might want to be. She would listen to her man over God any day. She would let her man be her god. After all, the infinitely wise God had given humans free will. Pegasus deviously smiled at the thought of how many women had turned from the one true God to follow their man.

Yet, Pegasus had not earned the leadership of legions without fighting many battles against the Lord's army of angels. He would not foolishly underestimate this battle. He had called four legions out of their other assignments just for tonight.

He would not be taken by surprise tonight.

Sergio sensed he had been strengthened and had feeling of sensual superiority coursing through him. He swaggered up to the door of Sheena's house with a confidence that he would win his woman's heart tonight. As he knocked on the door, Sergio somehow knew Sheena wanted him just as desperately as he wanted her. This understanding cut through the nervousness of seeing her for the first time in months. His own desire to have her by his side was met with an assurance of her desire for him as soon as he saw the look in her eye when she opened the door. She was unabashedly excited to see him. Sergio smiled coolly and calmly. He put his arm around her and pulled her into him. "It is wonderful to see you," he softly spoke into her ear.

She wrapped her arms around him and delightedly declared, "I am glad to finally see you too. It has been so long." He kissed her lightly on the forehead, and turned towards the car. "Let's go have some fun!" he exclaimed. They walked to the Mustang with arms around each other. Sergio opened the car door for her, and she smiled graciously at his gentleman like behavior. Sergio knew Sheena well. He was glad he had been able to keep the Mustang she loved. Getting her to trust him would be easy. Leading her would be a snap. Gently, Pegasus reminded his young man to take his time with the lovely young lady. There was no need in rushing a quarterback here.

As they drove into the parking lot of the miniature golf course, the battle lines in the spiritual realm were drawn. The angels of God had already covered the place, but the legions of demons were growing. Michael counted two legions roughly already there. He could see more in the distance. He dare not send a messenger back to the throne now. The demons were surrounding the legion of angels already. However, Michael knew that they had the one true and living God on their side and nothing could hinder Him. The angels assigned to protect Sheena encircled her closely. They really hoped the others were praying for her tonight.

The couple went into the golf course laughing about the last game they had shared together. Sheena asked Sergio to tell her all about his adventures on the backpacking trips. He had so much to tell her, he told story after story as they made their way through the game. When the game was done, they decided to go to a drive in for a hamburger. They wanted to be alone and not run into the gang, so they couldn't go to their soda shop. As they headed for the car, the angels knew the time was limited. In order to give Sheena the protection they could offer, they would have to fight and distract the demons now.

Michael assigned two more angels to go with the four previously assigned to her. They were fierce warriors and he knew they had the best chance of cloaking her from the demons. He signaled the others to the ready, and then gave the order to charge. The demons, delighted in the distinct advantage of numbers, held back and allowed the angels to come to them. Michael led his legion in a circular direction. He went straight towards the strongest section of demons. His legion of angles burst forward in each direction like fireworks shot into the sky. They expanded the circle of coverage over the parking lot and fought valiantly against the troops before them.

Sergio and Sheena got into the car unnoticed by the legions of demons. The distraction was working. The numbers were now to the six angels favor in the car. Sergio became a little anxious, but he had no idea why. He finally asked Sheena to tell him what she had been doing for the last few months. She smiled sweetly at him, and began to tell him of how she had met the King of Kings of the spiritual realm. He was shaking slightly as they pulled into the drive in. "So you mean to tell me, after everything we have seen and experienced together, that you have switched sides?" Sergio asked with a baffled look of disbelief.

"How could I not follow the one who rules over all? Not only does Jesus rule over all, but He gave his life for us." Sheena stated earnestly.

"You can't be serious!" Sergio responded with dismay. He looked at her and mockingly retorted, "You believe that Jesus died and came back to life?

His fingers began clinching the steering wheel, and his eyes narrowed. "You think He really is more powerful than Pegasus? You have got to be kidding me!" His lips and jaws drew tight.

The tone in Sergio's voice was surprisingly hurtful to Sheena. She had hoped and prayed that he, having known her since kindergarten, would at least be supportive and listen open mindedly. After all, she was not some church girl without a clue about the rest of the spiritual world. She was not mindlessly following her parents.

Seeing the hurt in her eyes pierced Sergio's heart. He softened and said, "I am sorry, but I am shocked that you have turned away from Pegasus after all we have seen."

The car hop came up to the window and asked if they were ready to order. Sergio asked for two burgers, a large fry, and two sodas. The girl smiled as she wrote the order down and then disappeared into the stand. Once the car hop was gone, Sheena said calmly, "You and I both know there are other spirits out there."

"Yes, but Pegasus has guided us for so long," Sergio stated. He reminded her, "He healed Josh." Then his head dropped and with hurt flowing through his voice he said, "We were building something beautiful together. It's almost like you betrayed us."

"Us?" Sheena looked into Sergio's eyes questioningly, "You feel like I have betrayed you?"

"Well.......yes. Yes, I do." Sergio stated gaining confidence again.

"Oh Sergio, You know I love you." Sheena put her hand on Sergio's arm.

"I love you too," Sergio admitted, then sadly added, "But it will not work for us to be divided like this." Then with a real sense of conviction he declared, "We need to be on the same team."

"And we can be!" Sheena replied with hopeful excitement. She continued, "Jesus didn't die just for me. He paid the price for you too."

"You can't expect me to believe that nonsense." Sergio said, frowning and in a low growl that revealed a sense of aggravation.

179

"Seriously, how can you believe he physically rose from the dead?"

Sheena could understand his cynicism about this part. She had struggled with the idea as well. She gently answered, "The proof is in the changed lives and the eyewitness accounts."

"There is nothing historical to prove that book." He scoffed.

"There are still millions being changed all over the world," She said softly, "I am one of them."

"Believe what you like." He stated sarcastically.

Sheena knew this was the end of the conversation for now. She looked down at her hands trying to think of something..... anything else she could talk about. Sergio turned and looked at the stand. The car hop came out just as he was about ready to push the call button. She smiled as she put the tray on the driver's side window and took the money from Sergio. His cross expression puzzled the girl, but she simply said, "Enjoy your meal," with a smile and walked back to the stand. Sheena was relieved, "Oh good," she said, "I was really getting hungry." She smiled reassuringly at Sergio, but he returned an irritated glare.

Now Sheena was a little nervous. This was not the Sergio she knew and loved. He had never really been angry with her before. She thought about how angry he was that night Tenicia shared her story. What would he be like now? Had she just lost her best friend? She ate in silence as she thought about what could happen next. Sergio was almost pouting as he ate the burger and fries. They finished the food and drove back to Sheena's house without a word spoken between them. They had often been together without talking, but not with such heaviness between them. All Sheena could do was pray. So she did.

When they pulled up in front of her house, she sweetly said, "I really enjoyed the game and the food. I am so glad we were able to catch up."

Sergio gave a halfhearted smile and said, "I have missed you the last few months. It was good to see you too." He got out, went around the front of the car, and opened the door once more. As Sheena stood up, he smiled a little bigger and said, "You know I love you."

When she smiled he caressed her face. Seeing the enjoyment of his touch in her eyes encouraged him. "Shall we go in the shop?" he asked.

"Not tonight." Sheena said a little sadly. He nodded, closed the car door, and returned to the driver's seat. Sheena followed him around the car. She stood at the car door, leaned over and kissed him on the cheek.

He said, "I'll call you." She nodded, turned and walked up to the door as Sergio drove away.

Sheena could feel the tears welling up in her eyes. She went in the house and straight to her room. She wept hard, grieving the loss of her best friend and lover. She knew things would never be the same.

Sergio kept driving. He wasn't even thinking about where he was going, he was just not going home. The thoughts were so jumbled in his mind. He had to clear his head. Just drive. He was angry, sad, hurt, confused, and even scared. Sheena had rejected Pegasus and chosen to follow this………. Jesus. She had not been as easy to lead back as he had expected. She was really different. How was this possible? She had experienced firsthand the power of Pegasus. He had to figure out how to talk some sense back into her. He had to show her who was more powerful. He had to defeat this…….. lie………….that's what Lisa had called it………….lie………….Christianity was a huge deception for generations to keep them under control……………a lie! He would prove it! But how?

Before he realized it, he was at the base of Rebel Hill. He was at their special place. Perfect! He really needed Pegasus to help him sort this out. This was going to be much more difficult than he had imagined. He turned the car up the dirt road and really smiled for the first time since Sheena had told him about Jesus. He knew Pegasus was guiding him even now. He raced up the hill as fast as the car could handle the rough road. He could hardly wait to get into the full presence of Pegasus.

Sheena finally cried out all the tears she had in her and went to wash up. She could not really understand how the heartache had been replaced with a deep sense of peace.

She just knew it was Jesus.

She did not know what to expect or do next. She decided to call Tenicia. She asked Tenicia to have her mom pick up the other phone, so all three of them could talk. Once both of them were on the line, Sheena told them everything that happened.

Both ladies were sorry to hear it, but they told Sheena how proud they were of her for not giving in to the pressure. They prayed with her about what to do next and that the Lord would somehow reach Sergio.

They prayed for the others from the circle as well. They prayed together on the phone for about an hour. Surprised by her own sudden understanding of how serious the situation really was, Tenicia gasped. Then Tenicia said, "You better call David. We're going to need him in on this. So many souls are at stake." Sheena agreed thinking back to the last encounter she'd had with Pegasus and Sergio's murderous tone when Tenicia had boldly witnessed to the whole circle. The ladies said good night, and Sheena immediately called David.

"Hello," answered the voice of the older woman again. It must be his mom, Sheena thought. "Hello, may I speak with David please?" she asked. "Sure honey, hold on," Nancy shook her head as she went to tell her son. She could not believe the boldness of young women today. When she was young, a proper young lady always waited for the gentleman to call. She announced the call to her son and went back to the kitchen to finish cutting the vegetables for tomorrow's stew. She loved the colder weather. "Hello," David finally answered. "Hi David; it's Sheena," Sheena said relieved he'd finally picked up the phone. Then she told him everything. They prayed. David had a deep sense of danger disturbing him.

"You know, I think we need the elders of my church in on this," David said.

"I don't know. They will think we're crazy," Sheena responded with heaviness.

David could understand Sheena's reluctance after all she'd been through with the other church. He encouragingly said, "These guys know what happened with me. They saw Lisa losing her mind that night. They know. They are trustworthy."

"David, the church I was going to couldn't handle it," the pain of the rejection brought a lump to Sheena's throat even as she said it.

"I know," replied David compassionately, "but these men are different."

He became more serious and stated, "The Holy Spirit is telling me this is far more dangerous than we realize. We can't take on the rest of the group ourselves. We need their covering prayers and wisdom."

"Do you have to tell them who we are?" Fear began to take hold of Sheena's heart like a vice grip.

David paused for a moment to seriously consider if it were necessary to tell them who was involved. "No, I don't think so," he said confidently.

Sheena breathed a sigh of relief and said, "Okay."

CHAPTER 12

Even as the young people were praying, the spiritual battle was raging over their small city. The warriors of God which had begun this battle grew in power and strength with each prayer. Yet, they still were outnumbered and fighting two to one. Though immortal, the angels and demons still felt the blows, the pain, and the fatigue. The wounded demons could fall back and let others take their place while they recovered. However being outnumbered, the angels had to keep fighting without rest through the entire night. Each time the believers prayed, more angels arrived to help battle the four legions Pegasus had called. Yet, there were still far more demons than angels, and they were ferocious warriors.

Pegasus sent the four other demons to the raging battle once he had Sergio alone on Rebel Hill. He had to drive the stakes of this game higher for the players. He had to show them what happened to his enemies. Pegasus spoke words of embitterment to Sergio, and his heart was filling with rage at the thought of losing Sheena.

He would take out the deceivers who had lured her away. He began to see how pleased Pegasus would be, how empowered he himself would become if he brought the virgin up here and sacrificed her. Pegasus began showing Sergio images of the powers he would be granted, powers far greater that Sheena had. Sergio could see himself moving objects with just a thought any time he wanted to, having women swooning over him, being able to plant thoughts in people's minds, and the power to hurt his enemies deeply with just a touch. As the visions of his own power growing flooded his mind, he smiled and then laughed with wicked delight.

He stayed in the trance for the majority of the night as Pegasus showed him the plan for luring Tenicia away from everyone else. He would deal with David once he had been empowered. David would be very sorry for turning against him, and turning Sheena away from him. Once she understood who really had the power, she would be begging to come back, he thought.

The following morning he began preparing the place for the ultimate sacrifice. The simple log alter was still intact from the last time they had come to sacrifice. He looked it over and realized he needed a flatter surface and a way to tie her down. He wanted her to know what she was dying for, so she would have to be conscious. It would be cruel to let her die a virgin, he thought, and began considering what he might do. "No," Pegasus declared firmly, "the blood sacrifice is far more powerful when pure. You will be able to have plenty of other pure girls for that kind of offering." He reached into his car to get the pad and pen from the glove box. He began writing notes on the tools he would need to bring up to the hilltop. There was a growing eagerness within him..........a primal urge.........a hunger to hunt and kill his prey.

While Sergio had been planning his sacrifice, David talked with his dad and they prayed together. This morning, they were going to see the pastor at his home together. They made the appointment without giving Pastor Dale much detail the night before. They had asked if he could call the elders too. Yet, they didn't know how many would be able to make it on such short notice. They needed to get together and pray with whoever could be there.

Samuel reminded him that Jesus said, "Whenever there are two or three gathered in my name, I am there in the midst of them."

This was a great encouragement to David. He did not understand the incredible sense of dread he felt. He had no idea how bad this could be, but he knew he had an overwhelming fear of the dangerous situation. He couldn't picture the horrendous thoughts Sergio was entertaining. David had no idea of Sergio's plan or love of power.

David understood that Sergio was highly competitive, but thought that Sergio had always been a good sport. He thought about how Sheena told him about the prayers against him. Maybe that was it, he thought, maybe Sergio doesn't realize what he is about to release. David was anxious to get to the pastor's home and begin praying.

When they turned the corner onto the pastor's street, David and Samuel were overjoyed at the sight of so many cars already there. "There's Roger's Charger," Sam said, "and Nick's van." He began calling out the names of the owners of several of the cars as he looked for a place to park his own. The excitement in his voice grew with each time he recognized another car. "Thank you Lord! They took it seriously, and *You* made the way for them to be here." Finally, they parked their own car and walked quickly up to the pastor's home. They greeted everyone as they walked in and asked them all to sit down. Samuel introduced his son and let David have the floor.

David began with a little trembling in his voice, "As many of you may remember from last year, there are several young people in town who have been involved in the occult. I praise God today that two of them have accepted Christ and repented from their involvement in witchcraft.

However, one of the young men, one of the leaders of this group, has basically threatened to murder one of the others. He is very angry, and we don't know how far he'll go. I can tell you I found out that they had prayed against me. When they did, I experienced all kinds of problems including breaking my ankle.

This was just after I shared Christ with the group. Now two of their members have come out of the coven, so I am sure they will pray twice as hard if not react physically. I can also tell you that I have a deep dreadful feeling." He paused and took a deep breath.

"I have never felt anything so fearsome in my life. This is why we are calling you together for prayer. I know we cannot win this battle alone, and there is so much at stake here."

Pastor Dale called David and Samuel to the center of the room. The elders and men of the church gathered around them. The closest men put their hands on David; the others put a hand on the shoulder of the man in front of them. They closed their eyes to focus and bowed their heads. David fell to his knees and the others followed. Samuel could feel an incredible rush within him, so he put both hands on the top of his son's head. David felt magnificent warmth flowing through him. The fear was being replaced with peace and joy. He sat back and began to just soak in the strength of the prayers. The men of God prayed for about two hours together.

As they prayed, some unseen barrier was broken in the heavens. Suddenly Pegasus' legions were completely surrounded by a tremendous number of God's army. A victorious shout went up from the center of the battle. The demons turned to defend themselves. The center legion of angels had been relieved just in time. The battle was quickly turned and the enemy was defeated once again. The Lord responded to the prayers of his people. Demons began fleeing from the fight.

On the other side of town, Sheena had gone out for a cup of coffee and change of scenery. She could feel something was stirring. Although she hadn't been at the coffee shop long, she could hardly wait to get home and be alone in the presence of the Lord. Something just wasn't right, so she got up to leave. She could feel a stare drilling through her as went to the counter and paid the check. She looked over her shoulder to see Lisa sitting with her mom. She smiled and said "Hi" politely. Lisa's mom asked, "Is that a friend of yours from school?" Lisa shrugged and replied coolly, "She used to be." Sheena could feel the disgust emanating from Lisa. She turned and walked out of the coffee shop towards her house. As she walked home, she could hear shrieks of torment and rage as demons flew past her. She shivered at the accusations and horrifying shrieks.

She began reciting the 23 Psalm as she kept walking. "The Lord is my shepherd, I lack nothing. He makes me to lie down in green pastures; he leads me beside quiet waters. He refreshes my soul. He guides me along the right paths for his name's sake. Even though I walk through the darkest valley of the shadow of death, I will fear no evil, for you are with me; your shepherd's rod and staff comfort me...."

As she continued reciting the psalm, she could feel the peace deep in her soul that she had come to believe was the peace that Jesus promised his followers just before he returned to heaven. She smiled with the assurance that He was with her. He heard her prayers; He really was living within her. The thought entered her mind to turn left rather than go straight at the next street. She asked, "Is this you, Lord?" She did not want to be deceived again. She had already given the enemy far too much of her life. She wanted to be sure this was the Holy Spirit, but she was not sure. She still had a full sense of peace, so she went ahead and turned left thinking, what do I have to lose? She asked, "Where are we going?" but heard nothing. She continued walking and praying that the Lord would show her what He wanted her to see....lead her in the right path like the psalm said.

She took a couple of more turns and walked for about 30 minutes. On the last turn she saw a street full of cars. She was puzzled. This was not a street near the mall or a school. What would be happening in the middle of the day in this kind of neighborhood? It wasn't the weekend. How did all of these people get off work? Suddenly, several men started coming out of the house. That is odd, she thought. Then, she saw David. She became nervous and didn't know which way to go. Would it be obvious if she turned around and began walking away? David noticed her and smiled. He quietly asked the men to stay for a little longer, and walked over to her. Sheena had frozen in her tracks.

The men talked quietly about everyday business looking as nonchalant as possible, glancing but not staring, smiles crossing their faces as they could see how fearful the beautiful young lady was.

One of the men walked back inside the house and called for Martha. When she appeared on the porch, Sheena felt a little more at ease; but she still was not comfortable.

"Hi Sheena, How's it going?" David asked with a friendly and inviting tone.

"Okay. How about you?" Sheena said with a nervous glance and a look of mistrust.

"I am great now! We just finished praying. It was amazing." David's whole face lit up with joy.

"That is what everyone is here for?" Sheena asked with a hint of suspicion.

"Sure, what did you think it was?"

"I didn't know, but I was wondering why so many people were here." Sheena's tone became pressing and serious, "David, something big is happening." Then with a touch of gratitude she said, "I am glad you guys were praying."

"I don't think it's an accident you are here right now." David's smile broadened as he asked, "Why don't you come in and let us pray for you?"

"David, I don't want them to know." Sheena said with hurt in her eyes.

Compassion filled David's heart, and he reached for her hand. He gently leaned in close and whispered, "Sheena, they will accept you. They all have a past too.....and they know it is only by the grace of God that they are saved."

Sheena pulled back and turned her head so David nor the others could see a few tears escaping. Unable to hide the grief in her heart, she sadly replied, "That is what the other church said, David, but when it came down to it; my sin was somehow worse than theirs." More tears welled up in Sheena's eyes as she thought of the way the people of the church had treated them.

The grief turning to a righteous anger she clenched her jaw. She turned back to him, looking him boldly in the eyes, and sternly argued, "Not only did they reject me, they rejected Tenicia and her mom as well for being friends with me." Then she sincerely warned, "These men will reject you if they know who I am, and you continue to be my friend."

"Some of them may," David admitted with his head dropped in embarrassment, "We cannot control that." He hated how they had acted, and knew full well there could be some people like that within his own church. He continued with re-assurance, "However, I know my dad won't. I know that Pastor Dale won't reject either us or them. Several of these men were with me the night we prayed at Lisa's. They understand. The timing of you being here is not an accident," David's face grew more serious and he earnestly said, "There is a huge battle happening right now, and you are in danger. You need the spiritual covering of their prayers."

Sheena searched his eyes for a moment before responding. She knew the battle was huge; she remembered the terrible screams of the tormented and enraged spirits as they flew past her just an hour ago. She didn't want to tell anyone of these people what she had just heard. They would all think she was crazy. Yet, she knew David was right. She needed their prayers. Maybe it was the Holy Spirit who had led her here after all.

"Okay," She forced out of her constricted throat. It was everything she could do to hold back the tears and fears, let alone speak. David smiled with a look of gratitude mixed with compassion and relief. He led her by the hand to the group waiting on the porch.

"This is my good friend, Sheena," he announced proudly, "She could really use some prayer. So if anyone can stay a little longer and pray some more, it would be greatly appreciated."

They each greeted her and introduced themselves. Several of them excused themselves to go back to work, but promised they would pray for her on their way. The much smaller group made small talk as they made their way back into the living room. Once they were settled, they asked Sheena to tell them her situation. As if a dam had broken, she poured out her life of the past few months including the details of the date with Sergio just a couple of nights ago. Had they not already heard of the unfolding events from David, and seen what had happened with Lisa; they would have been absolutely astounded! They would not have believed her.

However, having been in prayer over these things; they were mentally and spiritually prepared to be able to support Sheena with true grace and acceptance. She was so relieved.

Martha, the pastor's wife, suggested Sheena sit in the middle of the room so they could gather around her and pray. Sheena accepted and sat on the floor. Martha, David, Samuel, and Dale sat closest to her, putting a hand on her shoulder or taking her hand. The others sat behind them or on the couches and extended their hands also. They began praying first by giving thanks and praise to the Lord for all that He had done in her life. Sheena could feel the joy bubbling up in her heart as they praised the Lord.

A few minutes later, the prayer began to turn into a plain pleading tone. Pastor Dale led out with a heartfelt cry for the Holy Spirit to lead them and pray through them. Sheena found herself incredibly sleepy. She leaned back and they gently let her lay down on the floor. They continued to pray, though she had seemingly fallen into a deep sleep. Suddenly, David felt led to ask her, "Who is he?" Although she was certainly asleep, it was obvious she had heard the question by the puzzled expression on her face. Everyone grew very quiet as David asked again, "Who is he?" Sheena responded, "Pegasus." The group fell completely silent, but fervently prayed for her deliverance from the spirit. David asked again, "Who is he?" and again Sheena responded the same.

David repeated the question five more times. Finally, on the seventh time he repeated question, Sheena responded with a huge smile, and declared "Jesus!" The entire group breathed a collective sigh of relief.

Though they did not understand all that had just happened, they knew Sheena had somehow just been set free. None of them had known that deep down, she was afraid Jesus had rejected her. She was afraid that she still belonged to Pegasus. The accusation of betrayal from Sergio, the rejection from the church, the scriptures saying that witches were condemned, and the awful things the spirits were screaming at her had made her think that somehow it was really too late for her. Now deep within her soul, she had assurance she belonged to Jesus. She knew she was his!

Once the group of believers heard her sure acknowledgement of Jesus and saw the smile on her face, they knew she would be okay spiritually. They began to pray for her physical safety next. Prayers for Tenicia followed, and the fervency grew as the Holy Spirit revealed the danger she was in.

Tenicia was clueless about the prayers for her or the group which had gathered. She had no idea that the Spirit of the Living God had gathered the group of believers together, or that Sergio was planning to kidnap and sacrifice her. The image of a huge spiritual battle happening in the atmosphere above her city never crossed her mind that morning.

She had gone before the Lord simply to enjoy His presence as she often did now. She was filled with an incredible joy. It was only when she spent time in His Word, and in thanksgiving and praise, that she felt so alive. This feeling was better than anything the world had offered her. It was so much better than even the spiritual high she felt with Pegasus although it was incredibly different. She kept an ongoing conversation happening with the Lord as she went about getting ready to go to work. She put the finishing touches on her hair and face just before she walked out the door.

By the time Tenicia had arrived at work, Sergio had made it back to his house. He made sure everything he needed was in the car before he went to the store where Tenicia was working. He took a shower and dressed nicely. When he arrived at the store, he looked at the women's sweaters, then at the jewelry, then back to the sweaters. He meandered through the clothing slowly, pulling a sweater off the rack, pretending he was considering it, putting it back, and then moving to the next piece. The expression on his face was that of a man unsure of himself, lost, hopelessly trying to find the right gift.

Tenicia eyed him cautiously for a while, but couldn't resist the lost puppy look. She went up to him and asked him if he needed help. He smiled and feigned relief. He poured out his "dilemma" of not knowing what to buy Sheena for the holidays. Tenicia's understanding tone of voice delighted Sergio. Her sudden willingness to be helpful elated him. The trap was set. He had her in the target zone! During their conversation, he asked her nonchalantly when she got off work. Not knowing there was more to the question, she told him she was scheduled until 7 p.m. They continued discussing the perfect Christmas present, and then Sergio purchased two of the items she suggested. He looked over his shoulder and smiled his friendliest smile as he crossed through the storefront into the rest of the mall, completely disarming her.

Tenicia smiled and went back to work, praising God for softening Sergio's heart. She did not see any trace of the anger that Sheena had described, for which she was very thankful. Maybe he had really thought about what they had told him. Maybe he had decided they were right or at least that they could still be friends.

She returned a few items from the dressing room, picked up a few blouses that had fallen to the floor, and made sure the items were in the right display. She returned to the register to make sure the area was cleaned up there. A few more customers came in and she joyful helped each of them. Before she knew it, Sergio was back in the store. It was just a few minutes before her shift ended.

She looked at him curiously and asked, "Is everything okay with the sweater and bracelet you purchased?" He smiled and said, "Oh yes, everything is fine. I just saw this great necklace and earring set at another store that I want to get your opinion on. Would you take a few minutes after your shift to tell me what you think?" Tenicia smiled and said, "Sure, I'll be done in a few minutes. You can wait on the bench over there." She pointed through the same door he'd left by earlier. She thought, Wow! He must really like her, then reasoned, Well, they have been friends since kindergarten.

The supervisor came up and asked if she was ready to close out her register. They went through the process quickly; Tenicia's drawer was always right. She was very careful. Then she walked to the break room, clocked out, grabbed her purse and sweater, and headed out to meet Sergio.

They smiled at one another again, and Sergio took her over to an expensive jewelry shop in the mall. He showed her the set he was thinking about and asked, "Do you think she'll like it?"

"Oh, it's beautiful! She will love it," Tenicia replied admiringly, "but it's really expensive."

Sergio smiled big and confidently declared, "I have more than enough." Tenicia looked questioningly and he assured her as he said, "Those camping trips paid very well, and she is worth it."

"Then yes, it is perfect." Tenicia answered. She added with sincerity, "It will really show her how you feel."

"Thank you!" Sergio said in his most grateful voice, and then he exclaimed, "Hey, let me buy you dinner for the help."

"That's okay; it was my pleasure," replied Tenicia politely.

Sergio insisted, "No really, let me buy you dinner. I know a great little place not far from here."

"My mom is expecting me," Tenicia answered.

"Okay," Sergio said sounding somewhat disappointed. He hid how truly disappointed he was. He had to think quickly. He couldn't force her to go with him in public. Then an alternative idea hit him. He smiled and cheerfully said, "I know! We'll get a dinner to go from the food court here, and I will give you a ride home. Then you will still be on time."

Tenicia could not argue with that plan; she was pretty hungry. Besides, what could it hurt? Sergio obviously wasn't angry anymore. So she grinned and said sure. They headed over to the little pizza place, bought a small pepperoni pizza, and headed for his car. Sergio kept the conversation light. He told her about his wilderness adventures with the stars and how exciting it had been to meet each of them. He began to tell one of the better stories as they got into the car and buckled up. Just after starting the car he pushed the door lock button. Though she didn't know it, Tenicia would not be able to open the door. He smiled ruthlessly, and continued telling the story.

About the time Tenicia was helping Sergio pick out the

sweater, the believers finished praying. David offered to walk Sheena home after the prayer meeting.

They stopped by the soda shop, ordered a couple of burgers, and just hung out for a while, talking about everything. As they were turning onto her street, she felt a tinge of fear. Sheena prayed silently the one word prayer, "Help," and the Lord gave her more understanding. Tenicia is in trouble, the thought struck her mind as clearly as if someone had said it out loud. She looked at David, "Did you hear that?" she asked. "What?" he asked. "Tenicia is in trouble," she said, her heart racing a little faster. She had experienced things like this before and they always came true. "Let's call her when we get to your house," David offered, "then we will know if it is the Lord or not." They walked as fast as they could the rest of the way down the street. Sheena unlocked the door as quickly as she could and was almost surprised to see her parents sitting in the living room, watching TV together. She greeted them, introduced David, and said, "I'll be right back." She went into the kitchen to call Tenicia. Tenicia's mom answered the phone, and told her that Tenicia should be home from work any minute. The knot in her stomach grew tighter. She thanked Marcella, hung up, and immediately called the store to see if Tenicia had left. One of the other cashiers, a girl they knew from school, voluntarily told Sheena that Tenicia had left about fifteen minutes ago with Sergio. "Thanks," Sheena responded as the knot grew to epic proportions within her.

She walked back into the living room and said, "We're going to the mall for a little while." Her parents looked up, smiled, and said, "Have a good time sweetheart. It was nice to meet you, David." David returned the polite reply, got up, and opened the door for Sheena. She smiled, but he could see the concern in her eyes. He waited until they were halfway down the street to ask, "What is going on?"

"Tenicia left the store with Sergio, and they went into the mall together." Her voice was trembling.

"How long ago?"

"About 15 minutes ago. We have to hurry."

"Let's pick up my car. I only live a couple of blocks over."

They walked as quickly as they could another few houses and then David said, "Let's run." Sheena nodded and began running as fast as she could. David was far faster, but he made sure not to get too far ahead of her. He stopped in front of his house to make sure she was still in sight, then dashed up the sidewalk, rushed through the door to his room, grabbed his keys and wallet, rushing back out without a word to his parents. He unlocked the car and said, "Jump in!" as she was just coming up the driveway. Sheena did and they took off. Samuel saw their fear, turned to Nancy, and said, "Let's pray."

They drove to the side of the mall closest to the shop Tenicia worked in. They cruised through the parking lot looking for Sergio's car. They drove slowly through that section and went into the next. Across the parking lot, over by the food court, Sergio started backing out. Sheena spotted his car and screamed, "There they are!" David drove as quickly as he could through the lot to get close to Sergio.

As the two cars pulled into the exit lane, David and Sheena could see Tenicia was definitely in the car. Sergio turned onto the street and kept talking. David turned right behind him hardly stopping to look for oncoming traffic. He began honking the horn repetitively to get their attention. Sergio and Tenicia both looked behind them to see that it was David and Sheena causing the commotion. Sergio grew angry and silent. Tenicia became afraid.

They came to a stop sign, and Tenicia tried opening the door to jump out. Sergio's evil grin confirmed that she was locked in on purpose. She didn't bother to ask. Once they were away from the busier streets, Sergio started driving faster and faster, attempting to lose David. David's car was not as agile as Sergio's and he could not corner as quickly.

Sergio could see David dropping further behind on turns so he started making more and more turns until the other couple was no longer in sight. He made a few more turns to get out of the neighborhoods and onto a back road. He felt emboldened by the win, yet he knew his time was limited. With Sheena on their side, they would probably figure it out. There was no time to waste.

As soon as David knew he had lost Sergio, he drove straight to the police station. The officer at the front desk looked at the two young adults as if they were crazy as they reported the abduction in progress. He directed them to sit down while he called a detective. Neither of them could sit down and wait. They paced in the lobby looking for the detective every time someone on the other side of the counter moved.

Fifteen minutes later, David went back up to the front desk and asked the officer if he wanted to prevent a murder. The officer rolled his eyes, and redirected David to have a seat. David asked, "May I use your phone?" The policeman looked at David with a slight bit of annoyance, and then put the phone on the counter. David dialed his home. He told his dad where they were and what they had seen. The cop looked a little more interested as the young man earnestly explained to his father the evening's events. Samuel assured his son they would be right there.

Samuel called Pastor Dale before leaving the house to ask for more prayer, but he kept the conversation very short. Samuel told Nancy everything as they drove to the police station. Just before getting out of the car, they prayed together for the young girl. When they entered the police station, David hugged them with relief. Sheena dropped back from the scene, went to the farthest chairs, and sat down. David told his parents they were still waiting for a detective. Samuel looked over at the desk officer, who sheepishly looked down and said, "I'll try a different detective."

Sergio had gone the opposite direction while trying to lose them, so now he had to back track across the county on country roads. He looked at Tenicia and told her casually, "You know you have to die tonight, but do you know why?" He would not have enough time once they reached the top of the hill to tell her all he wanted to say. Tenicia had been praying silently since she understood the situation. Just as He promised in His Word, the Lord gave Tenicia the words to speak with power and boldness. "If I die tonight, it is for my gain. You want to kill me because I am a follower of the living Christ. Yet even if I die, I will surely live. For the Lord Jesus was crucified for our transgressions, buried in a tomb, and rose from the dead on the third day. Because he has conquered death, I now have an assurance of eternal life in Christ."

"Shut up! Just shut up!" Sergio began angrily shouting. Tenicia could not stop talking about Christ now. The words felt like stabbing swords to Sergio. He kept yelling at her and finally could stand it no more. He backhanded her across the mouth. The sting of the slap shocked Tenicia into a momentary silence. Sergio glared at her, and then looked back to the road.

Through a clenched jaw Sergio declared, "You will die tonight for betraying our circle and telling Sheena these ridiculous lies. Your blood will be her sacrifice. You will be my offering to Pegasus for Sheena, and for my own power. Once she sees how powerless your Jesus is to save you, she will come back to me….and Pegasus. That is why you will die."

Tenicia began praying silently again begging the Lord to help her. The two drove for the next ten miles in silence. As they began to wind their way up the mountainous roads, the thought occurred to Tenicia that if she had to die, she could take Sergio with her. She could at least spoil his plans to make her a sacrifice to the demons. She looked at Sergio and could see he was fully focused on the road.

She began watching the road and praying that the Lord would show her mercy if it was wrong. She simply could not just sit back and let him do this. They began a decent down one ridge and the speed pick up a little. When she saw the shoulder on her side was but a sliver of grass before the steep drop, she reached over and yanked the steering wheel hard.

The sudden turn took Sergio by surprise, and he could not keep the car from plunging off the road. He couldn't do anything but shut the engine off and hold on. The car flew out about 100 yards before it started dropping. They dropped for a good twenty feet before crashing into tree tops. The trees slowed the car, but not much. Unable to stop it, an angel flipped the little Mustang as it ripped off branches and leaves, and then smashed into the trunk of a Giant Sequoia on Sergio's side. The car slid down the tree stripping it of branches all the way to the ground, landing upside down on the roof. As the dust settled, the night grew darker, and forest grew silent around them. Tenicia groaned and looked over. Sergio was unconscious, possibly dead. She felt a sharp pain shoot up from her diaphragm, gasped and passed out.

At the station, the detectives were astounded at what they were hearing. The city's hero kidnapping a young woman to kill her in some kind of twisted revenge occult sacrifice seemed insane. Yet, they knew this family would not be just making this up. They began questioning Sheena more as she had been more involved.

One of the officers finally asked, "Where would he take her to do this?" Sheena thought for a moment before shouting, "Rebel Hill….He's taking her to Rebel Hill! It's our…" shame overcame her and her voice dropped to almost a whisper, "It was our sacred place." The detectives sent out the All-Points Bulletin to alert the city police in case they spotted the car. Then they called the Sheriff with the strange story requesting them to search the hill.

Knowing there was possibly going to be a murder, and not knowing how armed the young man was; the Sheriff's deputies prepared for the worst. They located the hill on the county map. Then they devised the plan to capture the guy and hopefully rescue the girl.

As they drove up into the mountains and deeper into the forest, they could see the tops of a few trees broken and burning. They radioed in to the dispatch requesting firefighters. As they came to the spot where Tenicia had grabbed the wheel, they could see brief skid marks. They parked and turned on the search lights. Not sure what to expect, they cautiously looked down the ridge. Because the flames on the tops of the trees provided extra light, they could see the wrecked car at the base of the Giant Sequoia. They radioed in for paramedics, before grabbing what gear they had. The deputies had rope in the trunk all the time.

They tied the rope to the steel bars attached to the front of their car, and began making their way down the side of the mountain, hoping they could get the young people out before the fire spread. As they reached the car, they looked up and were gratefully astonished that the fire was not spreading. The deputies were doubly amazed when they found the pair unconscious, but alive.

The following day Tenicia regained consciousness to see her mom sitting beside her. She realized she was in the hospital, and remembered what had happened. She smiled weakly at her mom whose head was bowed in prayer. Tenicia reached over, put her hand on top of her mom's folded hands and squeezed. Though the touch was light, Marcella's head shot up as if a bolt of lightning had struck her. "Thank you Jesus!" she exclaimed and called for the nurse. The assigned nurse came in and gasped in shock as she saw Tenicia's smile. She had not expected the girl to come out of the comma, certainly not this quickly. The nurse turned and went for the doctor.

As the group of believers in the waiting room noticed the sudden flurry of activity in Tenicia's room, they collectively took a deep breath and waited to hear some news. Had God answered their prayers with a yes, no, or something else? they wondered.

The doctor and nurses asked Marcella to step out for a minute as they examined Tenicia. With tears of relief streaming down her face she went to the waiting group. "She's awake," Marcella said through the tears. The group rejoiced with her, hugging, laughing, crying, and thanking God for His goodness. The group quickly quieted as the doctor came out of the room and approached them. "This is surely a miracle," he stated with an indication of awe in his voice, "She is conscious and appears to be just fine. We want to keep her for a little while to be sure, but...." He was drowned out by the believers' shouts of joy and adoration for their God. He smiled and watched for a moment before continuing. I will always remember this one, he thought.

Sheena broke away from the group and quietly asked, "May I go see her?" The doctor nodded and said, "Just for a few minutes though; she still needs a lot of rest." Sheena assured him she would not stay long, and went into Tenicia's room. Tenicia's eyes lit up with delight when she saw Sheena. Sheena went over to her and gently hugged her.

Sheena then looked her in the eye and said, "You have got to be either the craziest or bravest person I have ever known." Tenicia laughed and groaned at the same time. Sheena said, "I'm sorry," with sympathy. Afraid to even touch Tenicia for fear of causing more pain, she pulled back and sat in the chair by the bed. Then as Tenicia was able to breathe easy again, Sheena said, "I am so glad you're okay. The doctor said you are a miracle!" She placed her hand gently on Tenicia's arm and added, "He has no idea just how much of a miracle you are. I can hardly wait to talk to you about all that happened. For now though, just rest and get better."

Tenicia took Sheena's hand and squeezed it, "Thank you," she said softly. Sheena kept Tenicia's hand in hers and replied, "I am the one who needs to thank you. You introduced me to our King." The girls sat together a few minutes more in a comfortable silence before Marcella came back into her daughter's room. Marcella put one hand on each of the girls' shoulders and said, "When you're feeling better, you have a whole new family to meet. They have been here all night praying for you." Tenicia looked questioningly at Sheena. Sheena nodded, and said with a huge smile consuming her face, "They have been praying for us for quite a while."

Tenicia smiled with a deep satisfaction at the thought that Jesus had been preparing a family for them before they knew of their need for one. She closed her eyes and allowed her head to relax into the pillows underneath her. Sheena asked, "Is there anything I can get you?" with a little concern coming through her voice. Tenicia squeezed her friend's....her sister's hand reassuringly and said softly, "I just need to rest now." Sheena leaned over and gave Tenicia a gentle hug, not wanting to hurt her, and whispered, "Okay friend, rest. I will be back soon. I will not quit praying for your complete healing."

As Sheena stood, Marcella gave her a hug and said, "Thank you. Get some rest yourself." Sheena replied, "Ditto." They smiled at each other, then Sheena turned and left the room.

She walked over to the waiting group and filled them in. They praised God together and prayed one more time before they each headed home. Although they were tired, they were all in awe of their God and the true miracle they had just witnessed.

CHAPTER 13

As Sheena and David started to leave the hospital, she could not help but go to the other section and peek into Sergio's room. David too, was concerned about his friend and teammate, so he went with her. Gilberto and Oriana sat next to him with deep apprehension showing on their faces. Sheena looked at Sergio lying there, his face bruised and swollen with several deep cuts stitched closed. He had hit the door window as the car hit the tree. He looked bad!

Sheena's heart grieved for him and his family. "Lord, have mercy on them. Forgive him," she whispered. David whispered "Amen," then they respectfully and quietly walked away.

David drove Sheena home and told her he would check on her tomorrow. Sheena thanked him and retreated into the house. She was exhausted. She realized she hadn't told her parents anything, but they were both off at work anyway. Good, she thought, I'm so tired. She went to her room and collapsed on the bed.

She would tell them everything.....soon. Her eyes were too heavy to keep open. She could feel the muscles in her body letting go as she took in and let out a deep breath. She quickly fell asleep.

Sheena heard her mom in the house and turned to look at the clock. 6:00 p.m. or a.m.? she wondered. She felt horrible, almost as if she had been in the car herself, her body was sore all over. She got up slowly and thought, I wonder if I can talk to the two of them together, or if it would be better to talk to them separately. Sheena prayed, asking for courage and wisdom.

The smell of roast started drifting in her room. Her stomach rumbled a little. She realized she hadn't eaten since lunch the day before. "Thank you, Lord," she whispered. Her mom had cooked family dinners several more times the past month than she had in couple of years. Maybe talking to them over dinner would be a great way to help ease the shock, she thought. "Do you need any help?" Sheena asked with joy radiating from her face as she entered the kitchen.

"Sure!" replied her mom, pleasantly surprised to see her. "You can set the table."

They made small talk as they finished getting dinner ready. As her dad came in, she went over and gave him a hug. He smiled as he hugged her tightly and said, "I'm so glad it wasn't you in that accident." Sheena smiled as she realized they already knew at least that much. She stepped back and asked, "So what have you heard?"

"Not too much, just what was on the news." Oscar said in a matter-of-fact tone with burrowed eye brows.

"Oh, I just got incredibly nauseous as I saw Sergio's car flipped upside down and smashed into that tree!" exclaimed Eileen.

"I wondered if there were other cars involved," said Oscar, "but they reported there weren't any others."

Tears formed in Eileen's eyes and she softly said, "I was terrified the hospital would be calling us. The longer we waited...." she turned her head as her voice dropped off.

Her dad filled in the silence as he solemnly stated, "They didn't release the name of the girl, but when I called the police..."

"You called the police?!" Sheena interrupted.

"Of course," replied Oscar, "We recognized the car and were very worried about you."

Sheena suddenly understood her mother's tears and feeling sick had been because she thought it might be her in the car. She realized that though they hadn't said so in such a long time, her parents really loved her. She went over to her mom and hugged her. "I'm sorry. I should have called you and told you that I was okay. I love you,"

"We love you too" Eileen responded and held her close for a moment.

Sheena stepped back, looked into her mom's eyes, and said, "I have a whole lot I need to tell you guys. I am glad we're having dinner together."

Eileen and Oscar glanced at each other looking to see if the other parent had a clue. "Well, perfect timing! Eileen cheerfully chimed. She checked the roast and stated, "Dinner's ready. Let's have a seat, and you can tell us everything."

"We're all ears," added Oscar with a large grin as he walked up to her chair and pulled it out for her. Sheena sat down, looked over her shoulder, smiled affectionately, and said "Thank you," as her dad slid the chair in. She loved being treated like a lady. Oscar did the same for Eileen before sliding into his own seat at the head of the table.

Sheena talked to her parents more than she had since she was about ten years old. She told them everything she had experienced with the spirits, and how she'd just recently come to know Jesus. Her parents said very little, occasionally asking a question as they marveled at what their daughter was telling them.

For the first time in a very long while, Sheena felt as if the house she lived in was truly home. She felt free and secure. She was so grateful for her mom and dad and the time they had together that night. She didn't know what they would do or how they would respond, but they seemed to take it all in calmly. They both expressed again that they loved her, and how glad they were that she and her friend were okay. They even agreed to go to church with her the following Sunday.

When she had finished, Oscar simply said, "Don't worry about the kitchen ladies. I've got it under control." Mother and daughter gladly left the mess to him, and they headed towards their rooms for the night. Sheena's mother hugged her tightly one more time and kissed her forehead gently. Sheena smiled and said, "Good night Mom," as she turned to her bedroom door. Sheena had a deep assurance everything would be okay, and easily fell back to sleep.

The following day Sheena went to visit Tenicia in the hospital. Tenicia was sitting propped up by the inclined bed and pillows. She was looking stronger. The girls smiled at each other as their eyes met. Tenicia happily reported that she was in pretty good shape. There were no broken bones, and no internal bleeding.

She had some deep bruising and a severe concussion, but she would be going home in a little while. Sheena told Tenicia a little more about the group praying for her, and how good they were to come to the hospital right away. Tenicia was grateful and looked forward to meeting them. Tenicia closed her eyes, but assured Sheena she wasn't asleep. Just as Sheena was telling Tenicia about the dinner with her parents, a nurse walked in.

"Hello ladies," the nurse said cheerfully, "before we can release you, the police would like to talk with you. Are you up to it?" Then she moved closer and with a proud protectiveness she said, "I can make them go away. Just say the word."

Tenicia smiled and replied, "It's okay. I want to tell them everything."

"Alright then." The nurse replied with a bit of a smirk. She saluted Tenicia and left the room with an exaggerated march, making the girls giggle.

Within a few minutes, two detectives entered the room. They asked Tenicia to tell them everything she could remember. They scribbled notes as quick as they could only raising an eyebrow every now and then as Tenicia told the story. Although it was clear Tenicia was getting tired, they asked a few questions before leaving to file the report. Then they stated that with Sergio still unconscious, there wasn't much else they could do. Although Tenicia told the police what had happened, the news reporters only knew that Sergio had lost control of the car, and it was a miracle the two young people were alive. Everyone agreed it was best to keep it that way.

Marcella arrived just a few minutes later. She was happy about taking Tenicia home, but had a lot of questions for the doctor. She wanted to make sure she did everything right so Tenicia would completely heal. She also wanted to know what to do if something didn't seem right during the next few days.

Sheena gave her friends both another hug before leaving. Once again she walked to the other section where Sergio's room was. She peeked in to see if anyone was there. Sergio's mom looked up at just the right moment, and their eyes met. The heartache for Sergio was shared between them without a word. Sheena gave a slight, respectful nod, and Oriana motioned for Sheena to come in as she softly said, "Come sit with me." Sheena didn't like what Sergio had done, but she loved him. She also had a great compassion for his mom.

She went in and gave Oriana a hug then sat beside her. She understood he was not acting completely on his own. She silently prayed again, "Lord, please have mercy on him and his mother and father. Heal him and give him another chance. Please don't let him die without another chance to know you. Please give his whole family understanding of who you are. Thank you, Jesus."

On the way back to her house, she stopped to see if David was home. She was able to tell him Tenicia was going home and update him on Sergio. They agreed to ask everyone to pray for Sergio. They hoped that the other believers would share their heart for him and his family. Several of the others agreed to pray for him, but not all of them could forgive him so easily.

Sheena kept going to the hospital every day for the next week. She went up to Sergio's room and gave Oriana and Gilberto a break. She would sit with him and pray for him, while they went home for a shower and a meal. His mom had such a hard time not being there every minute of the day. However, having Sheena there with him, gave her enough comfort to leave for a couple of hours. One afternoon, Aaron and Josh walked in as Sheena was praying for him. They waited quietly until Sheena stopped.

"Why can't you heal him....like you did me?" Josh asked curiously.

"I don't follow Pegasus anymore, and even if I did; I don't know if I could heal this?" Sheena responded sadly. It was painful for her not to try to use the power she once knew to heal him.

"Well, didn't Jesus tell his disciples they would do what he had done and even greater things?" Aaron asked with an undeniable sarcasm.

Then he put his hand on his hip, looked at Sheena with an "I dare you" kind of look as he said, "Why don't you heal him like Jesus healed others, if your Jesus is so much more powerful than Pegasus?"

Despite the sarcasm and challenge, Sheena thought, maybe Aaron is right. Maybe I can still heal through Jesus. Yet, she wasn't sure she could or even if she should try. She sat there for a minute, looking down, asking the Lord what she should say or do.

Aaron looked a bit disgusted and said, "I didn't think so. You should never have left Pegasus. Look at what you've done. This is all because of you. Come on, Josh, let's get out of here."

Sheena looked up at Josh and Aaron. Josh gave her an "I'm sorry" look, then dropped his head as they turned and walked away. Suddenly, she was shaken in her belief of what was right. She honestly didn't know how to answer them. Why hadn't Jesus already answered her prayers? Pegasus had answered so quickly when she had prayed for Josh. She felt powerless. She felt guilty. She felt abandoned. She felt confused!

She was relieved when Sergio's parents came back in. She couldn't get out of there fast enough this time.

Why? She asked Jesus again. Why aren't you healing him? She kept walking yet her heart was sinking further down into her stomach. Finally, one thought came which gave her some encouragement. She knew his mom and dad were praying to their gods too. Sergio was not being healed by them either.

Although it relieved her feeling of guilt that she was not the only one who couldn't heal Sergio, it seemed to only bring more confusion and questions. She went to the park and sat quietly under a tree. She took her questions to the Lord with an open and honest heart. She wanted to understand why Sergio was still not healed. Why didn't she feel healing power working through her like she had when following Pegasus? Why, with several people praying, did the Lord seem to be ignoring their heart felt request?

What was the problem? Did God want to punish Sergio for eternity because of what he'd tried to do to Tenicia? Was that what was happening? Or was it something altogether different? She prayed, "What is going on Lord? Why don't you heal him?" Sheena didn't receive a direct answer, but she felt a strange comfort and peace that made no sense. I will have to search the scriptures, she finally concluded, maybe I will find the answer there. "Even if I don't, I trust you Jesus," she declared.

As Sheena was praying under the tree, Sergio's parents were praying at Sergio's side, Josh and Aaron were praying together, David was praying as he worked, Tenicia and her mom were praying together, and many others were praying throughout the small city. They prayed to different gods, and for many different things, but they were praying.

In response to those prayers, many angels and demons actively did what they could. The warrior angels and demons stood guarding their people, warily watching each other, and waiting for commands. For the larger requests they had to have approval before they could act. Dispatches had been sent. The small city was in a spiritual standoff.

Upon hearing the news, Satan, the ruler of all the demons, roared with rage. "This is not happening again!" He yelled, "You let two of them go! This young man couldn't carry out a simple order! And now they're praying specifically for him! KILL HIM!" Satan raged.

"We cannot your majesty. There are mighty angels guarding him," Pegasus replied with his head dropped, "There are several praying for him."

Satan left the Earth enraged, went to the highest heavens, and entered the throne room of the Living God. "What are you planning to do with this one they call Sergio?" asked the serpent boldly as he approached the throne.

"What would you like me to do with him?" The Father asked Satan calmly, already knowing what the evil one intended.

"He's mine already. Let him die." Satan said confidently and caustically.

"Why? Don't you intend to use him further?" God asked with chagrin at the pure hatred in Satan.

"Would you attempt to save this murderer?" Satan spewed with contempt for Sergio, "Would you have mercy for this evil man who would take one of your precious jewels, a virgin no less, and kill her to gain power?? He would have done far worse to her than that if **My** servant had not restrained him," Satan laughed dreadfully and turning to the angels present he said, "You heard his thoughts! He is a vile one!" as he tried to gain support for his position. He did not see the smaller soul hidden behind the huge angels.

At that moment, Jesus, who had stayed seated at the right hand of the Father, stood and spoke, "Abba, you sent me for such as these. What will one more chance hurt if he is as hard hearted as Satan accuses him of being?"

"Surely you don't think a little car accident will change his heart?!" Satan retorted.

"Abba, please listen to the hearts of your children who love him despite what he has done. Hear them praying even now." Jesus pleaded earnestly.

"Aaaahh yes, look how even his parents and friends who are my servants are praying too," Satan slyly switched his argument, "Yours will not be the glory; it will be mine!"

"Don't be so sure Satan," Jesus replied with blazing eyes, showing the serpent the holes in his hand as a reminder.

Satan shrunk back with a pained expression and a reclaimed, "He's mine. He accepted my servant, Pegasus, willingly. When the girls turned, he stayed with me, growing in hate and vileness."

Jesus looked straight into the Father's eyes and with love and grace pleaded, "Abba, if you will give him to me, you know I will not lose him."

Everything in the throne room became completely silent as the entire court listened for the proclamation. The Lord Almighty said, "We will see how hard hearted he is. I will give him another chance.

Satan he has pledged allegiance to your Pegasus, you may tempt him as you see fit; however you can't physically harm him any further." Satan bowed, thanked the Lord and departed from his presence.

Then the Father turned to His Son and lovingly smiled, "If he is willing, he is yours."

At that very moment, Sergio's eyes opened slightly. He felt dazed and was unsure where he was. Focusing was difficult. Everything was hazy. He looked to the right and saw his mother sitting there in a chair beside him asleep. He closed his eyes and tried to remember what had happened, but nothing made sense. He had just been someplace incredible beyond belief, and now he was in this hazy room. His mom asleep in a chair beside him made him think, I must be in bad shape. He closed his eyes again and drifted back into a deep sleep.

Sheena finished praying for Sergio and got up from under the tree. She decided to go check on Tenicia before heading home. She wondered how Tenicia would feel about her praying for Sergio to recover. Will she be angry like Sergio had been? After all, it was her he'd tried to kill. Will she tell me we can't be friends anymore when she knows I'm praying for him...that I've asked others to pray for him? She silently sent another prayer to heaven. Lord, please go before me and help Tenicia forgive Sergio and me. She prayed for Tenicia as she walked to her house. She was hopeful as she walked up the now familiar sidewalk. She knocked and stood waiting for what felt like several minutes before the door opened.

"Hello Sheena. It's so good to see you," Marcella greeted her with a joyful smile and a hug.

"It's good to see you too," Sheena relaxed in the hug, "How are you two?"

"We're doing much better now that she's home," Marcella acknowledged as she released Sheena and showed her in, "I am finally catching up on some sleep. Tenicia's getting stronger every day. How about you?"

"I am good," Sheena replied, "My mom and dad are making a point of being home more, and they even went to church with me last Sunday!"

"That's wonderful! I can hardly wait to meet them." Marcella smiled.

"We might be able to go this coming Sunday. I think she'll be strong enough by then." Tenicia's mom said hopefully.

Tenicia heard Sheena's voice and got up out of her bed. She put her robe on and slowly walked out into the living room. Her face lit up like the sun as she greeted Sheena. It was so good to have a friend come to see her. She hadn't left the house yet and was glad to have company. Her mom had been incredible over the last week, but after it just being the two of them all week; another friendly face was like a refreshing breeze blowing on a warm summer day.

"How are you girl?" Tenicia asked excitedly.

"I am just fine," Sheena replied, "The important question is; how are **you**?"

"I am getting stronger. I have been up for a few hours today, and I am able to concentrate on a puzzle. It's weird how tired I get just doing that sometimes, but I am glad I can. There were a couple of days I could only talk or watch TV for a couple of hours, and then I would be so tired I would have to sleep. Trying to focus on something, make my mind think, was almost impossible." Tenicia shared with humble honesty, "I don't know what I would have done without my mom."

"That's what moms are for," said Marcella lovingly, "I am glad I could take the time off work and be here with you," she turned to Sheena, "Would you like a glass of tea?"

"I love your tea!" Sheena exclaimed, "That would be wonderful." She waited until Marcella was in the kitchen before telling Tenicia, "I have something I need to tell you."

Tenicia smiled at Sheena's sense of secrecy and said, "We'll go into my room after Mom brings the tea."

Tenicia smiled as she grabbed Sheeena's arm and said, "Come see this puzzle, Sheena. Maybe you can help me find a few of the difficult pieces. I think I am going to glue it when it's done."

212

"Don't wear yourself out to much," Marcella cautioned. She was glad Sheena was there but concerned that Tenicia would overdo.

"Okay mom," Tenicia replied with a roll of her eyes and a touch of annoyance.

This was the first person she'd seen in a week besides her mom. She could take a nap after Sheena left, she thought.

"I won't stay to long," Sheena said reassuringly.

Once in the room, the girls talked a bit about the puzzle and found a few more pieces. Sheena agreed that it was a beautiful picture and the significance of it being the first puzzle of Tenicia's recovery made it a good idea to glue it together. Finally, Tenicia could not wait any longer to know what was on Sheena's mind. "So what is it you need to tell me?" Tenicia asked with curiosity.

Sheena looked at Tenicia seriously, determining if she were really up to hearing what she had to say. She'd been trying to think of something else to tell her, but couldn't think of anything. So, with a little hesitancy she confessed, "I have been sitting with and praying for Sergio every day." She watched Tenicia's face closely for reaction.

Tenicia just stared blankly at her for a moment then calmly asked, "How is he?"

"He's in bad shape. He was still unconscious when I left today. His poor mom is there all the time, unless I come in and sit with him," Sheena compassionately answered.

"That's sad," Tenicia replied coolly. She could feel a little sympathy for his mom, but not him. She knew and understood that Sheena and Sergio had been best friends all those years, becoming lovers over the past summer, but after all this; how could Sheena have even a shred of compassion for him? Tenicia could not help the anger rising within her.

"I keep praying that the Lord will give him another chance…. that he won't die and go to hell," Sheena said, hoping the reality of hell would strike a soft spot in Tenicia's heart. "I just hope it's not too late for him or his family."

"Well, Jesus did die for all the sins of the world," Tenicia knew it was the right thing to say, but her heart was cold towards them.

"God so loved the world..." her voice trailed off, she turned away, and she just stared out the window.

"Are you okay?" asked Sheena placing a hand on her shoulder.

"I'm fine. I'm just tired now," Tenicia replied. She looked over her shoulder and gave a fake smile. "I think I need a nap."

"Alright, I told you're mom I wouldn't stay too long," Sheena hugged Tenicia and said, "I will come see you again in a few days. We're all still praying for you to heal completely and quickly too."

"Thank you," Tenicia replied earnestly with a real smile. She knew they were and was truly grateful for it. She loved Sheena and the others, but wondered how they could really pray for him. He'd planned on killing her! Maybe if they'd heard the hatred in his voice or felt the back of his hand like she had....deep in her heart, she hoped he did die and go to hell.

Yet, she knew that wasn't right to say. She simply smiled and said, "It was great to see you. I can hardly wait to see you again. Come back soon." After Sheena left, Tenicia cried into her pillow, and asked the Lord to let him die. Finally after weeping for a while, she felt a pleasing peace wash over her. She grabbed a few Kleenex and wiped the tears and runny nose away. She laid down and fell into a deep and restorative sleep.

Early the following morning, Sergio woke up again. His mom was right there. She was praying for him. Things looked a little clearer than they had the last time his eyes had opened. He was able, with a bit of concentration, to move his hand over to his mom's hand and take hold of it. Her head shot up with surprise.

She just stared unbelievingly for a minute at him as he gazed lovingly at her. Then she shouted with joy, "You're awake! You're awake!" He smiled a weak smile, and she stood up, bent over him, and hugged him gently as she whispered in his ear, "I love you." Then she stepped back and started laughing and crying all at the same time. She sputtered, "Oh, it's so good to see you awake again!"

The floor nurse came rushing in after hearing the commotion. "Oh my! Well, welcome back Mr. Santiago," she said with a satisfied sound. She checked his vitals and turned to his mom saying, "Good strong heartbeat; everything looks good. I'll give the Doctor a call and let him know."

"Thank you. Can you please send someone to tell his father?" "He's in the cafeteria, getting us breakfast," pleaded Sergio's mom.

"I will go," replied a nursing assistant who'd come into the room, "I know what Mr. Santiago looks like, and it will be a pleasure to deliver such good news." She walked out of the room briskly, almost running through the halls, to the elevator.

Sergio tried to say, "Thank you" but could hardly whisper. He gave a slight smile to the nurse. It was all he could do right then. He felt very weak, even though she'd said his heart was strong and everything looked good. He didn't really remember what had happened, or how he'd ended up here. He was becoming more aware of his body though, and it hurt badly. He let out a low groan.

"I'll see if the doctor will authorize something for pain while I have him on the phone," the nurse said sympathetically as she left the room.

Oriana came back over and held his hand. She soothingly stated, "It will be okay. I'm right here with you. They'll take good care of you," then with resolve she declared, "I will make sure of it."

Sergio smiled and whispered, "I love you, Mom." Then he closed his eyes and drifted back off to sleep for a while.

When Sheena came to the hospital to give Mr. and Mrs. Santiago a break, they excitedly shared the good news. He had been awake twice that morning for a short time. The doctor had come in and examined him. The doctor explained that Sergio had not gone back into a coma, but would need a lot of sleep as his body continued to heal. He also warned them even with the best treatments available, Sergio would probably never be the same. They didn't know exactly what that meant yet, they were just thrilled he was alive and would recover.

Sheena rejoiced with them. She didn't tell them she hoped he would accept Christ; she knew it wasn't the right time.

She simply was happy that Sergio had come out of the coma, just as they were. They thanked her for coming to the hospital faithfully as they left for their break.

Once they were gone, Sheena thanked the Lord for this miracle. She asked if it be the Lord's will that Sergio would heal quicker than doctors could explain as well as more completely than they could hope. She asked that the Lord use this to glorify his name and do things that were undeniably him so everyone could see how good he is. She began praying for others' eyes to be opened through this situation as well.

As she prayed, Sergio woke up again. This time as his eyes looked to see his mom sitting next to him, he was shocked to see Sheena. He wasn't sure why he was surprised, but he was glad she was there. He reached over and put his hand on top of her bowed head. He loved the feel of her soft hair. She picked up her head, smiled, and said, "Hello. It's good to see you awake again. I know a lot of people who are going to be happy to hear the news."

Sergio smiled back at her and strained to whisper, "It's good to see you." Sheena barely heard him. She could tell he had strained to even say that so she encouraged him to just relax and not try to talk right now. He smiled a grateful smile for her understanding. She explained that his parents would be back in a couple of hours when he started looking around the room for them. She also told him that Josh and Aaron had been there to see him the day before. She shared she would have to make several phone calls as a lot of people were praying for him. Sergio suddenly had a suspicious look on his face and began to feel a bit uncomfortable with her there. Yet, he had no idea why. He asked, "Nurse?" in a strained whisper. "Of course," replied Sheena and she jumped up to get the nurse.

She stood back towards the door as the nurse came in to see what she could do for Sergio. "Water, please" he whispered. The nurse smiled and promised she would return in a moment.

Sheena was relieved it was just water he needed. The nurse returned with ice chips and put just a couple in his mouth. She explained that he could only have the ice chips right now to relieve the thirst without overwhelming his system.

The ice was refreshing on his parched tongue. He had not had any water orally in over a week. Although the hospital had supplied all his nutritional needs through an Intravenous solution, his mouth and throat were very dry.

Sheena decided it would be better to talk about random things than to bring up spiritual topics right now. She gave him a couple more spoons of ice chips as she talked, and was happy that his parents returned while he was still awake.

They were excited to see him awake and taking ice chips. They started talking to him about having the house ready for their winter celebration. They assured him they would wait until he was ready to go home before celebrating.

Wow! Sheena thought as she left them, this would be her first Christmas as a Christian. She knew it would be different, and much more meaningful than ever before.

What an incredible gift she'd been given! She was full of joy at the thought of it. Yet, there was a mix of sadness because she could not share any of this with Sergio's family. She said goodbye, and headed home.

Her first phone call was to David. She told him the good news about Sergio and asked him to help make the phone calls. He was glad to. She called Josh next, knowing he'd be happy for Sergio, and asked him to call Aaron. She didn't want to personally call him right now. She didn't need any discouragement or hatred. Then she knew she had to call Tenicia. She stopped and prayed for the Lord to give her the right words and give Tenicia grace.

When she called, Tenicia's mom answered. Sheena felt a bit relieved, and told her in a subdued voice that Sergio was in rough condition, but he was awake. Tenicia's mom was not as cold as Tenicia had been about Sergio, but she wasn't overjoyed either. She replied she would tell Tenicia when she woke up, and then protectively asked if the police had been notified. Sheena wasn't sure. Tenicia's mom said, "Well, make sure you call them."

Sheena assured her she would. Suddenly Sheena was torn about Sergio waking up. She knew he had to face the consequences if he were able, but it didn't feel good to be the one to call the police. None the less, it was the right thing to do. She got her purse and dug out the detective's card. She called and left a message.

There was so much uncertainty about Sergio's future now, but she was thankful he'd have another chance to hear the truth about Christ. She prayed that his heart would be ready the next time someone would tell him about God's love and forgiveness. She asked that the Lord would save his parents too, and then she prayed for the rest of her circle.

Finally, she called Pastor Dale and his wife Martha, asking them if they could get together and pray. They had begun to have a prayer meeting every week at their home, and they invited her. She was excited about going.

Over the next few weeks, the believers met together to continue praying. So much good was happening all over their little city. Sheena's parents accepted Christ and began going to church regularly too. Tenicia healed. She and Marcella became part of the group of believers. They began growing in Christ and becoming stronger in the Word. They grew in boldness as well, and began telling others about the love of Christ. Many people began to accept the Lord and the group grew.

Sheena continued going to the hospital to see Sergio as well. Oriana was finally able to go home at night, but would be there early in the morning. She was always appreciative of Sheena coming to stay with Sergio while she went home for a little while. Gilberto had to go back to work, so he could only be with them in the evening, and she needed to have some semblance of supper. She would put supper in the slow cooker, clean up and return to Sergio's side as quickly as she could. Sheena assured Oriana she could take her time. Sergio was often asleep most, if not all of the time she was there.

This day would be different. After weeks of praying faithfully for her friend, she still did not expect what the Lord was doing.

After Mrs. Santiago headed home, Sheena pulled out her Bible and began reading softly yet out loud. She had been doing this since the Lord had given her the idea about a week before. When she finished reading the chapter, she began praying for Sergio.

As she was praying, Sergio was squirming sporadically. Suddenly, Sergio sat straight up, staring straight ahead; he couldn't help but scream from the scary scene he alone had just seen.

Sheena reached over as she softly began speaking reassuringly, "Sergio, it's okay. I'm right here. It's just a dream."

Sergio looked at her still in shock. He looked around the room searching for the fearful beasts he'd seen, took a deep breath and lay back beginning to relax as he realized he was back in the hospital room. He looked back at her with the concern still showing in his eyes and told her, "It was not a dream. I was there. I was really there."

Sheena looked deep into his eyes, reading them; she could tell he really did experience something beyond a dream. "Tell me about it," she softly encouraged.

"I was standing before a grand podium with a huge book on it. There on the other side of the podium stood a man, though he looked quite different than us, he was bright with white light. He was looking through the entries as he asked me my name. I told him, and he nodded as he continue the search. After turning and searching hundreds of pages, he finally concluded my name was not written in the book.

He looked very sad as he told me to go to the end of the line to the left. Sergio looked off to the right upper corner of the room as the memory came flooding back. He looked back at Sheena, then looked down with a fearful look in eyes. He paused for a moment longer, swallowing the lump in his throat.

Sheena sat silently, but reached over and put her hand on his in a show of support. He smiled weakly, gently took hold of her hand, and continued, "The line seemed to move by itself like we'd been put on a conveyer.

At first it moved a large group of us rather rapidly away from the man at the podium. Then it slowed down, way down, until it stopped." Sergio took a deep breath and asked, "May I have some ice. " Sheena got up, retrieved the cup of ice chips and handed it to him. He put a little in his mouth, allowing the ice to melt. Still holding onto the cup, he began again, "Then it began to move forward again, slowly. As the line moved forward, I could hear screams of torment and anguish." He grimaced.

He took another deep breath and continued, "The further the line move forward, the louder the screams got. I turned to go back, but there was nowhere to go. There was now a huge gulf between the man at the podium and us. It was getting hotter too. I turned back around and could hardly believe what I was seeing.

Two huge creatures that looked like something out of an evil alien movie were tossing people into this molten hot lake of fire! It was horrible! There was nowhere to go to escape it. My heart was pounding faster and faster as I was getting closer to the creatures. I kept looking for a way out, but there wasn't one. I couldn't see anything, but there where invisible walls. I yelled back to the man, but he told me there was nothing he could do.

There were only three people left in front of me when I was suddenly rushing out of there in a wind current. The current was faster than any ride I have ever been on. Everything was just a blur of streaks of brilliant colors. As I came slamming back into my body, it all stopped. I think that's when you told me everything was okay." He looked at her now searching her face to see if she believed him. He was relieved to see that she did.

"Wow!" was all Sheena could manage to say. She sat there wide eyed in shock. It took a full two minutes of silence before either of them said anything. Sheena finally uttered, "You've been given a unique vision and an incredible opportunity."

"I know," Sergio responded with sincerity. He pointed to the large book in her lap and asked, "Does that book tell you about the book of names and the lake of fire?"

Sheena looked down, smiled, and looked back up at him. She had a joyful twinkle in her eye as she replied enthusiastically, "Yes....yes it does. Would you like me to leave this one with you?"

"Yeah," Sergio responded.

"I am going to put this book mark in the beginning of the book of Mark. I'm not sure exactly were, but I know it's in there. We can talk more about it when I come tomorrow if you like."

"If you want someone who really knows it far better than I do, maybe we can call David." She gently gave him the Bible.

He took it from her and just looked at it a minute. Then he looked at her, smiled and said, "Thanks. Sure, call David."

His face became puzzled and he asked, "Do you really think this is the truth?"

"Now more than ever!" She responded, her face glowing with joy.

"Alright, I'll try to read it when Mom goes home tonight. Would you put it in the drawer?" he asked as he handed it back to her. She took it from him and put it in the drawer.

"How's everyone else doing?" he asked. Sheena began telling him what she could about the others. He was relieved when he found out Tenicia was okay and confessed he really felt bad for doing that to her. Sheena was thankful to hear him say so. When his mom came in, they all talked for a few minutes before Sheena had to leave. Mrs. Santiago could see a change, a huge improvement in Sergio and she was thrilled.

Sheena left the hospital feeling as if she were floating on a cloud. She didn't know what would happen next, but Sergio had been given a second chance. The Lord had answered her prayers in a surprising and powerful way. She could hardly wait to get to the prayer meeting and tell them of all that God had done.

The dramatic turn of events and the time spent in prayer bonded Sheena to the believers in a way she had never experienced. She felt far closer to them than she had even Sergio, as she shared the news with them. They were glad he had been given this second chance. They all intensely hoped he would come to know the Lord.

"He will be locked up for a few years," the District Attorney said when they spoke with him later that week, assuring the girls their testimony and the evidence in the car was undeniable.

Sheena decided she would not quit praying for him. Just as the Lord had forgiven her, she forgave and loved Sergio. Tenicia agreed to pray also, although it was difficult and painful; she too forgave him.

Pastor Dale and Martha remarked they were impressed with the girls' maturity as young believers. They encouraged them to keep following the Lord no matter what happened. Sheena responded, "Who else would I follow? Jesus is the King of Kings and Lord of Lords! Now that I know him, I love him so much! I can hardly believe it sometimes. It's absolutely amazing that even while I was deep in my sin, He loved me."

A Note from the Author

I have experienced the realities of the spiritual realm, and like several of the characters in this story; I have come to know Jesus personally. He is very real and alive! He has completely

 transformed my life. I walked away from witchcraft in 1989 to follow the King of kings and Lord of Lords, Jesus, The Christ.

It's been an amazing adventure I will never regret. If you've been involved in spiritualism, witchcraft, New Age, or anything other than a vibrant relationship with the One True Living God, I invite you to consider who Jesus is.

If you know someone involved in the occult and are concerned for them, also know there is hope! If I can help you and walk with you through your questions, decisions, prayer needs, or next steps please let me know.

Have you been impacted by this story? Do you have questions or comments after reading this story? Do you need prayer? I would love to communicate with you and will gladly pray with/for you.

Contact me @
Sarah.sheena65@gmail.com

For inspirations, poetry, and more by the author follow one of the social media pages or sign up for the free email.

www.facebook.com/sarahsheenasjourney

or

https://www.google.com/+SarahSheenasJourney

55856178R00141

Made in the USA
San Bernardino, CA
07 November 2017